ALWAYS WITH YOU

HANNAH ELLIS

To Arlene, Jess, Lizzie and Mandy,
my Kununurra family.

And in loving memory of my mum,
always with me.

PROLOGUE

LIBBY TAYLOR

Mum didn't tell me about my father until she was dying, and by then I felt like it was too late to ask any questions. Growing up, I'd just accepted that I didn't have a dad. It wasn't a big deal. As a teenager, I'd asked a few questions and Mum told me that she'd had a fling. By the time she'd realised she was pregnant, she couldn't even remember his name. It was a mistake, she'd said, with laughter in her eyes, but it was the best mistake she'd ever made. I didn't push her. It had always been my assumption that tracking him down would have been impossible, even if I'd wanted to – which I never had.

I was twenty when Mum started her descent towards death. It felt so surreal. One minute she was fit and healthy and we were completely unaware of what was taking over inside her. Six months later, she was gone. In those last months, I tried to absorb every detail of her. I hung off her every word, terrified they'd be her last. The realisation that she wouldn't be around forever stirred a million questions in me. There was so much I wanted to know, and it was all locked inside her. I was terrified that once she was gone, all the questions I'd never asked her would haunt me. From the mundane – did I even know her favourite colour? – to the overwhelming – did she have any regrets?

Strangely, questions about my father still weren't at the front of my mind. They should have been. If she'd told me everything, it would have made things much easier later.

Mum went from healthy to frail so quickly that I couldn't bring myself to ask all the questions which danced around my head. It was as though the diagnosis had made her ill, not the disease itself. She seemed fine until they told her she was ill. That was hard to get my head around. What if no one had ever mentioned it? Couldn't she just have carried on with life until the cancer admitted defeat and went away, tired of being ignored?

So I didn't ask my questions but waited, sitting with her and telling her all my usual gossip, biding my time until she'd start talking. And she did start talking. Because she was scared too. Not just of dying, but scared of moving on from the world and leaving nothing but me. Just little old me who didn't even know everything about her.

She started with her childhood, dissecting her relationship with her parents, much of which I already knew. Then, over the months, she talked about her schooldays and her friends; for a while she became obsessed with the ornaments in the house, adamant I should know any stories behind them.

Then one day she mentioned Australia – the outback town of Kununurra where she'd lived when she was twenty-one: the year before she had me. The first time I heard her utter Joe Sullivan's name, her eyes glazed over, and I knew there was a whole story she'd never told me anything about.

By then it was too late; she was slipping away, and it seemed as though the story would be lost forever.

HANNAH ELLIS

Chapter 1

EVELYN TAYLOR – May 1994

Travelling alone around Australia was the biggest adventure of my life. Every day brought new people and exciting experiences. My journey started in Sydney and took me north along the extensive coastline to Cairns and then even further north to Darwin. I had a visa for a year, and after two months I already knew my time in Australia would go too fast.

It was in Darwin that I heard people talking about doing farm work to extend their visas. Three months of farm work could add another year. Immediately, I knew that was my next step. With my funds starting to run low, I'd already been thinking about finding a job. This sounded perfect.

I scoured noticeboards in the hostels close to where I was staying in search of others doing the same and offering a ride. Three days later, I found myself in the back of a Ford pickup, travelling the bumpy road from Darwin to an outback town called Kununurra. I was with a couple of British guys and a French girl, whose names I forgot as soon as we parted. When we finally arrived in Kununurra after a ten-hour drive, my companions were underwhelmed by the small rundown town and decided straight away they would only stay for a night and then continue further west to Broome. I, on the other hand, was charmed. I'd become used to life on the main tourist track where things were well maintained and everything began to look the same. Kununurra was rough around the edges.

We arrived at the Walkabout Hostel on the edge of town and were told they could only offer a communal room for one night. After that, they were fully booked. The girl in charge told me there was another hostel in the middle of town which I could try if I wanted to stay longer. She curled her lip as she warned me that it wasn't the nicest place.

Early the next morning I walked into town. My fate lay in the hands of the hostel in the heart of Kununurra. If they had rooms, I'd stay; if they didn't, I'd continue on to Broome while I had the chance of a ride. The town was quiet, but I still felt it had a buzz about it. It was hard to put my finger on why, when the place was so sleepy, but somehow the ramshackle little town seemed to be talking to me and drawing me in. The hostel was easy to find: slap bang in the centre, opposite a pub called Kelly's Tavern. I ventured through a rusty archway where a weathered sign announced the Kununurra Croc Backpacker Resort. It didn't really have a resort feel, I thought as I meandered along the path through the overgrown gardens. A building finally came into view. It certainly wasn't anything like what I was used to. The lizard that ran across my path startled me, and I said hello to it when it stopped to look at me.

"G'day," a gravelly voice replied as the lizard scuttled away. The voice belonged to an old guy with tanned, leathery skin and a slow but sturdy gait.

"Hi," I said as he opened the door to the office and wandered inside.

"You're a bit early for check-in," he called over his shoulder.

"I just wanted to see if you had any rooms available," I said, following him into the cramped office.

He introduced himself as Stan. "I've got rooms," he said, gesturing to the price list which hung on the wall behind him.

I studied it for a moment. "That's reasonable," I remarked.

His eyes glinted in amusement. "It's pretty basic."

"You know, I think I'll treat myself and get a single room." It was the same price for a single as it was for a dorm room in the other hostel.

"Go crazy, little lady, you only live once. How long you staying?"

"I'm not sure," I said, looking around and feeling somehow at home. "I might stay a while."

"Wait until you've had a look around!" he said, a cautionary tone to his voice.

"I think I'm gonna like it here. I feel it in my bones!"

"You're very cheerful," he said, shaking his head.

"Oh, I'm very sorry," I said, attempting to frown dramatically. He was right, though; I felt unusually happy for so early in the morning.

"Room two," he said, throwing me a key. I fumbled to catch it. "Next to the kitchen. Bathrooms

11

are at the end. I'm writing you up as an indefinite stay, but I reckon you won't last a week."

My eyebrows knitted together. He was an odd character, but he wasn't unlikeable. "I heard there are fruit-picking jobs around here . . ."

His whole body vibrated through his throaty chuckle. "You're not built for fruit-picking. It's hard labour, you know."

"I'll manage," I said, my steely glare challenging him to argue.

"Register over at the Job Shop. There are pick-ups daily, and they take you out in the morning and bring you back in the evening."

"Thanks!" I left to go in search of my room.

"I'll buy you a drink if you manage more than a day on a farm," he shouted after me.

"You're on," I said, reaching the door of room number two and stepping into my new home.

He was right; it *was* basic. I held the door and moved aside as a speedy little lizard shot out from under the bed. Closing the door after it, I checked to see if he had any friends around the place, but the coast was clear. A room to myself was a luxury, and I lay for a while staring up at the ceiling fan. The room contained a bed, small wardrobe and a desk. The flooring was terracotta tiles, which were cool beneath my feet. It wasn't spectacular, but I liked it. Not having to listen to other people snoring and people coming and going at all hours would be a treat.

After dragging myself up, I set off to explore and sign myself up for fruit-picking.

Chapter 2

EVELYN – May 1994

It was early the next morning when the minibus rattled over uneven ground and on to Jenkins' Farm. My fellow passengers were mainly male. In fact, out of ten of us, only two were female. I'd introduced myself to Tina as we waited to be picked up. She wasn't particularly friendly, but I sat with her on the minibus regardless and found that she'd been fruit-picking on and off for six months at different farms scattered all over Western Australia. That explained her muscular physique. Tina looked down her nose at me and although she didn't say it, I was sure she thought I wouldn't last a day. I was slightly concerned about being out in the open fields and melting in the heat, but the work didn't scare me; I was fitter than I looked and was sure that lugging my backpack around for the last two months must have built up some muscle tone.

I wasn't prepared for the slave driver who owned the farm. Len Jenkins was a big man whose face was set into a cold, hard frown. He was waiting out in the field and glared as the minibus came to a halt. I'd been surprised by the lack of conversation on the drive. Whenever I tried to chat, I was met with shrugs and odd looks. I'd expected a camaraderie between the workers and hoped they would warm up as the day went on. Maybe it was just too early. The sun was only just rising.

"You'll hate pumpkins by the end of the day," a low voice whispered in my ear. We'd disembarked to join another group of workers standing around three tractors. The tall, blonde Dutch guy introduced himself as Johan. I was happy to have someone to talk to.

"I was starting to think I'd come out with a bunch of zombies," I said.

"Once we set off, you'll have to learn ventriloquism if you want to chat. Talking is not allowed." I waited for him to laugh, but his tone was serious. "Len's always watching." He pointed to a nearby lookout post – a tall wooden frame with a shaded seat at the top, similar to a lifeguard's chair. There were more spread out at regular intervals across the fields. "He spends all day up there with his binoculars. If you talk too much or take too long for a break, he'll fire you, just like that."

We were split into three groups and each given a pair of secateurs. The rough-looking guy who'd driven the minibus gave me brief instructions on picking out the bad pumpkins and good ones.

"Find the good ones, cut them at the stem and throw them up to me," Johan said as he climbed onto the contraption behind the tractor and stood among the huge plastic bins.

"Sounds simple," I said.

"It is simple," he agreed. "But it's not easy."

I was cheerful enough for the first hour. Walking behind a tractor throwing pumpkins up to Johan wasn't so bad. There was something satisfying about it. An honest day's work, I'd say. The swing of my arms as I launched the pumpkins up to Johan was a good workout, and it soon became clear how he'd gained his athletic build and surfer-dude tan.

By 8 a.m., sweat poured down my body, and I wondered how I would cope at the hottest part of the day when the sun was high overhead. With every pumpkin thrown, I managed a smile for Johan. *It wasn't so bad*, I told myself repeatedly.

At the end of the row, water was handed around and we had a ten-minute break, which seemed to be timed to the second.

"How you doing?" Johan asked as I leaned against the massive tractor tyre and gulped down water.

"I'm okay."

"Hard work, isn't it?"

"It's pretty much what I expected," I said, loath to admit that I was exhausted after just a couple of hours. I flexed my fingers, which ached from the effort of cutting through the stubborn pumpkin stems.

"Well, the good news is that you get to be up on the tractor now!" He grinned at me as our group was rallied back into action. The tractor turned and I clambered up to take Johan's spot. I was happy to give my back a break from all the bending and lifting.

Catching pumpkins wasn't the easiest thing in the world either, though. Johan worked fast; I'd barely placed one pumpkin into a bin when another was launched at me. He had a good throw, and it took a while for me to get used to the force of the heavy pumpkins being fired at me. Flies tickled my skin and I barely had time to waft them away. The temperature became gradually less bearable, and my thirst rose by the second.

"Can I have some water?" I shouted to the guy in charge.

"At the end of the row," he told me in no uncertain terms.

"Is it legal for them not to provide water on demand?" I asked Johan.

"Probably not," he muttered as he tossed another pumpkin my way. It was a large one, and the weight of it almost knocked me off the tractor.

"How long have you been working here?" I asked him a little while later. A bit of chat might take my mind off my aches and pains, which were developing at an alarming rate.

"I'll talk to you at lunch," he said. Everyone took the no talking rule very seriously. The mention of lunch perked me up a little bit at least.

As the sun got hotter, the pumpkins got heavier and the flies more persistent. Time slowed and my body began to scream at me: for water, for food, for a rest. The field stretched out and the end of the row seemed to get further and further away.

"Still okay?" Johan asked when we finally reached the end of the row to be rewarded with more water. It struck me that he took amusement in watching me being gradually worn down by the gruelling work.

"I'm okay," I said, trying my best to sound convincing. All I wanted to do was sit in a cool bath and then curl up in a dark room.

"Lunchtime," he said cheerfully. I followed the crowd onto the minibus, which drove us the short distance to the house. A table was laid with sandwiches, fruit and soft drinks. Everyone tucked in with gusto.

"So how long have you been working here?" I asked Johan again.

"Four weeks," he told me and then slipped into a whisper. "You chose the absolute worst farm to work on."

"Really?"

"The work's all the same, I guess, but from what I hear, the conditions here are the worst around."

"Why are you still here then?" I asked. Four weeks certainly seemed a very long time to me, and it occurred to me that perhaps Stan was right; I could never hack three months of farm work.

"I don't have a work permit," he confided. "And Len doesn't care about that sort of thing."

Johan stopped talking abruptly and cast his eyes down, concentrating on his lunch. The stern voice behind me took me by surprise. "You need a lift back to town?"

I turned to find Len glaring at me. Confusion wrinkled my face.

"Seems like you weren't managing too well out in the field," he said.

"I'm fine," I replied. "Good to recharge," I added, waving my sandwich weakly.

"You're slow. You expect me to pay you when you're so slow? If you're not up to the job, you're no use to me."

A glance showed me that my co-workers were suddenly taking great interest in their plates. I was on my own. "I'll go faster," I told him. "I was just getting the hang of things."

He stared at me for a moment. "Work faster. Talk less. Got it?"

"Got it," I said.

"Back to work," he shouted. Everyone moved at once.

Len's eyes bored into me as we moved back to the minibus. In fact, I felt his unseen eyes on me all afternoon. I worked faster and only swapped the odd word with Johan when we had a break at the end of the rows. It was hell, and Stan was right – I wasn't built for farm work.

By the end of the day, I was broken. My spirit was broken, and my body was broken. There was no way I'd make it back the next day. That I'd survived one day seemed like a massive achievement, and I still wasn't sure whether I might collapse and die before the day was done. I'd never been so excited to get to bed and sleep in all my life.

"At least I won't have to pay you," Len grumbled when we finally finished for the day.

"What?" I asked, as Johan slinked away from me.

"I pay cash on Fridays. But you won't be here then, will you?"

I wanted to cry. I'd just done the hardest day's work of my life and I wouldn't get paid for it. The thought of struggling through a whole week of this torture was too much to bear, but his smug look enraged me. With no energy to argue, I got into the minibus and rested my head on the filthy window the whole way back to town.

Everything ached when I stood under the shower. I thought I might fall asleep standing naked under the soothing water. My limbs had decided to ignore my brain's instructions for them to move. Finally, I switched the water off and forced myself into clean clothes. Every movement was painful.

"Fun day?" Stan asked, his amusement obvious.

All I could manage was a groan as I walked past him and into my room, where I collapsed onto the bed and fell fast asleep.

HANNAH ELLIS

Chapter 3

EVELYN – May 1994

When I woke, it was with a raging hunger that forced me, painfully, from my bed. The first movements were the worst, and every muscle ached with a heaviness I'd never known. My body felt like it was made of lead as I trudged into the kitchen. The bacon and egg sandwich was the most delicious and satisfying food I'd ever eaten. It wasn't light out yet and everything was quiet. I was surprised when the kitchen door swung open.

"Well, I have to say, I'm amazed," Stan said. "You've surprised me."

I grunted my confusion.

"I didn't think you'd be able to stand up today, never mind go back to the farm. Good on ya, girl!"

"A lot of people underestimate me," I told him, rinsing my plate and putting it away. "Guess you'll owe me a beer this evening."

"I'll have it ready for you," he promised.

Oh good God, what are you doing, Evelyn? I sauntered past Stan, ignoring the pain that shot through my body. *Admit defeat. Another day might*

21

actually kill you. It's not worth it.

I should have listened to that sensible inner voice instead of deciding I had something to prove. The group at the collection point looked surprised to see me, as did the driver, who happily told me so.

"Bloody hell," Len said when we reached the farm. "What are you doing back?"

"I'm here to work," I said.

He seemed to mull things over for a moment. "If you can't keep up today, you're out of here."

I nodded and the day began just as the one before. My body was being pushed to the limit, and with every pumpkin I threw, I thought of quitting. As there was no talking, I developed an inner monologue which mainly consisted of me arguing with myself about whether or not I could manage a week. I tried to focus my mind on other things. I thought of my parents and my friends back home. Thoughts of my best friend, Mel, distracted me for a minute or two, before the blister on my hand burst with the action of the secateurs. My left hand didn't have the strength to cut, and after a few attempts while forcing the handle into an open wound, I asked for a plaster. I was surprised to be given one without fuss and got back to work. The pain was searing, even with the protection of the plaster.

Dizziness set in just before lunch, and every time I stood my body threatened to give out. I was on the verge of collapse but still refused to give up. Lunch was a welcome sight and gave me a small boost.

"You should just give up," Johan whispered. "Len's had his eye on you the whole time. He doesn't like you. I don't think he's going to pay you no matter what."

"If I make it to Friday, he'll have to pay me." It was only Tuesday, and Friday seemed like a far-off destination.

"He'll fire you on Thursday . . ."

"He wouldn't," I said.

"Girl." Len's grainy voice drifted over my shoulder. "Are ya trying to make a fool of me or what?"

"No," I said, turning to look at him.

"But you think it's okay to come onto my farm and slack off?"

I took a deep breath. "I wasn't slacking off."

"And you're going to sit and argue with me while you eat my food? You're really taking the piss now!"

Sometimes you have to know when to give up. I gave up. Standing, I took a final bite of my sandwich. "Here," I said, "have it if you want." I threw the remainder of the sandwich, and it bounced from his broad chest to the ground. Disbelieving intakes of breath were the only sounds to be heard. I hoped he stuck to psychological abuse and didn't delve into physical punishment. I had the distinct feeling I was about to be launched across the fields. "I think I'll leave now."

I dodged around him and set off down the driveway away from the house. It was a relief to know I wasn't going back to the pumpkin fields. I didn't care if I didn't get the money owed to me; I just wanted to get out of there. I expected Len to shout abuse after me, but all I heard was him yelling at everyone else to get back to work.

I was free, and I was proud of myself as I marched

off Len Jenkins' property with my head held high. Adrenalin buzzed through my system, and I laughed out loud as I recalled the look on his face when I'd thrown the sandwich at him. When I reached the road, I marched purposefully in the direction of Kununurra.

My plans for a visa extension were fading fast. It definitely wasn't worth enduring that torture. Maybe I could brave a different farm, but the thought of just staying for one year suddenly seemed okay. A year in Australia had been my original plan, and there was nothing wrong with sticking to it.

After ten minutes, my glee at throwing sandwiches and walking off the job was replaced by a raging thirst and my brain attempting to calculate how far it was back to Kununurra. It hadn't taken that long to drive out, had it? Half an hour maybe? But that would take a long time to walk, and I was already struggling. I turned and looked back; the road stretched out in both directions, shrubs dotted either side of the dusty road to create a stunning landscape of rich greens and rusty reds. I could just make out the fence post at the farm. Turning back seemed defeatist, but continuing on seemed like the road to my slow demise.

I could actually die out here, it occurred to me.

Chapter 4

LIBBY – July 2017

On the first anniversary of Mum's death, I lay in bed listening to the bustle of my aunt and uncle's lively house. Spoons clattered in cereal bowls and feet pounded up and down the stairs. Cupboard doors and drawers banged into place. Four familiar voices drifted up with varying volume – a constant hum interlaced with the odd shout. Every morning was the same, like a song stuck on repeat. Bickering kicked in like a familiar chorus.

I waited for Aunt Mel's voice to be directed my way. Every morning she'd shout that I needed to get up. Apparently, she still thought I was ten years old and unable to get myself out of bed in the morning. There was no prompt for me this morning, though; Aunt Mel was quiet.

Dragging myself out of the comfort of my bed, I felt the familiar tightening in my chest, the crushing in my throat. I inhaled deeply and waited for it to pass. I just needed to get through the day.

A shelf full of Lego creations caught my attention, and I righted the Lego man who'd been lying on his side. I'd been staying in eight-year-old Alfie's room for almost two months. It was a wonder he didn't complain about the situation more than he did. What was more amazing was that he'd been moved in with his older brother, Josh, who'd never said a word about it. Not in my earshot, anyway. I'm sure no seventeen-year-old would be happy about sharing with their little brother.

I should find somewhere else to live.

"Morning!" I said when I ventured into the kitchen, showered and dressed for work. Working as a chambermaid in a local hotel wasn't really my life's ambition, but it was okay as a stopgap. I just needed to figure out what was at the other side of the gap. The hotel job was at least comforting as I'd worked there every summer since I was sixteen. It was familiar and mostly stress-free.

"Morning, love," Aunt Mel said softly as the rest of the family descended into silence. "How are you doing today?"

"Fine, thanks." I reached for the cereal box. Josh mumbled something about getting dressed, and I dropped into his vacated seat. Alfie's eyes ping-ponged between his mum and dad, who were no doubt exchanging meaningful glances.

I felt Uncle Rob's eyes land on me. He cleared his throat. "Maybe you should stay home today," he suggested, failing miserably in his attempt to sound casual.

"I'm fine," I told him cheerfully. My focus shifted back to my breakfast. The silence was deafening.

"Why's everyone acting weird today?" Alfie asked.

Mel shuffled behind me. "No one's acting weird," she said, her voice too high and too insistent. "It's my day off, Libby. Why don't you ring in sick and we can have a girlie day?"

Alfie's eyes widened hopefully. "If Libby's staying home, does that mean I don't have to go to school today?"

"You're going to school," Rob replied. "Run upstairs and brush your teeth."

"How come Libby doesn't have to go to work today?"

Because my mother died and everyone thinks I'm going to fall apart, that's why. I caught Alfie's eye. "Don't worry, I'm going to work."

"Good," Alfie said. "Because it's not fair if you stay home and I'm at school."

Rob nudged him. "Go and brush your teeth."

"You really don't need to go to work today," Mel said as Alfie's footsteps receded up the stairs.

"I'm fine." My chair scraped when I stood. "It's just another day. Same as all the rest."

"Oh, Libby." Mel's voice caught in her throat, and her eyes filled with tears quicker than should be humanly possible. She turned away from me as the tears overflowed. The sob that erupted from her made my chest tighten again. Ignoring the lump in my throat, I gently rubbed her arm before making a quick exit out of the kitchen. I couldn't deal with her emotions. Rob would have her enveloped in a bear hug before I reached the stairs.

"You all right?" Josh asked, looming over me at the top of the stairs.

"Don't you start," I snapped, manoeuvring past

27

him to get to my room. *Alfie's room.*

"If you don't want to go to work, we could always spend the day in the pub . . ."

"That's a generous offer. You're so selfless. I can't believe you'd sacrifice a day of school to look after me. In the pub!"

"Anything for you, sis!"

"I'm not your s—" I stopped. He only called me *sis* to wind me up. The more I remind him that we're not in any way related, the more he calls me *sis*. Mel and Rob aren't my real aunt and uncle; I'd just grown up calling them that. My mum and Mel had been best friends since they met on their first day of school. So many of my childhood memories were from Rob and Mel's house. The garden of Mum's house had backed on to Rob and Mel's garden, and they'd always joked there was a Libby-shaped gap in the hedge that had grown as I did.

Their house was my second home, which had been amazing for so many years. But it turns out that second homes are only really amazing if you've actually got a first home. With Mum gone, along with the house I grew up in, I wasn't sure where to call home any more.

But that was exactly the sort of thinking that would ruin my day.

"What?" I muttered, letting go of my necklace that I'd been fingering absent-mindedly.

Josh looked quizzical. He'd asked me a question but I'd missed it. "Can you drive me to college?"

"If Mel doesn't need the car," I said. There were three drivers in the house and two cars, so I didn't drive as much as I'd like. Getting a car was second on my list of things to do – right behind finding somewhere else to live.

"She'll let you have the car," he told me confidently. "You can get whatever you want today."

He pulled the door closed as he walked away, and I sat at the desk, which doubled as my dressing table. My make-up was scattered between Alfie's Playmobil figures. Apparently, there'd been a battle between the pirates and the emergency services, and it was unclear who'd won. Certainly not my make-up, I decided as I reached for my foundation, which was lying on its side, having been pushed off the battlefield.

Mel tried her best to give me some space and privacy in the house, but there just wasn't enough room. Until two months ago, I'd been at university and living in halls of residence. Completing my degree after Mum died seemed to shock everyone. Repeatedly, I'd been told I could take some time off and finish uni the following year. It was difficult for me to figure out what they expected me to do though – sit around and cry, I guess. Since that wasn't an appealing option, I threw myself into my studies and got my degree. If that made me cold-hearted and unfeeling, so be it. It was certainly easier than thinking about the fact I'd never see my mum again and that I had no family other than my elderly grandmother.

After university, Mel and Rob assumed I would move in with them. For lack of any other plan, I went along with it, but I was adamant it was only temporary. Growing up, money had always been a struggle, but after the house had been sold there was a bit of money for me. I could use that to get my own

29

place. The idea played on my mind constantly, but for some reason, I was avoiding actually doing anything about it.

"Don't spend forever trying to make yourself look pretty," Josh shouted through the door. "There's not enough make-up in the world! Hurry up."

I smiled at my reflection as I heard Mel chastising him for teasing me. He'd have been briefed about being nice to me today. Poor fragile little Libby: that's what they thought of me. I hated it.

With a minimal amount of make-up applied to my freckly face, I gave my hair some attention, brushing the frizzy blonde mess back and twisting it before securing it to the back of my head with a sturdy clip. I ignored the wisps that fell down around my face.

Glaring at myself in the mirror, I took another deep breath and steeled myself for the day ahead.

Chapter 5

LIBBY – July 2017

My best friend, Heidi, was waiting in the staff room when I arrived at work. The room was otherwise deserted, and I was glad I didn't have to make polite conversation with anyone. Heidi was lying on the couch in the centre of the room and looked about twelve with her ridiculous pink hair in pigtails. Her hair was a different colour every few weeks, depending on her mood. Her fluffy purple jumper was partially covered by the awful grey tabard that was standard issue for hotel staff of a certain level. We had the glamorous title of chambermaids. I was sure they would soon have to update that description to something more modern and less ludicrous. I'd probably feel much better if I were referred to as a room technician or a bedroom attendant. Perhaps not the latter.

"I'm going to come straight out and ask," Heidi said, pausing from filing her nails. "Do you want a hug? We could just sit here and cry for the morning if you want? I'd deal with anyone who tried to interrupt."

I chuckled lightly as I started the process of extracting my outer layer of clothing and readying myself for a morning of making beds and cleaning up after a bunch of strangers. "No, thanks!"

"We can find a minibar to raid if you want?"

"I don't think so."

"A regular-sized bar then, if you insist!"

"Did Mel message you?" I asked, pulling on the ugly grey tabard and switching my shoes for a pair of well-worn Crocs.

"Only like a thousand times," Heidi said, swivelling to sit upright on the couch. "She told me to look out for you today. As if I don't look out for you every day! She's actually driving me a bit crazy. You know she had the cheek to invite me over for dinner tonight?"

"She is awful sometimes," I said, deadpan. "What a cow."

"But why does she think I need an invitation? Is she trying to make a point about all the times I come around without being invited? Like every Friday night for the past ten years! I'm family. Why do I suddenly need an invite?"

"Well, you're not *actually* family," I reminded her.

"*They're* your family, and *I'm* your family, so I'm related to them through you."

"Just two small flaws to that equation," I said flatly. "I'm not related to them or you!"

"I'm your best friend!" she said, outraged. "We're bound by the knowledge of each other's deepest secrets and most embarrassing moments. It's more of a tie than blood, that is. And of course Mel and Rob are your family. You say the weirdest things sometimes. I don't know why you insist on identifying as a poor little orphan girl."

"I don't!" I spluttered. Heidi stared at me, her eyebrows at odd angles. "I'm not even an orphan," I mumbled. "I have a father somewhere."

Heidi settled herself back into the couch. "Let's talk about him."

"Let's not." Sometimes I wished I'd never mentioned my father to Heidi. The snippets of information I'd found out about him before Mum died had played on my mind for a while, and I'd confided in Heidi at the time. I still knew little more than his name. Heidi had been more excited by the revelation than me. She'd spent time searching for him on the internet but hadn't found out much, other than that he still lived in Australia – where my mum had met him. Heidi had wanted to get on the first plane and go track him down. The more Heidi encouraged me, the more I laughed it off as a crazy idea. After all, I'd managed perfectly well without a father for twenty-one years; why did I need one now?

Because you don't have a mother any more, the annoying voice inside my head reminded me.

"We should pack in our jobs and go search him out," Heidi said excitedly. She suggested this approximately once a week. "We could do with an adventure."

"Come on," I said, pulling the door. "Let's clean some hotel rooms. That's quite enough adventure for me."

Heidi followed with a sigh. "You're really boring. If you'd listen to me sometimes we'd have way more fun!"

I decided a change of conversation was needed. "So, you're coming for dinner tonight?"

"I don't know. It's awkward now Mel's invited me. I feel like I'd have to bring something – flowers or a pudding or something. It's not good etiquette to turn up empty-handed if someone's invited you for dinner."

"You're probably right!"

"Sod it. I'll just come, shall I? If she's expecting flowers she'll just have to be disappointed."

Chapter 6

LIBBY – July 2017

I thought I'd done so well. It was as though I'd switched my emotions off. Actually, it was better than that; I'd been cheerful and happy, and I hadn't even thought about biting anyone's head off. Apparently that's how my grief usually channelled its way out of me.

Heidi had come home with me after work and we'd helped Mel cook. The six of us had eaten dinner together and – ignoring the sympathetic half-smiles that Aunt Mel kept giving me – it was the usual mix of chatting, bickering and laughing. Mum would have been proud of us.

Josh left as soon as he'd eaten. It was Friday night and he was off to a friend's house to play computer games. That was the story, anyway. He'd actually be going to a pub to indulge in some underage drinking. Mel and Rob knew that too, though went along with the pretence that he was soberly sitting at a friend's house under parental supervision. It was fairly standard behaviour for a seventeen-year-old.

Heidi didn't hang around long either. She offered

to stay and watch films with me, but I knew she was dying to get out and meet up with the guy who she'd been dating for a few weeks. I told her I was tired, absolving her of best friend duties.

It was when I was alone in my room that evening that the silent tears appeared, as though a tap had been turned on. I ached for my mum, and the grief wrapped itself around my throat, making it hard to breathe. Burying my head in the pillow, I waited for the feelings to pass, as they always did, eventually.

Surprisingly, I managed to calm down without slipping tearfully into an emotionally exhausted slumber. I dragged myself from the bed and rooted in the wardrobe for the photo album which I'd avoided looking at for more than six months. After Mum died, I'd spent hours poring over it, until I'd decided it was becoming an unhealthy obsession and forced myself to leave it alone. I was suddenly drawn to it again and sat on the floor hunched over as I slowly turned the pages.

I'd looked through the album so many times, it was like looking at old friends. Joe Sullivan's smiling face was etched into my brain. I'd searched his face for some part of myself. Despite us having the same hair and eye colour, I struggled to see any real resemblance. His blonde hair was a similar shade to mine, but his was straight and smooth whereas mine was frizzy.

I didn't even know if Joe Sullivan knew I existed. Had he known and wanted nothing to do with me? Or had Mum never told him about me? She hadn't managed to tell me the details, but the way she spoke his name made him sound like the loveliest man on earth. So why wouldn't she have told him about me? Why had she left Australia and never looked back? It didn't make sense.

I needed to know, I realised. The questions had niggled at me for a year, and I began to understand that they would never go away. The unanswered questions would eat away at me until I couldn't take it any more. I had to do what Mum had asked and find this mysterious Joe Sullivan. She had told me a few days before she passed away that I should find him. Up until then, I'd dismissed it as a drug-induced deathbed request which could definitely be ignored.

I snapped the album shut, scooped it up and went downstairs. Alfie was already in bed and the house was still for once.

"Do you want a drink?" Rob asked as we met at the bottom of the stairs. He had a beer in one hand and a red wine in the other.

"No thanks," I replied, following him into the living room.

"I thought you were already asleep," Mel said, managing to avoid asking if I was okay.

"Do you know anything about my father?" I asked. Mel's eyes darted from the TV to me. Rob hit mute and the room fell silent. "I think this is him," I told Mel, perching beside her on the couch and opening the photo album to a picture of Joe; he was sitting on a bar stool and beaming at the camera.

I'd never shown Mel the album or told her that Mum had spoken to me about my father. She calmly took the album from me and flicked through it. Rob hovered, glancing at the photos with an odd look on his face.

"This is from when she was in Australia," Mel mused without looking at me. She closed the book to look at the cover before turning the pages once more. The puzzled look on her face told me she didn't have any answers for me. "Why do you think he's your father?"

"Mum told me before she died . . ."

Mel looked sympathetic. "You know she didn't always know what she was saying at the end, don't you?"

"Yeah. But she was adamant about this. She told me to find him. She talked about this little town in Australia. She wanted me to go."

Mel's smile was condescending but she said nothing, just scanned the photos.

"You must know *something*," I prompted. "She was your best friend. She must have told you."

"She *should* have told me," Mel said. "It was one of the only things that ever caused any real friction between us. She wouldn't tell me, and it hurt me that she wouldn't confide in me. She used to say she'd gone home with some guy after a night out. I didn't believe she couldn't remember anything about him, that she couldn't track him down somehow."

"So you think this guy could be my dad?"

She shrugged. "She was different when she came back from Australia. We weren't as close. I always thought she felt sorry for me – she'd been on this big adventure and I'd stayed here, getting on with my boring life."

"Thanks!" Rob said, from the arm of the couch.

She smiled up at him. "We'd planned to go to Australia together, but then I met Rob and changed

38

my mind. She was annoyed but went alone. When she got back, things weren't the same. I was shocked when I found out she was pregnant. She kept to herself and I barely saw her. Then she called me after you were born and we got back to how we had been."

She paused, deep in thought. "Whenever I asked her about your father she'd clam up and wouldn't talk about it. Eventually, I realised it was something I would never know and accepted it. I stopped asking."

"This is him," I said, touching the familiar photo of Joe Sullivan in the book. "And I want to find him. I need to know what happened."

Rob's laugh made me jump. "No." He shook his head as though I'd said something stupid. He was the one who was usually on my side. I'd often been able to sway Mum or Mel to my way of thinking if I'd had Rob nearby to back me up.

"No?"

"I'm sorry," he said, standing to pace the room. "You're not flying halfway around the world on a wild goose chase. You've no idea who this guy is. Your mum was drugged up to the eyeballs – there's no way she'd actually want you to try and track down some long-lost relatives. If she'd wanted to know your father, she had plenty of time to do something about that while she was alive."

"But she didn't," I snapped. "And I want to know. I might have lots of family out there who I know nothing about."

"You've got us! We're your family."

"Of course you are," I said gently. "But we're not actually related. Not by blood. I want to find my real family, if I have any."

39

"I understand," Mel said.

"You're not going to go along with this craziness, are you?" Rob snapped.

"It's not crazy," she insisted. "I think it's perfectly natural. But let's take some time and think things over. We'll find out what we ca—"

"No," I said firmly. "I just want to go and find him."

"No way!" Rob said.

"I'm an adult!" I reminded him, though at that moment I'm fairly sure I didn't sound like one. "And I've got the money. I'm not asking your permission." Tears welled in my eyes. I never argued with Rob, and I hadn't expected this to be such a big issue.

"Think it through for a minute," Rob said. "How do you think this guy is going to react if you turn up on his doorstep claiming to be his daughter?"

"Rob!" Mel looked at him sternly, and he inhaled deeply before sitting beside me.

"I'm sorry," he said, brushing my hair off my face to look at me. "I just don't want you to get hurt. And I don't want you to waste your money flying round the world looking for someone who shares your DNA."

"It's not just that," I confessed, as the tears spilled from my eyes. I was descending into a blubbering mess but was powerless to stop it. "I need to get away. I want to get out of Alfie's room and out from under your feet. I'm sick of being in the way. I need a change."

"You've never been in the way," Rob whispered, pulling me to him and fighting off his own tears. "We should have cleared out Alfie's room – made it yours. The boys don't mind. You staying here wasn't

40

supposed to be a temporary arrangement. You're part of this family the same as any of us."

I sobbed into his shoulder, mortified he could think I hadn't felt welcome when I always had.

"I know," I managed.

"You're not going anywhere," Rob said, kissing the top of my head. "You're just having a bad day. I'll clear all that bloody Lego out of your room and you'll feel better."

"Uncle Rob!" I called when he got up. "The Lego isn't the problem." The stairs creaked under his weight, and I wiped at my eyes. "Has he really gone to clear the room out *now*?"

Mel chuckled beside me. "You know what he's like once he gets an idea in his head!"

I sighed and lowered my head to my hands.

"This place looks beautiful," Mel said, flicking through the album once more. She stopped on a page full of pictures of waterfalls. Mum and her friends lazed in pools, beer bottles in their hands. Mum glowed with her bronze tan and the happiness that radiated out from the pictures. "I think you should go."

I caught Mel's eye, never expecting her to agree with me on this one.

"Keep an open mind. This guy might not even remember your mum. But why not go on an adventure? It might do you good. Go to the places that your mum went, see the things she saw and maybe meet some of these people. If they're still there. Just don't forget that we're your family and we're always here for you."

"What about Uncle Rob?"

41

"He'll come around. You're his little girl. He'll just be worried you won't come back."

"I'll always come back. I do appreciate everything you've done for me." My eyes welled up again. "I love you. All of you."

"I know," she said, pulling me to her in a warm embrace. "And we love you. So much."

Once the decision had been made, I was relieved. The urge had been there for a long time and ignoring it hadn't worked. I would go to Australia and find this little outback town. And maybe I'd find the mysterious Joe Sullivan while I was at it.

Chapter 7

EVELYN – May 1994

What the hell should I do? It was hard to think rationally, sitting at the side of the road in the blistering heat. No great ideas came to me so I stayed where I was, thinking that at some point I'd have to swallow my pride and walk back to the farm. Ten minutes later, a vehicle came towards me, throwing up dust as it approached. I jumped to my feet and waved in a half-hearted attempt to flag down the battered old pickup truck. *Please don't be an axe-murderer.*

The tyres crunched on the gravel when it slowed, and I moved to peer gingerly into the passenger window. The girl looked about my age – early twenties – and her smile immediately put me at ease. Her eyes sparkled, and my first thought was that she was absolutely beautiful. Not in the face-full-of-make-up-and-trying-too-hard way but really naturally beautiful. Her light-brown hair looked like silk and complemented her lightly tanned skin. She wore a pretty, pale pink dress that hugged her slender frame.

"You all right?" a friendly voice asked from the

43

driving seat. The guy also looked to be about my age and had kind eyes. Tufts of soft blonde hair poked out from under his cap. They certainly looked like respectable citizens. In fact, they were such a stunning couple that they could've been a pair of Hollywood stars who'd got lost on location.

"Yeah," I said, looking up and down the road, weighing up my options once more. "Well, actually, I've been better."

"Need a ride?" the girl asked.

"Yes, please," I said without hesitation. I did not want to go back to the farm.

"I'm Joe," the guy told me as I climbed in. "And this is Beth."

She moved over to make room for me, and I fumbled to put my seatbelt on.

"There's a knack to it," Joe said, leaning over and clicking it into place for me.

"You weren't at Len's place, were you?" Beth asked as we rolled down the dusty road with the warm air blowing through the windows. It was suffocating.

"Air con's knackered," Joe said, reading my mind and pointing to the footwell, where bottles of water rolled in unison.

I reached for one and gulped it down, not caring that it was probably hot enough to make a cup of tea with. "Yes," I finally replied. "But I've decided farm work isn't for me."

"I'm not surprised," Beth remarked.

Joe glanced at me, raising his voice as the truck rattled over potholes. "Len has a special kind of regime. It's not the norm. I thought they'd stopped sending girls up there."

"It was awful," I said. "Thank goodness you came along."

"You were lucky," Beth said. "There's not usually much traffic out this way. Where're you from?"

"England," I said, launching into the usual conversation about myself. By the time we approached Kununurra, I'd found that Joe and Beth both lived in Kununurra and had gone to school together. Joe worked at a camping shop and Beth had a job in the beauty salon, though she wanted to run her own salon one day. They'd had an unexpected day off together and had been swimming at nearby springs. I felt comfortable with them immediately. They seemed so in love and were the sort of couple who would finish each other's sentences and know exactly what the other was thinking. It should've been sickening, but they were actually very sweet.

"You're staying at Walkabout Hostel, I presume?" Joe asked, as we turned off the highway and into town.

"No, the Kununurra Croc."

His eyes widened. "You've been working at Len's place *and* you're staying at the Croc? You don't have high standards, do you?"

"To be fair, this was only day two at the farm. And Walkabout Hostel was full so I didn't have much choice."

"There's always the hotel," Beth said. "You could probably get yourself a job there too."

"I didn't know there was a hotel," I said. "Not that I could afford it anyway."

Joe parked outside the Croc and leaned on the steering wheel. "They have accommodation for staff."

"I actually don't mind the Croc." It definitely wasn't the nicest place I'd stayed, but it had its charms.

"Weirdo," Joe said with a laugh.

My brow creased but I couldn't help but smile. He spoke to me as though I were an old friend and not some hitch-hiker he'd just picked up on the road.

"Thanks so much for the lift. I'd probably just be a puddle on the side of the road now if it weren't for you."

"Anytime," Joe said as I hopped out of the truck.

I looked at Beth. "It was nice to meet you both."

Her smile lit up her face.

"See you around," Joe said.

Hope so, I thought as they pulled away.

***

The next couple of days were mostly spent lounging by the public pool, the water soothing my aching limbs until I started to feel normal again. I spent an evening in Kelly's Tavern – referred to simply as the Tav by the locals – and tried not to think about my dwindling funds. At least the accommodation was cheap. I needed to make a plan of what to do next, but every time I thought about it I came up blank. Broome would be the obvious next stop, but I was reluctant to get back on the road and was enjoying having a room to myself.

"You should get a swimming pool here," I said to Stan when I sat beneath a tree, having a picnic lunch on Saturday afternoon.

"Too expensive," he said flatly.

"But if you had a pool and did the place up a bit – made the rooms nicer and tidied up the garden – then you could charge more and you'd make the money back."

"Full of ideas, aren't you?"

"You could have a little bar by the pool, serve cold beers and cocktails and a few snacks. You could even have themed nights."

"I'd have to employ someone if I did that."

"But you'd make more money so you'd be able to."

"I like things how they are," he said.

"This place has so much potential. The garden could be a real feature if you jus—" I jumped up to follow him as he walked away. "Honestly, you should get a gardener. The place could be incredible."

"I manage the garden quite well myself," he said huffily, stopping in front of a large shed. "In fact, I'm going to mow the grass, so I'll ruin your peace. Maybe you should head off for a walk or go and find someone to talk to in the Tav . . ."

"Are you trying to get rid of me?"

"You talk a lot," he said, rolling a cumbersome old lawnmower past me. I looked into the shed at the array of tools and junk.

"I could help you," I suggested, reaching for a pair of shears which hung on the wall. My body seemed to produce an involuntary negative response to the tools, but I ignored it. I could probably never look at a pumpkin again, but I could manage a bit of gardening. "I could trim the hedges."

Stan looked dubious.

"I can't really mess it up, can I?" I said. "It could hardly look any worse."

"Now you're being offensive!"

I fluttered my eyelashes at him. "Come on, let me help."

"I'm not paying you."

"You don't have to. I'll work for the satisfaction of making the place look nice."

"I could probably stretch to a beer, I suppose."

"Perfect!" I said, setting off with the rusty old shears. "I'll start around the main path to make it more appealing when people walk in."

He waved me off and brought the lawnmower to life with an almighty roar. I'd expected it to be satisfying, hacking back the thick shrubs and bushes, but I soon realised my mistake. My hands hadn't quite recovered from the farm work, and I struggled to grip the shears properly. Then there was the heat: sweat trickled down my body as I fought with the foliage. The shears were old and rusty and not really up to the task, even if I'd been working at my full strength. Back in the shed I searched for another pair, but the ones I found weren't much better.

"S'ppose you're gonna blame my tools when you can't manage the job?" Stan asked as I set off for round two.

"I'll manage!" I shouted over my shoulder. Nothing made me more determined than someone telling me I couldn't do something. After an hour, though, I'd barely made a dint. I was tired and thirsty and my arms looked like I'd been mauled by a wild animal. I'd hardly registered the bushes which scraped my skin, but glancing down now I looked like I'd

ALWAYS WITH YOU

been attacked. I was fairly sure I had a scratch across my forehead too.

"The bushes won then?" Stan remarked when I wandered into the office.

"For today, yes. But tomorrow is another day. It's too hot now, but I'll start early tomorrow and the place will look great in no time."

"I'm not paying you," he reminded me.

"I know that, grumpy pants! A little thanks wouldn't go amiss."

"I didn't ask you to hang around here getting in my way," he said. Reaching into the fridge beside the desk, he produced a can of Coke and passed it to me. "You know, if you want someplace fancy to stay, it'd be much easier for you to get a room at the hotel than try and makeover this place. You could get a job there too."

"You're not the first person to suggest that," I said. "I'm being helpful, though. I'm not sure why you're in such a rush to get rid of me."

"I don't need help," he grumbled. "I managed fine before you got here, didn't I?"

"That's debatable," I said cheekily, taking a swig of the blissfully cool drink. "I suppose I will go and check out the hotel. I'm going to need a job if I'm going to stay around here. And I really don't feel I can leave you!" I flashed a mischievous grin.

"I'm sure Arthur will tempt you with his lovely staff accommodation. En-suite bathrooms and everything over there. If you can put up with him, that is – he's a miserable old fart."

"Well, that says a lot coming from you! Don't worry, I'm only going to ask about a job. I'm not

49

leaving this place until it's shipshape."

"It's fine as it is," he shouted after me as I waltzed out the door.

Chapter 8

EVELYN – May 1994

Kununurra was unlike anywhere I'd been before, and it fascinated me. When I'd quizzed Stan, he told me he reckoned there were about three to four thousand permanent residents in the town, though that number would rise if you included people on surrounding farms and stations. There were also a lot of tourists buzzing around, he told me with raised eyebrows. Considering his livelihood depended on tourists, you'd think he'd have a bit more patience for them.

I was happy when he told me there were a couple of clothes shops over by the big Coles supermarket. I planned on treating myself to some new flip-flops. Stan had looked at me funny when I'd shown him how worn out my current pair were. He insisted they were called thongs, and I explained that thongs should never be worn on feet. It was an amusing conversation that left Stan blushing.

The Kununurra Hotel was located on the other side of town, just before the petrol station. It was set back from the road and fronted by a row of palm trees, which gave the place an exotic feel. I found the front desk unmanned and the place quiet. There were no signs of life until I reached the bar area in a large courtyard at the back of the hotel.

A familiar face beamed at me from the edge of a small swimming pool in the middle of the open space. It was Joe. "We meet again!" Water dripped from his hair and glistened down his toned torso.

"Hi!" I said, making my way between the tables towards him. I smiled at Beth, who was sitting nearby with another girl. "I thought I'd take your advice and see if I could find myself a job."

"And a nicer place to stay?" Beth asked.

"No. Honestly, I like it at the Croc. And I promised Stan I'd help him out with some gardening." I looked down at my arms. "Although, it's not going well so far."

"Jeez," Joe said, standing and rubbing a towel over his hair. "You're one for punishment, aren't you?"

"Maybe! Do you know who I should ask about a job?"

"Arthur. If you dare!"

"You have to be thick-skinned to work here," the girl beside Beth said. "Arthur's not the easiest of characters."

"Can't be worse than Len Jenkins, can he?"

"You worked for Len?" she asked with an approving nod. "Maybe you'd cope with Arthur then. I'm Leslie, by the way."

"Evelyn," I said, thankful that not all the young people around here were stunningly beautiful. Leslie's dark curls matched her dark skin and deep brown eyes. She was pretty, but in a less obvious way than

Beth, who perhaps ought to be preserved in a museum somewhere. I actually found it hard not to stare at her.

"You want a beer?" Joe asked, moving to the bar.

I nodded. "You work here?"

"No. But we're friends with the owner's son. Todd's around somewhere – he'll be back in a minute."

"You went to school with him," Leslie said, looking at Joe. "I think calling him a friend is a stretch."

"Don't be mean," Beth said. "Todd's all right."

I'd just taken a seat beside Leslie when a booming voice rang out around us.

"You better be paying for that!" An older man stood glaring at Joe, who'd just taken a beer from the fridge behind the bar.

"Of course," Joe said casually.

"That's Arthur," Leslie told me quietly.

"Where the bloody hell is Todd?" Arthur asked.

"Store room, I reckon," Joe told him. "There he is."

A young skinny guy came in carrying a crate. "You need me?" he asked, looking at Arthur.

"Tuck yer bloody shirt in. You look a scruff. And don't go wandering off all the time."

"I'm restocking the fridges," Todd said, tucking in his shirt hastily.

"I'm going out for a while," Arthur told him. "Try not to run the place into the ground while I'm gone." He turned back to Joe. "And it's not a bloody social club, you know?"

"We just stopped in for a quick drink," Joe told him cheerfully. I took a swig of the beer he'd put in

53

front of me and tried to look inconspicuous. The rumours about Arthur were right, and I was happy he was leaving. "Mr Kingston," Joe called, stopping Arthur in his tracks. "This is our friend, Evelyn. She's looking for a job if there's anything going?"

I plastered on a smile as Arthur looked me up and down. "I might have something coming up. One of the cleaning girls is leaving. You need a place to stay as well, I suppose?"

I shook my head. "I only need a job."

"Come and see me on Monday," he said, before stalking away.

"Seems as though he likes you," Joe said, knocking Leslie's feet from the chair to sit down. "He's grumpy but if you keep your head down, it's probably not such a bad place to work. There's air con anyway!"

I was startled by a voice behind me. "You worked in a hotel before?"

"This is Todd," Beth told me.

Todd glared at me as he waited for me to answer. His tone was unfriendly and there was something unsettling about him. He was too thin and his dark eyes were set close together.

"No," I told him as he hovered awkwardly. "I really need a job though."

"It's not as easy as you'd think," he said.

"C'mon," Joe jumped in. "It's a cleaning job! Making beds and tidying up – it's not exactly rocket science, is it? You Kingstons really know how to make people feel welcome."

"I didn't mean . . ." Todd hesitated, looking flustered. "It's just that people always think it's an easy job. I'm only saying it's not that easy."

"Thanks for the warning," I said. "But I'm not afraid of hard work. I plan on giving the Croc a little makeover, and I don't think that will be easy either."

I earned myself a round of snorts and chuckles. "Stan won't like you messing with the Croc," Leslie said. "He's a big softie but he's set in his ways."

"I think the place could be amazing," I said. "I made a start trimming back the hedges, but his gardening tools are antiques."

"I used to help him out now and again," Joe told me. "But he just doesn't seem to care about the place any more."

"It makes the town look bad," Todd remarked. "He ought to give it up and retire. Dad would still buy the place."

Joe looked at me. "Arthur's been wanting to buy the Croc for years, but Stan says he'd rather run the place into the ground than let him get his hands on it."

I took a sip of my beer. "Well, he seems to be doing a good job of that."

We chatted until I finished the beer, which Joe insisted on paying for. I promised it was my round next time since I already felt in their debt for saving me from the side of the road.

I just hoped that meant I would be seeing more of them.

Chapter 9

EVELYN – May 1994

"You make friends quick, don't you?" Stan said when I arrived back at the Croc after an early morning swim on Sunday. I frowned quizzically. "Joe dropped some things off for you." He nodded over to the office, and I saw a selection of gardening tools propped up by the door.

I smiled to myself. "These will make life so much easier," I said, walking over to check them out. Not a hint of rust in sight.

"You're not giving up this idea then?"

"No, it's my project. Once I set my mind to something, that's it, I'm afraid."

"So you didn't get the job at the hotel?"

"Not yet, but I have an interview tomorrow."

He leaned against the office doorway. "You'll be leaving me then, I suppose."

"No chance," I said, winking at him. "I'd better get on." I threw my bag on the ground, picked up the shiny new shears and headed down the garden.

"Joe said he'd come and help you later," Stan called after me. "He's a good kid, that one."

I worked for two hours solid and was amused by the array of lizards I disturbed. Occasionally they made me jump, but generally I enjoyed watching them scuttle around. Cute little things. Stan brought me water at regular intervals and gave me a few gardening tips but showed no interest in helping me. When my arms got tired, I collapsed on my back under the shade of a tall tree, closing my eyes and listening to the birds singing gleefully.

They stopped abruptly when the roar of machinery filled the air. When I looked up, Joe was grinning at me with an electric hedge-trimmer held aloft. I laughed and wiped the sweat from my hairline. He took over at the part of the hedge where I'd stopped, moving at a steady speed, branches falling all around him. His khaki shorts showed off his deep tan, and the muscles in his back and arms flexed as he worked.

"A hedge-trimmer seems like cheating," I told him when he sat beside me half an hour later.

He grinned and handed me a can of beer. "It's a great invention, isn't it?"

"I would've managed it my way."

"Sure you would," he said. "Eventually!"

"It looks good, anyway." The gardens already looked bigger. I glanced around, weighing up what I'd do next.

"So you're planning on staying in town a while?" Joe asked.

"Yeah, I think so. If I get the job at the hotel anyway."

"And you plan on staying at the Croc?" He looked around.

"I like it," I said. "It's rough around the edges but

58

there's just something about the place. And I like Stan."

"He's a good guy. He lost his wife a couple of years ago, and I think he still doesn't know what to do with himself."

I frowned, suddenly seeing Stan in a different light. "That's sad."

"Yeah. It's nice that you're helping him out. I should come around more often. Right after Linda died, I was around here a lot, but I stopped coming so regularly. It just tailed off, you know? He didn't seem to want any help."

"He's a hard one to read," I said thoughtfully. "Sometimes I feel like I'm in his way but other times he seems to like the company."

"I'm sure he's enjoying having you around," Joe said, picking absent-mindedly at blades of grass. "Most people don't stay more than a night or two. He pretends he likes it that way, but I don't think it's true."

Stan came into view, ending our conversation. "Well, you've made a right bloody mess!" he said, looking at the discarded foliage strewn along the path.

"We've not finished yet, you old slave driver!" Joe told him, putting his beer can to one side. "Come on," he said to me. "Looks like the break's over!"

***

My job interview on Monday lasted about three minutes. Arthur sat behind his huge solid wooden desk and asked me a couple of questions before telling me I could start the following Monday. Todd spent the whole time lingering in the corner.

"Fill in these papers and bring them with you when you start," Arthur said gruffly. "Arrive on time every day and get the job done properly and we'll get along fine. I'll see you next week." He glared at Todd, who opened the door for me.

In the hallway, I cast my eyes over the papers. "That was easy," I said to Todd.

"Like he said, work hard and you'll be fine."

My eyebrows knotted together. Todd was an odd character. He seemed so unsure of himself, as though he wanted to be like his dad but couldn't quite pull it off. Although why anyone would aspire to be like Arthur was beyond me.

"Did you have a good weekend?" I asked, hoping to lighten the atmosphere.

"I run a hotel," he said, pompously. "Weekends are busy."

"You must get some time for fun?"

"Of course."

"I better go," I said, edging away. "I've been doing some work at the Croc and I want to get on with it. Joe kindly lent me some tools, so it's a bit easier now."

"He's got a girlfriend," Todd said. "Don't start causing trouble."

I lowered my eyebrows, unsure how to answer. It was an odd comment and I wanted to laugh. "I'm not . . . I mean, I know he's got a girlfriend. I met Beth, remember?"

"I'm just saying, that's all. Joe's too friendly for his own good sometimes."

"Thanks for the warning," I said flippantly. "See

you around, I guess."

I left the hotel with the distinct feeling that getting a job there might not be the best decision I'd ever made. Arthur and Todd had both put me on edge, and I got the impression that Todd was probably right: working there wouldn't be easy. Or, at least, working for the Kingstons wouldn't be easy. I'd give it a go and if it didn't work out I'd pack up my things and hit the road.

My brain was still whirring over Todd's warning when I bumped into Joe. He was across the road from the Croc, standing in front of a shop: Bushcamp Stores. It was the first time I'd really noticed it, but it was hard to miss now.

"So this is where you work?"

"Yep," he said, grinning at me. "My dad owns the place."

"How is it working with your dad?"

"It's fine. Most of the time. Sometimes I think he's going to drive me mad, but most of the time we get along well. It's easier since I moved out. Living together and working together wasn't ideal. Did you get the job?"

"Yes! I start next week."

"Congrats!" he said. "Off to celebrate then, are you?"

"Something like that. Stan's got more jobs for me!"

"You'll have that place looking great in no time." He paused. "I'm having a party on Friday. You should come and we can celebrate then?"

I accepted gratefully, happy to have something in my social calendar.

Chapter 10

EVELYN – May 1994

The next week was glorious. I enjoyed helping Stan out around the Croc, and he even left me to man the office one day while he went fishing. It was nice to see him relax a bit, especially after what Joe had told me about him losing his wife. My little stint at running the place wasn't exactly challenging. Some newly arrived guests asked me where the post office was, and I was happy to be able to answer their question. You could practically see the place from the Croc.

I also made my room a bit cosier that week, including buying a couple of cheap photo frames to display a picture of my parents. And one of Mel and me pulling silly faces on a night out before I left. I'd been sending Mel letters regularly and was excited to fill her in on my latest news – and to be able to give her an address for me. It would be fun to receive mail. When I'd first set off on my great adventure, I was annoyed that she wasn't coming too – as had been the plan – but the more time went on, the happier I was that I was doing it alone. Having Mel with me would have been good, but I got the feeling it would have been an entirely different adventure.

I saw Joe a couple of times that week when I was coming and going from the Croc. He always greeted me warmly and stopped to chat for a few minutes. On Friday, I treated myself to a haircut and was returning from the hairdresser when I saw him again.

"Hi!" I said, crossing the road to talk to him.

An older guy stepped out of the shop.

"This is my dad," Joe told me as he caught sight of him.

"Mick," he said, holding a hand out to me.

"Evelyn," I replied.

"So you're the one who got the job at the hotel?"

"That's me!"

"We put bets on how long people will stick it out there. If you can make it a month, I'd appreciate it!"

"Hey!" Joe said. "You're not allowed to influence her."

"Split your winnings with me and you've got a deal," I said.

"I like this one," he said to Joe. "I better get back to work, seeing as you're slacking off today."

"You're the one who said I could leave early," Joe protested.

"I know. Get off then, and don't go crazy just because it's your birthday!"

I fell into step with Joe as he shouted goodbye to Mick and walked towards his truck.

"You didn't tell me it's your birthday."

"It's my birthday!" he said with a boyish grin.

"Happy birthday then! I'm afraid I didn't get you anything."

"You could always help me and Leslie get ready for the party?"

"Okay," I agreed. "Where's Beth?"

"She's working," he said. "She always seems to be working. She'll join later."

The radio came on with the engine, and Joe opened the windows as we set off.

"Did you ever think about getting the air con fixed in your truck?" I asked. It felt like sitting in an oven.

He shook his head and grinned. "It's a ute! And yes, I've tried but it's beyond repair."

"Maybe it's time for a new *ute* then?"

He sucked air through his front teeth as though I'd said something offensive. "There's still life left in her yet," he said, patting the dashboard affectionately.

I smiled at Joe's attachment to his ute and was amused by the Aussie language too. I was picking up new words every day.

A few minutes later, we arrived at Leslie's house to find her waiting on the front porch.

She greeted me with a smile as she climbed in next to me and then leaned over to hug Joe. "Happy birthday, cousin! Twenty-two! Aren't you getting old and grown up?!"

"Don't need to act like it though, do I?" he asked.

"Not today, you don't!" she agreed.

***

It was hard to keep up with Leslie in the supermarket; she whizzed the trolley around, flinging in assorted snacks. She didn't consult Joe until we reached the alcohol aisle. He picked up a couple of cases of beer, a few bottles of wine and some soft drinks. With that done, we loaded everything into the back of the ute and drove to Joe's place. It was a small, ground-floor apartment in a convenient location, not far from the hotel.

"Do the neighbours mind you having parties?" I asked as I followed Joe and Leslie into the open-plan living room with a kitchenette in the corner. It felt quite homely for a bachelor pad.

"They're cool," Joe said. "It's all young people. They'll just join the party."

Leslie beamed in excitement. "I've got some very tacky birthday banners! Where do you want them?"

"Wherever you want," Joe replied as he filled the fridge with beers. Leslie looked to me.

"On the front door?" I suggested. "Maybe one above the TV and one on the opposite wall?"

"Perfect!" She rooted around in a bag and produced a bunch of banners and streamers.

"They look fine, don't they, Joe?" I asked a while later when we'd balanced precariously on chairs to hang the banners. Leslie looked unsure. They did look a little naff, but I didn't think anyone would really notice them anyway.

"They look great," Joe said reassuringly. "And after a few beers they might even look straight!"

Leslie gave him a playful shove and grabbed her bag. "Time to get changed. People will start arriving soon!" She seemed far more excited than Joe, and I guessed she was a few years younger than him.

We sat outside, sipping beers in silence until Leslie reappeared in a white mini-dress and high-heels. I gave an internal sigh as I looked down at myself. It hadn't even occurred to me that I wasn't dressed for a party.

"What do you think?" Leslie asked, giving us a twirl.

"I think you look fantastic," I said. "And I think I need to go and get changed!"

"You don't need to," Joe said kindly. "It's all pretty casual."

"I'd like to." It would be nice to at least have a shower and put on clean clothes. Not being a big sweaty mess was my aim for the evening.

Joe offered to drive me, but I was adamant I would walk. The shower was refreshing, and I threw on my trusty denim mini-skirt and a low-cut top with sequin detail. A pair of wedge sandals finished the look nicely, and I was glad I'd made the effort to come back and change. I felt ready for a party.

When I returned, Beth was outside the apartment, sitting on Joe's knee with a glass of wine in her hand. She wore a long flowing skirt and simple T-shirt but looked stunning as always. They were deep in conversation with a group of people and when they didn't notice me, I slipped inside in search of Leslie.

I found her in the kitchen and volunteered to help her dish up snacks. She was easy to be around. She introduced me to a few people, and I spent a while chatting to Joe's neighbour, Cam – a well-built guy with broad shoulders and several tattoos down his arms.

"When did you sneak in?" Joe asked when he eventually came inside for a beer.

"About an hour ago," I told him.

"I thought you'd decided to get on with your

gardening or something!"

Beth appeared beside him and gave me a hug. "Great to see you again," she said. "Congratulations on the job!"

"Lots to celebrate today," Cam said, slipping into the conversation. "We should do shots!"

I'm not sure if it was the heat or that I was tired, but the shots went straight to my head, and before long I found myself sitting outside, looking up at the stars, my head spinning as the party buzzed around me.

"Are you okay?" Beth asked, smiling down at me.

"Fine," I said. "But the shots have done me in. I think I better go home." When I stood, the earth swayed and I stumbled. Beth caught my arm and I giggled. "Sorry!" Out of the corner of my eye I could see Leslie attempting to do cartwheels on the thin strip of lawn in her mini-dress, so I felt comforted that it wasn't only me who was drunk.

"Don't worry," Beth said. "One of the boys will walk you back."

"I'll be fine," I said.

"I can walk you back," Joe offered.

"No! It's your party."

Cam appeared by my side. "I'll see you home," he said. "I wouldn't mind checking out the action at the Tav anyway."

Leslie's eyes flashed with excitement as she stumbled over to us. "I'm coming too!"

"It's Joe's birthday," I said. "You guys should stay here."

"Don't worry about it," Cam said. "This party will be going long after the Tav closes."

Joe thanked me for helping out and promised he didn't mind me stealing his friends. The walk sobered me enough that I accepted an invitation to join Cam and Leslie for another drink at the Tav. I was surprised at how busy it was. I wasn't sure where everyone had appeared from, and it was an interesting mix of locals and backpackers. Everyone seemed to be having a great time, and the atmosphere was jovial.

Until then, my time in Australia had mostly been spent with other backpackers from all over the world, so it made a refreshing change to spend time with locals. I had a definite feeling I was going to enjoy my time in Kununurra.

Chapter 11

LIBBY – August 2017

The flight passed quicker than I expected. I'd resigned myself to the fact it would take approximately forever, and my slight exaggeration meant it didn't seem such a long trip after all. It was hard to believe I was really going to Australia, and on my own too. Persuading Heidi that I needed to do this by myself had felt a little mean. She'd been quite understanding in the end. It helped that she couldn't really afford the trip. The goodbyes had been hard, but I felt a weight lift as soon as I boarded the plane. I would do some exploring and find some answers to my questions. Then I could move forward with my life. I'd be back in the UK before I knew it.

On the plane, I'd flicked between watching films and listening to music, dozing in between. I let my mind wander, imagining Mum making this same trip all those years ago. She would have been much chirpier than me. She'd have had the odd glass of wine and chatted to the people around her, telling them about her big adventure. Although maybe she'd thought of Mel too. Was she angry that Mel had left her to come alone? Maybe she spoke to no one and sank deep in her own thoughts, just as I was. Had she been scared about travelling alone? I think she'd have been excited. She was always so confident and positive. Mel backing out wouldn't have dampened her spirits for long.

The cabin lights were dim as we made our approach, and I gazed out at Sydney, lit up in the darkness. From where I was sitting, it dazzled and buzzed with life. *Mum had loved her time in Australia. I wonder what's in store for me.* I could be anyone, I realised. No one knew me, and I could reinvent myself as whoever I wanted. If I was going to walk in my mum's shoes, I should probably do it her way. No moping around for me – I'd be outgoing and sociable and have the time of my life, just like her. I'd try not to get pregnant, but otherwise I'd follow her example.

The strap of my backpack dug into my shoulder as I dragged it towards a waiting taxi outside the airport. The sun had only just risen and the air was chilly. I shivered when I climbed into the back of the taxi. *I thought Australia was supposed to be hot.* I gave the driver the name of the youth hostel I'd found online and relaxed into the journey, thankful he wasn't the chatty type. I'd put my sociable and outgoing plan into action once I was settled.

The cute guy at the reception of Sydney Backpackers asked me about my plans. Smiling weakly, I told him I was heading north, along the coast to Darwin. He nodded. It was the popular route, he informed me cheerfully. I didn't mention that I planned to continue to a little outback town in search of the father I'd never met. All he saw was a young girl on a gap year looking for an adventure. He didn't need to know otherwise. I rounded off the conversation with my complaints of jet lag and he handed over a key attached to a wooden fob, the number eight written haphazardly in marker.

The room contained two sets of bunk beds. Two girls around my age stood between them, chatting as they rummaged through their backpacks. Declining their offer to join them for sightseeing, I crawled into bed. Sleep came in an all-consuming wave of black, leaving me confused and groggy when I woke more than four hours later.

My roommates arrived back to find me showered and revived. I was keen to get out and explore, but the day had worn on and instead I joined them for a barbecue and drinks in the courtyard of the hostel. It was a nice scene: a canopy of dried palm leaves shaded the bar, and the outdoor furniture was crafted from untreated wood, giving a rustic feel.

"You on a gap year?" Carol, the girl with a blonde bob and a hint of a Scottish accent, asked me.

My mind raced through my complicated story before I made a decision. I could be whoever I wanted to be. Did I want everyone I met over the next few weeks to hear the story of my dead mother and my long-lost father? Did I want to see their reactions and encounter the inevitable uncomfortable silences? No, thanks. In fact, I didn't want anyone to know. Not one person. Lying didn't come naturally to me and would make me uncomfortable, but a twist of the truth would be okay. A smile tickled my lips as I realised I could finally shed my grieving daughter coat and just be me

HANNAH ELLIS

again. Whoever that was.

"Yes," I said. "I just finished uni and decided I'd see a bit of the world before I tied myself down to a proper job."

"You'll have a brilliant time," red-headed Jenny said, her eyes lighting up. "We've just done the coastal route up to Darwin. I want to do it all again now."

"How long have you been travelling?" I asked.

"Six weeks," Carol replied. "And we're getting low on money so we'll have to look for jobs when we reach Perth."

"Is that where you're heading next?"

They nodded in unison. "We blew the last of our savings on tickets for the Indian Pacific," Jenny said, joyfully.

"This one's quite excited," Carol said, patting Jenny's knee. "I'm not quite sure how I feel about spending sixty-five hours on a train."

"A historic train across the Nullarbor Plain!" Jenny said, her eyes glazing over. "Doesn't it sound romantic?"

"It does," I agreed, wondering for the briefest moment about the nature of Jenny and Carol's relationship. When Carol reached over to kiss Jenny tenderly, my question was answered. Sipping my tequila sunrise, I caught the eye of the barman, blushing when he winked at me. In that moment, the world was a wonderful place. This adventure was exactly what I'd been in need of. I'd find myself, find my dad, find some peace, find some closure. But first, I'd drink cocktails and dance the night away with my new friends while stealing glances at the dishy barman.

Chapter 12

LIBBY – August 2017

Daylight burned my eyeballs, and I grunted at the person gently shaking my shoulder.

"We're going," Jenny said. "We've got to catch the train."

Confused, I battled to make my dry mouth produce the right words. "Today? You're leaving today?"

"Yeah. Why don't you come with us?" Carol said.

"To Perth?"

"Yes!" Jenny said. "Come with us."

"Can't," I muttered. "Going up to Darwin. And I can't move."

"You're such a party animal!" Carol teased. "What time did you get to bed in the end?"

I rubbed my eyes as memories of the previous evening hit me in flashes. A jumble of faces and voices, snippets of conversations. I'd danced, I'd laughed, I'd had fun. "No idea," I said. "Too late."

"We've got to go," Jenny said with a frown. When she leaned down to hug me awkwardly, I felt a pang of regret. It would have been fun to spend more time with them. The idea of travelling alone seemed suddenly lonely. I wished the three of us were heading in the same direction.

Carol patted my arm. "Go back to sleep. We left our email addresses on top of your bag. Keep in touch, won't you?"

"And look us up if you find yourself in Perth," Jenny said as she lugged her backpack onto her shoulder. "We'll probably be there a few months at least."

"I will! Have a great time."

"We will!" they promised. The door closed behind them, and I was asleep again within minutes.

When I came round, it was the middle of the afternoon, and I cursed myself for wasting so much of the day. I was slightly perturbed by the book and hairbrush which lay on the adjacent bunk. Someone had been in the room and I hadn't even stirred. My new roommate had obviously arrived and then left to explore for the day without me noticing. I didn't even feel refreshed by my mammoth sleep; a hangover lingered and my head was banging. The bottle of water beside my bed was a welcome sight, and I gulped every last drop before moving to the bathroom and sticking my mouth under the tap.

With great effort, I made myself presentable and dragged myself out, intent on seeing something of Sydney. Two familiar young guys sat in the foyer of the hostel, huddled over a map.

"You look like I feel," the taller of the two said, glancing up at me as I hovered in front of a wall full of flyers advertising an array of tourist attractions and day trips. I swiped at my hair. Perhaps I wasn't quite as presentable as I thought.

The second guy gave me a puzzled look. "We were dancing last night, weren't we?"

"Yeah." *If you say so.* "I'm Libby."

He reached to shake my hand. "Phil."

I turned to his friend and offered my hand. "Max," he told me before gesturing to the map spread out on the table. "Got any hot tips?"

"I just arrived. I don't know where I'm going myself."

"Hangovers don't help, do they?" Phil said. "Let's just wander and see what we find."

As they attempted to refold the map, I resumed staring at the tourist wall.

"You wanna come with us?" Phil asked.

With a shrug and a nod, I followed them out into the bright Sydney sunshine. As with Jenny and Carol, it didn't take long for me to become attached to Phil and Max. They were best friends from East London and were easy-going sightseeing companions. Over the next three days, we roamed the dazzling city, taking in the Opera House, Bondi Beach, Circular Quay, Darling Harbour and an array of fantastic places.

We drank beers in glorious sunshine outside a trendy bar overlooking the harbour. We got lost, defiantly resisting the urge to turn on mobile roaming data, instead bickering over the map and pointing out street signs before marching on, only to find ourselves even more lost. I developed private jokes with Max and Phil, and they teased me about the shade of green I turned at the top of the harbour bridge after they talked me into doing the bridge climb with them. We had our photo taken at the top, huddled together as though we were old friends. A bar close to the hostel offered nightly drink specials so that was where we spent our evenings.

On day four, they got on a bus to Melbourne and I felt as though I'd just come out of a long-term relationship. *What will I do without Max and Phil?* I remembered how we'd laughed at Phil's sunburned nose. The memory of dancing with Max as we made our way from the bar to the hostel after too many cocktails brought a smile to my lips. *But what now? I don't want to travel alone. I want Max and Phil or Jenny and Carol.* It was rare to meet people and have such an immediate connection.

My plans to go to Kununurra became hazy. Maybe all I really needed was a change of scenery and to let my hair down. Finding long-lost relatives sank lower and lower down my list of things to do in Australia.

Alone in the hostel bar the evening after Max and Phil left, I met Jamie. She was American and intrigued me immediately because I'd never known a female Jamie before. She was confident and fun. By the end of the evening we were firm friends, and desperate not to lose another friend, I accepted her invitation to travel north with her the following day.

Leaving Sydney behind, we made slow progress on a Greyhound bus. When we finally arrived in Byron Bay we had another new friend: Mieke, from Holland. Her English was excellent and she had a wicked sense of humour. We checked into a hostel just a few minutes' walk from the beach and then went out to explore, just as the sun was setting over the water. I'd been determined to have an early night but we ended up at Cheeky Monkeys, a popular tourist bar, and danced on tables until the early hours. It was just too much fun to leave.

The next few days were a blur of swimming and sunbathing, drinking and sleeping. Mieke carried on northwards and was replaced in our dorm by Jess and Lisa, sisters from Ireland. A few days later – with hugs and a heavy heart – I left Jamie in Byron Bay and continued up the coast with my Irish friends. We stayed together through the bustle of Surfers Paradise and Brisbane, with some more relaxing and less touristy stops in between. We parted ways in Brisbane, and I spent a day exploring the city alone before hopping on a bus to Noosa.

It was the first time in weeks I'd stopped to think about the reason I'd come to Australia. I'd been too busy blending into the backpacker scene and enjoying my time as a normal twenty-one-year-old. As far as anyone around me was concerned, the only baggage I carried was the hefty backpack which seemed to fluctuate in weight depending on how much I'd had to drink the previous evening. I was still a fair way from Darwin, but it began to play on my mind what I would do from there. If only I had a crystal ball to show me what I would find in Kununurra. I just needed a clue. Was it a good idea or not? Whenever I'd spoken to Rob on the phone, he'd told me to forget the idea – that I should just enjoy my holiday and then come home to them. He was pleased when I agreed that he was probably right.

Chapter 13

EVELYN – May 1994

The first shock in my new job was the uniform.

"Oh my goodness. Are you kidding?" I asked Mrs Kingston as she held it out. *Surely they're having a joke at my expense.* Mrs Kingston didn't seem like much of a joker though. Arthur's wife looked to be at least ten years younger than her husband but had the same cold manner. She hadn't offered her first name and treated me like an inconvenience in her day.

Glaring at me, she instructed me to change in a curtained-off corner of the room. *She wasn't joking about the uniform, then.* I squeezed into the too-tight and too-short black skirt and pulled the frilly nylon blouse into place as best as I could. My cleavage was very much on display, and I frowned when I looked down at myself, hoping that this *was* just a cleaning job; I was dressed more like a hooker.

"It's quite small," I remarked, emerging gingerly from behind the curtain.

"I'll see if we have a bigger size. That will do for today though. It looks fine."

I tugged at the top in an attempt to decrease my

cleavage and increase my dignity. It had little effect. "A bigger size might be better," I agreed. *A bigger size? Yeah, right, because it's the fit that's the problem. Am I really going to degrade myself like this? Do I really need a job that much?*

"Where do I start then?" I asked, disgusted at myself but deciding that I really needed a job – and an income – for a little while. It didn't seem like the sort of establishment where you could argue about the uniform on the first day. Or any day, come to think of it. So far, the Kingston family all seemed to be sadly lacking in compassion and people skills.

"Follow me," Mrs Kingston said, aloof and impatient. "Let's make sure you know exactly how to do the job and hopefully tomorrow you can be left to do it alone."

At the front desk, she showed me how to check which rooms were being vacated and would need a thorough clean and which were still occupied and only in need of straightening out. Next, I had a tour of the stock cupboard and loaded up a trolley with supplies before continuing to the first bedroom of the day. Mrs Kingston stood in the centre of the room, giving instructions and watching my every move. She checked that everything was done meticulously, haughtily smoothing wrinkles from freshly made beds and compulsively turning toiletries to stand at an exact angle. Joe had been right; it wasn't rocket science, but Mrs Kingston made it seem like the most important job in the world, and having her shadow me the whole time was exhausting.

"It seems like you'll be fine on your own tomorrow," she told me when I finished the last room of the day. I guessed that was the closest to a compliment I would ever get from Mrs Kingston. "I do regular checks, so don't think you can cut corners."

"Of course not," I said, eager to get out of the awful uniform and away from the place, which suddenly seemed stifling. Mrs Kingston left me in the staff room with a curt nod and a warning about always being on time.

Back in my own clothes and heading back through the hotel, I passed Todd. "Survived the first day then?" he asked in a tone that implied he wasn't sure I would have lasted this long.

I squinted up at him. "I managed," I told him lightly. "Are you working on the bar again today?"

"I go where I'm needed," he said. "Anything that needs doing, I do it. I'll be running this place one day. It's way more than a bar job for me."

"Okay." I'd only intended to pass the time of day; I didn't actually care what his duties were. He'd definitely inherited his parents' air of superiority. "See you tomorrow then!" I said, desperate to get away from him.

"Don't be late," he warned, his voice suddenly an octave deeper. My curtsy came out of nowhere, and the laughter erupted from me involuntarily. I wasn't sure I was going to last long in the employment of the Kingstons.

***

"Hi!" Joe called as I walked back to the hostel. He was busy unloading boxes with Mick from a truck

85

outside of Bushcamp. "How was the first day?"

"Better than working for Len," I said. "Sorry, Mick, I'm not sure I can cope with that uniform for a month!"

A look passed between them.

"What's wrong with the uniform?" Joe asked with a cheeky grin. "I always think it looks pretty good!"

"You would," I said, rolling my eyes and continuing on my way.

Back at the Croc, I admired my handiwork as I walked up the path. It was unbelievable the difference cutting back the hedges had made. The borders had been overgrown and full of weeds, and I'd managed to pull them all out. Now all I needed to do was put some life back in with some healthy plants. It would have to wait though, because first on my agenda was lunch and then a refreshing dip over at the swimming pool.

Working in the mornings and lazing around the pool in the afternoons would be my daily routine, I decided when I pulled myself out of the pool a couple of hours later. I was utterly content as I got on with the strenuous task of lying on a sunlounger under the shade of a palm tree.

"Hello!" I said to the little lizard which shot past me. "You're a little cutie."

"Talking to yourself?" Leslie asked, appearing beside me.

"The wildlife," I said, happy to bump into her.

"Joe said you were over here," she said, settling herself on the sunlounger next to me. "I'm afraid there are no secrets in this town. How was work?"

"Okay," I said, thoughtfully. "She's a battle-axe,

isn't she? Mrs Kingston?"

"Oh yeah, she's awful. Sometimes I think she's even worse than Arthur. Weird family. I bet the uniform looked good on you though!"

"Oh my God!" I said dramatically. "It's hideous. I thought it might be a joke at first."

"The Kingstons don't joke!" Leslie said, laughing. "I can't believe they still have that awful uniform."

"I'm not sure how long I'll last there, to be honest."

"There are worse jobs," she told me. "I currently work on the checkout at Bush Tucker!"

I failed to hide my feelings and let out a groan on her behalf. Bush Tucker was a small supermarket; I'd been in a couple of times for supplies, but it seemed to attract a dodgy clientele so I'd taken my business to the larger Coles supermarket. "How long have you been working there for?"

"Just a few months, since I finished school. I'm trying to save some money, then I want to go to college in Broome."

"What do you want to do?" I asked, reaching for my almost-empty bottle of water.

"I want to be a teacher," she said wistfully. "I help out at the kindy on Friday mornings. It's the best day of my week!"

"I bet you'll make a great teacher," I said. "I wish I knew what I wanted to do. I studied Art and Design, which my dad thinks is ridiculous. And he might be right. I don't really know what I'll do with it. I had these grand ideas about being a famous clothes designer."

"That sounds amazing! You should do it."

87

"Maybe," I agreed.

"We should do something tonight," she suggested. "Celebrate the first day of your new job. How about drinks at Joe's place?"

"Won't he mind?"

"No! I spend half my life there. There or at Cam's. I think Beth's working late, but she usually calls in after."

"Is there something going on with you and Cam?" I asked. They had seemed very close when I spent time with them at the weekend.

"No. He's just a mate. He's a nice guy though. Why? You interested?"

"No," I said, hastily. "Just wondered. I thought he liked you."

"No way. We've been friends for years, that's all."

***

Cam's apartment was right next door to Joe's, and they were sitting outside when we arrived. They didn't seem the least bit surprised to see us. Leslie had come back to check out my room while I changed and insisted on taking me to Chicken Treat – the only fast-food restaurant in town. I hadn't quite decided whether it really was a treat or not, but it filled me up nonetheless.

"Good," Cam said, taking the beers we'd bought. "We were just saying we're running low."

"It's always the same around here," Leslie told me. "A constant argument about whose turn it is to get beers."

"It's his!" Cam and Joe said at once, pointing at each other.

"You could've at least worn your hotel uniform," Cam said, handing me a cold beer. "I'm sure it looks good on you!"

"Let's not talk about the uniform," I said. "I'd rather not think about it."

"If I were you," Cam said, "I'd work there for a week and then give it up."

"You in on this bet too then?" I asked.

He grinned at me. "Don't know what you're talking about! Just stay a week."

"How long have you got me down for?" I asked Leslie.

"Two weeks!"

"Wow, nobody thinks I can hack it?"

"Nobody likes working there," Leslie said. "Don't worry. Joe reckons you'll stay forever."

My eyebrows shot up when I looked at him. "Forever?"

He looked sheepish. "Everyone else was betting days or weeks. I just thought I'd go to the other extreme. I think I actually said five years."

"Five years would *feel* like forever," Leslie said.

"Well, I'll be kicked out of the country long before then anyway," I said before turning back to Joe. "How late does Beth work?"

He shrugged. "Usually until eight or nine. Depends."

"Depends who it is she's trying to make look pretty," Cam quipped. "It can be a long job!"

Leslie reached over to slap him as he laughed.

It was a fun evening and time flew by. Beth didn't turn up, and I was surprised when I looked up to find the night sky hanging over us, illuminated by a half-moon and an incredible blanket of stars intersected by the misty Milky Way.

"Stunning, isn't it?" Joe said, breaking the silence. Cam and Leslie were in the kitchen, giggling away.

"It's amazing," I agreed before glancing at my watch. My eyes were heavy and tiredness swept through me. "I should get going."

"I was just going to suggest shots!" Leslie said from the doorway.

"Guess who doesn't start work until lunchtime tomorrow?" Cam said, pointing at Leslie.

Leslie grinned mischievously. "I'm going to crash here, okay, Joe?"

"Since when do you ask if it's okay?" he said, shaking his head. "I'm going to walk Evelyn home."

"I'm fine," I said. "You don't need to walk me."

"You can't go alone," Cam said seriously. "It's not safe."

"Let Joe walk you back," Leslie said. "Don't walk by yourself at night."

"Okay," I agreed, feeling like a burden. I was sure I'd be fine walking back alone.

We set off in silence, and I was soon glad that I had an escort. Shouts drifted from a nearby house and streetlights were few and far between. There was an eerie feel to the place.

"It's not really a nice place to walk alone at night," Joe said quietly.

"It's kind of creepy," I agreed.

"How long do you plan on staying?" he asked as

we passed the hotel.

"I have no idea. There's still a lot more of Australia I'd like to see. But I also like the idea of staying in one place for a while."

We walked on in an easy silence and my tiredness, combined with the alcohol in my system, made me wobble slightly. For a moment, I almost linked my arm through Joe's before I remembered his girlfriend. I felt suddenly awkward about being alone with him. Maybe I should've got Cam to walk me.

Joe escorted me right to my door. The bright light outside my room attracted a host of creepy-crawlies. Moths of varying sizes crashed into the light, bouncing off and going back again. The ground moved with bugs, and geckos wandered the walls.

"I don't think I'll ever get used to this," I said to Joe, looking at the hive of activity around my door.

"I'm surprised it doesn't freak you out," Joe said.

"I struggle with the spiders in the shower," I confessed. "And what's with the frogs in the toilet bowl?"

His eyes danced with amusement and the smile lit up his face. "I don't know. It's all pretty normal to me."

"It's crazy," I said as I opened my door. "Thanks for walking me home."

"No worries," he said. "I'll see you around. We always have drinks on Friday night, if I don't see you before."

"Sounds good," I said.

I watched him walk back towards the road. When he turned at the last minute, I was embarrassed that he had caught me watching him. He waved and turned the corner.

I was glad to have made friends with the locals. It felt like a proper Aussie experience. I just needed to see some crocodiles.

Chapter 14

EVELYN – May 1994

My week at work was far less painful than I'd expected. The uniform was hideous, but aside from that it wasn't so bad. I learned to listen out for the Kingstons and try to avoid crossing paths with any of them. They were courteous and professional to customers, but any time I heard them speaking to each other, they were awful. And I overheard Mrs Kingston screaming at one member of staff over a stained napkin. I got on with my work and got out as quietly as possible. The trick was to become invisible.

On Friday evening, I ended up outside Joe's apartment again with him, Cam, and Leslie. Apparently Beth was at some function at the beauty salon and Joe was supposed to meet her there. He was complaining that he didn't want to spend the evening with a bunch of older women getting their nails done and drinking fizzy wine. We had a laugh when he insisted they all flirted with him. I could just imagine it. Leslie said she'd gone along to the regular event once and decided it wasn't her thing either. Every time Joe muttered about leaving, Cam would pass him another beer and he'd swear he was leaving after that one.

"I'm going home," I said eventually, swaying as I stood. "I have to work tomorrow."

"I'll walk you home," Joe offered. "Then I'll go and find Beth."

"You're in so much trouble," Leslie said, giggling. "You're so drunk and you're so late."

"You're so dead!" Cam added cheerfully.

"It's fine," Joe said, his words overly jolly. His eyes were drooping and he had a dopey look about him as he grinned at nothing in particular. "Come on," he said to me.

"You're going to be in trouble, aren't you?" I asked lightly as he struggled to walk straight.

"I'm in so much trouble!" His broad smile took over his face. "But she'll forgive me."

"How long have you been together?" I asked.

"A long long time," he said slowly, bumping into me as he swayed. "Sometimes I think . . ."

"What?" I asked when he trailed off.

"I don't know," he slurred. "Never mind. Did they move the Croc? It seems further away."

"That's 'cause you're zig-zagging!"

"All right, Little Miss Sober."

"Some of us have to work tomorrow."

"Oh, crap! Me too!" he said. "I'm not going to this bloody beauty party. I need to get to bed."

"Right, well, we made it," I said as we reached the Croc. "Off you go!"

"I'll see you to your door," he said. "I'm a gentleman."

"A very drunk gentleman," I said with a laugh.

"You ought to get Stan to do something about all these bugs," Joe said when we reached my door.

"What's he gonna do?" I said. "I've asked them nicely to leave and they don't listen to me. Why would they listen to Stan?"

"You've been talking to the bugs?" he asked, swaying under the bright light.

"Mainly the geckos." I turned to the wall. "Good evening, Mr Gecko."

"You're as drunk as I am!"

"I'm really not! And you ought to move, you're attracting moths standing under that light . . ." I reached to swat at the winged insect which fluttered around him, and my hand landed squarely on Joe's chest. He smiled lazily and covered my hand with his. My heart rate quickened. After the briefest moment, he took a step back.

"Bed!" I said, attempting a smile.

"I'm going," he said, raising his hand in salute before turning and stumbling away.

When I fell into bed, I was thinking of the moment my hand had touched Joe's, and I wondered if he felt the electricity too or if it was just me. *Do not fall for Joe.* I wouldn't though; I was only drunk. He was with Beth. And Beth was perfect.

***

Work the next morning seemed to drag on forever.

"Are you hungover?" Todd asked sternly when I walked past him on reception. I think I *had* probably drunk too much. I hadn't even noticed as we'd chatted and laughed all evening.

"I'm quite capable of cleaning with a hangover," I snapped. "It's not like I'm performing surgery."

Mrs Kingston appeared, and I guessed she'd been lurking around the corner. "I'll be checking all the rooms this morning, Evelyn. Why are you standing around chatting?"

With a forced smile, I hurried past her to the staff room. The uniform made me want to cry, and cleaning hotel rooms to Mrs Kingston's standards suddenly felt about as likely as me performing surgery. It crossed my mind to quit. I tried to remember who would win the bet. *Not Joe.* The thought made me smile as I forced myself to get on with work.

Relief flooded through me when I finally finished my shift and walked out of the hotel. I felt better immediately. Surprisingly, I'd managed to clean the rooms without any major complaints from Mrs Kingston.

"Evelyn!" Stan shouted as I reached my room, intent on having a nap.

Please don't ask me to help with anything. "Yeah?" I asked, doubling back to the office door.

"Phone for you," he said, holding the receiver out to me.

"Oh!" I'd never got a call here before. Whenever I called home, it was me who called them using a pre-paid phone card, which involved dialling approximately seven hundred numbers before the number I wanted to call. Or so it seemed.

"Do you want to come to Ivanhoe with us?" Leslie asked quickly down the line.

"Yeah, sure," I said, without knowing what I was agreeing to.

"Great. We'll pick you up in five! Bring your bathers."

"Okay," I said, pleasantly surprised by the phone call. I handed the phone back to Stan. "Thanks!"

He nodded, and I went to grab my things.

"How you feeling?" I asked Joe when I sat beside him in the back seat of Cam's ute.

He frowned. "Not great. Don't shout."

"I didn't shout."

"He wants us to whisper," Leslie said.

"You look awful," I told him.

"Thank you very much, girl who talks to lizards!"

"Hey!" I said, swiping to hit his leg and narrowly missing when he moved at the last moment. "Did you get into trouble with Beth?"

"No, not really," he said. "She's back at work again all day. She's got no time to worry about me."

"It's a shame she has to work so much," I remarked.

"She loves it," Leslie said. "She'd rather be at work than doing anything else."

"Imagine enjoying your job!" Cam said, clearly puzzled by the very idea.

"My job's all right," Joe muttered before pulling his cap down over his eyes and resting his head on the window.

I leaned forward to Cam and Leslie. "Where are we going?"

"Ivanhoe Crossing," Cam said. "It's a causeway over the river. The water should be low enough to drive across."

"Okay," I said, still unsure what we were doing.

"It's fun," Leslie said. "We thought we'd show you around a bit. We've got a picnic and beers."

Joe groaned at the mention of beers.

"You're really pathetic, mate," Cam said, glancing back.

It didn't take long to get to the river. Cam slowed to a stop.

"You can't really drive over that, can you?" I asked. The river was wide and fast-flowing. I'd expected it to be a few centimetres of water, but I watched a ute drive over ahead of us and its tyres were almost completely submerged.

"This is nothing," Joe said, peeking out from under his hat. He and Leslie opened their doors. "Come on," he instructed with a flick of the head. I followed them and took Joe's hand when he offered it to pull me up onto the truck-bed. My heart fluttered at his touch.

"Better view from out here," Leslie said.

"Hold on!" Cam shouted and we moved to steady ourselves on the roof of the cab. The road disappeared into the water, and we drove slowly across the broad stretch of river. To the right there was a drop of a couple of feet, creating a small waterfall as the water rushed over.

"Is it safe?" I asked, talking loudly over the noise of the water.

Joe shrugged beside me. "Safe enough. I wouldn't fish here though." He looked at a guy nearby standing thigh-deep in water with a rod in his hand. "He looks like croc food to me."

"Idiot," Leslie said.

As always, the sky was a brilliant blue. The river was strewn with huge rocks, and trees were dotted along the riverbank. It was a stunning part of the world.

"Picnic time," Leslie announced when Cam parked at the other side of the river. We clambered over the rocky riverside until we reached a flat patch by the edge of the river. Leslie spread a blanket on the ground while Joe pulled his T-shirt off and headed for the water. The many large rocks along the river formed natural pools where the water was almost still.

"What about the crocs?" I asked, as he sat in one of the pools.

Joe grinned. "I'll ask them politely to leave me alone and go chomp on the crazy fisherman!"

"Should be all right here," Cam told me seriously as he joined Joe in the water. "You gotta be careful though."

"How?" I asked, confused.

"Well . . ." Cam glanced at Joe and laughed. "Just don't get eaten! That's the usual plan."

"You're all crazy," I said, joining them in the water.

Cam grabbed at my leg and thrashed it around under water. "Just don't lose a limb!"

"The sensible thing is to stay out of the water," Leslie said, perching on a rock.

"It's so hot though," I complained, enjoying the feel of the cool water on my skin. I watched as another pickup drove slowly across the causeway. "It's amazing that you can drive over there."

"You can't always," Cam said. "In the wet season, the water's too high."

"You'd love the wet season," Leslie said. "You'll have to stay until then at least."

"I can't imagine it here in winter," I said and then watched the looks pass between them, their mouths twitching at the corners. "What?"

"It's not winter," Leslie said.

"It's the wet season," Cam added.

"Yeah, but . . ." I trailed off as Joe gave me a kick under the water.

"Don't say anything else," he said. "You'll only embarrass yourself! Just stay for the wet season and you'll see."

I will. I wanted to see everything there was to see. It was all so different, and every day felt exhilarating. I never knew what new and exciting things I'd encounter next. The wildlife fascinated me, and the scenery was stunning. I'd stay for the wet season because I wanted to know everything there was to know about the area. I didn't want to miss a thing.

The next incredible sight came soon after. Standing on the back of Cam's ute as he drove back across the causeway, Joe leaned over, and with his face close to mine, pointed downriver to a croc lazing on a rock, motionless and eerie.

The sun was setting as we drove back to town, and everything glowed orange and red. We passed several of the distinctive boab trees, which I'd heard were unique to the Kimberley region. I loved the shape of them with their swollen trunks and spindly branches.

"The trunks are hollow," Joe said when he caught me staring at them. "They used to use them as prisons."

"Really?" I said, looking at the trees in awe.

"So they say."

I'd never seen anything like them, and I couldn't drag my gaze away. "I love them."

***

It was early evening when Cam pulled up outside the Croc. Beth was standing outside Bushcamp talking to Mick, and she smiled widely when we arrived.

"Hope you didn't have too much fun without me?" she said, moving to Joe as we congregated on the pavement.

"You shouldn't work so much," Joe said, kissing her. "We missed you."

She wrapped her arms around his waist and rested her head on his chest. They were so cute together.

"How's everything going?" she asked me. "This lot being good tour guides?"

"The best," I said. "I'm having a great time. I love it here."

"Really?" she asked, seeming surprised. "What about the wildlife?"

"Takes a bit of getting used to . . ."

"She chats to lizards," Joe said. "I think she's okay with it all!"

"I lived in Perth until I was thirteen," Beth told me. "I'm still not used to life in the outback."

"I love it," I told her as we moved into the gardens of the Croc. We still had beers left and decided to continue our picnic on the grass in front of my room.

"I guess it's different if you're just passing through," Beth said as we walked side by side. "Can you imagine living like this permanently? The heat and the snakes, lizards and spiders. And the dust."

"You really don't like it?" I said, amused.

"It has its good points, I guess." She glanced at Joe. "I want to move to Sydney one day. Set up my own business."

"You really love your job, don't you?"

"I want to have my own chain of beauty salons. Maybe I'm ambitious, but I have to try."

It was endearing to hear how passionate she was about her job. I wished there was something *I* wanted to do that much. In that moment, I couldn't even imagine being back in the UK, never mind what I might do for a job.

Joe sidled up and draped an arm around Beth. "You telling Evelyn all about your plans to leave me and start your own beauty empire?"

"Of course not," she said, giving him a big kiss on the cheek. "I'm taking you with me!"

Chapter 15

LIBBY – August 2017

In Airlie Beach, I met the most unlikely backpacker so far. Yvonne had approximately the same figure as me. Okay, not quite. But if you pulled me to twice my height and skimmed off any fat which might still be present after such a stretch, we'd be similar. Talking to her involved craning my neck to an uncomfortable angle, and standing beside her made me feel podgy and unkempt. One thing I'd really been enjoying on the backpacker trail was that my frizzy hair and unmade-up face were perfectly acceptable. My outfits were entirely thrown together. I was currently in khaki shorts and a vest top over a bikini. My standard attire. I'm not sure how Yvonne managed to look so glamorous. The only luggage she had was a small suitcase on wheels, which seemed to weigh nothing at all. Not that it mattered because over the next few days I found that every time she bent to pick it up, some attractive guy would swoop in to save her the trouble.

My first instinct was to get as far away from Yvonne as possible. Hanging around with such a stunning creature would do nothing for my self-confidence. We met one morning in the Bush Village Hostel and I clumsily introduced myself. She really was beautiful – and so unlike anyone I'd met on my travels that she was quite a curiosity.

She looked as though she was about to go out for the day, but she lingered while I made my bed – the bunk above hers. I said goodbye when I walked into the bathroom, presuming she'd be gone by the time I'd showered, but she was still there. Returning her shy smile, I felt awkward and wished she'd leave.

"Have you got plans for the day?" she asked when she finally spoke. She wore a flowing maxi dress with a bright floral print, and I wished I had something similarly stunning to wear. I'd been rotating through three pairs of shorts and five T-shirts, and I suddenly felt like a change. There were a couple of sundresses and a skirt or two tucked in the bottom of my backpack which I saved for evenings out.

"I was just going to have a wander around and check the place out. Then I'll make a plan for the next few days." It was my usual routine when I arrived in a new place. Usually I ended up being swept along in other people's plans.

"Do you want to hang out together today?" There was a sudden vulnerability to her, and I felt panic rise as I tried to think of an excuse. My assumption was that she'd want to spend the day shopping, and I couldn't cope with that. She didn't look like someone who'd be interested in sightseeing. I definitely needed to negotiate a day to myself.

"I need to do some washing and then go and find a bank. Boring stuff. Shall we meet later? We could make dinner together in the kitchen downstairs?" *Because I really don't want to be seen out in public with you.*

Her big puppy-dog eyes pleaded with me. "Will you come to the beach? I heard about this beautiful, secluded beach. It's supposed to be a local secret that the tourists don't know about . . ."

I smiled cheekily. "Except *you* know about it."

"It's supposed to be amazing."

I pulled a face. "Is it far?"

"I think it's about forty minutes in the car. I don't want to go alone . . ."

"I really need t—"

She snatched at my hand. "Please! You can do your washing later. Please come."

There was an awkward silence, and she kept my hand clutched in hers. "Okay." I sighed. "You've talked me into it."

"Yes!" She reached for an oversized tote bag and a wide-brimmed straw hat. I found a towel and my sunscreen, shoving them into my day bag: a scruffy old backpack which had belonged to Josh once upon a time. I enjoyed having the little reminder of home.

"It really better be a deserted beach," I said, looking down at myself and then at Yvonne. "I'm not sure I like the idea of lying next to you in a bikini!" My tone was light-hearted and Yvonne, to her credit, looked confused. "I meant that in the nicest possible way," I told her with a grin. "It's just that you've got such a gorgeous figure and I feel a bit frumpy next to you."

"You're not frumpy," she said, scrutinising me. "You're so pretty."

She was genuine, and for a moment it crossed my mind that she might be flirting with me. It took a huge effort for me not to laugh out loud at my own train of thought.

"What?" Yvonne asked, catching my smirk.

I shook my head. "Sorry. I just had a weird thought. Ignore me."

"You're funny," she declared.

"It's a good idea to rent a car," I said as we stepped out onto the street. "Get off the beaten path a bit. My budget wouldn't really stretch to it."

"I don't have a car," she said, glancing down the street and looking at her watch.

"I thought you said—"

"It's not *my* car," she explained. "I met these guys last night and they invited me along with them. It sounds wonderful. I'm so glad you can come. I didn't want to go alone with them – I only met them last night."

"You didn't tell me that!" I glared up at her, but she was busy looking around for her date. "I don't want to gatecrash."

"You're not. I invited you. Anyway, I really like this guy, Simon, but his brother's really nice too. It'll be fun. A double date!"

"That's what I'm worried about. I'm not dressed for a date. And I don't *want* to go on a date!"

Yvonne waved enthusiastically as an open-top jeep pulled up to the curb in front of us. I'd missed my chance to get out of this day trip.

A tall, blonde-haired guy jumped out of the driver's seat and greeted Yvonne warmly.

"This is my friend, Libby," she told him. "She's

going to come with us."

"Great!" he said.

Turning to the jeep, Simon shooed his brother into the back and gestured for me to follow.

"I'm Libby," I said, buckling myself in.

"Andrew," he replied with a smile. He was very easy on the eye, with similar looks to his brother but darker hair.

This might just be a fun day.

We rolled out of town and weaved our way along a quiet coastal road. It was almost an hour's drive and conversation didn't go well. Words got lost on the air that rushed through the jeep. They were brothers from the north of England, Andrew told me. He was travelling for a couple of months and Simon had a visa for a year. That was all I got before we smiled at each other and gave up.

HANNAH ELLIS

Chapter 16

LIBBY – August 2017

Leaving the car in a pull-in by the road, we wandered along a sandy path through dry shrubs. Eventually we reached a line of low sand dunes which gave way to a stretch of white sand. As promised, it was deserted, and I paused for a moment, watching the tranquil waters lap gently onto the shore.

"Not a bad beach, hey?" Simon said. He had a cool box in one hand and a towel slung over his shoulder. He'd peeled off his T-shirt when we exited the car and his physique was almost as breathtaking as the beach. I averted my eyes. There was definitely a lot of beauty around me.

Andrew chose a spot for us halfway down the beach and spread his towel out before stripping off to his low-slung board shorts. I was self-conscious as I lay on my towel in my bikini.

"I couldn't hear a thing in the car," Andrew said. "You'll have to tell me your life story all over again."

"Not much to tell," I said casually.

Simon sat beside me in the sand. "Let me guess. You just finished studying and are having a year out before you go back to find a proper job and lead a sad, boring life!"

"You got me," I said, amused. It did seem to be a common theme among the travellers I'd met. "Though I've also met a few people who are trying to" – I did the obligatory air quotes – "find themselves."

"You're not old enough for that," Simon pointed out. "You have to live your sad, boring life for a while before you need to find yourself."

"Good point!"

When Yvonne suggested a swim, we ambled down the beach together. The sea was amazing: crystal clear and perfectly refreshing. I bobbed around on my back, splashing at Simon when he dived into the water beside me. When Andrew headed back up the beach to sunbathe, I followed him, leaving Yvonne to flirt with Simon. I sat on my towel and watched them splash around in the water. Their laughter drifted up to me, along with the sound of the waves breaking against the shore, but otherwise everything was still and quiet. Andrew seemed to be having a nap.

Without warning, thoughts of Mum popped into my head, and I imagined her in this exact same spot back when she was my age. Maybe she'd been right here, playing around in the sea with some cute guy. I think she'd have been a big flirt back then. She'd have had all the guys hanging around her.

Glancing at Andrew, I was surprised to find him looking at me. His gaze shot down to the shore. "It's a nice necklace."

I was unaware I'd been fiddling with it. "Thank you," I murmured, pressing it to my chest.

110

"Can you do me a favour?" he asked, sitting up and reaching for the bottle of sunscreen. "My back feels like it's burning."

"Sure." I shuffled over on my towel to make room for him. My hands glided over his back. *His lovely silky smooth and perfectly toned back.* There was a small birthmark on his shoulder blade in the shape of a diamond. Even his imperfections were attractive. *Get a grip, Libby. The last thing you need is a holiday romance. You've got enough to think about as it is.*

"Done!" I told him, with a final swipe.

"Thank you," he said, moving back to his towel. "How long are you travelling for?"

"I've got a visa for three months," I said vaguely. "I just landed in Sydney a few weeks ago and I don't really have much of a plan. I'm just going with the flow . . ."

He nodded his head slowly and I felt suddenly uneasy, as though I were lying to him. "This place is beautiful," I went on, changing the subject. "I've been having such a great time the past few weeks, but sometimes it feels like I'm stuck on a designated backpacker path and I'm missing some hidden gems. With a car, you probably see so much more."

He laughed. "It's Simon's attempt to impress Yvonne! You're right though – it *is* nice to see something less touristy."

When Simon and Yvonne re-joined us, lunch was produced from the cool box. We spent a lazy afternoon sunbathing and swimming, and I was content when we packed up late in the afternoon and set off back to the car.

"Simon's great, isn't he?" Yvonne whispered to

me, slowing her pace to distance us from the boys.

"He's lovely," I agreed.

"He invited us for dinner tonight . . ."

"Us?" I laughed. "I don't think you need a chaperone any more."

"But Andrew will be there too."

"I don't know," I said. "It feels a bit weird. Shouldn't you and Simon go on a date alone?"

"I think Simon's worried about ditching Andrew."

The conversation stopped as we caught up with the boys.

"Shall we head back into town and find somewhere for dinner?" Simon asked.

Yvonne's eyes pleaded with me as Andrew climbed into the back of the jeep. "Why don't you two go alone?" he said to Yvonne and Simon. "You don't need us cramping your style, do you?" He turned to look at me. "Sorry, unless you wanted to?"

"I really should go back and get some washing done," I said, trying my best to hide my disappointment. Of course I didn't want to go when Andrew clearly didn't. But it felt distinctly like rejection and stung just a little. I told myself I was being ridiculous.

On the drive back, I managed to put it out of my mind. The warm wind blew through my hair gloriously. The sun and the scenery and driving along the Australian coast with these people who I didn't even know the previous day made me feel that anything was possible.

I loved the adventure I was on.

Chapter 17

EVELYN – July 1994

My birthday in Kununurra didn't seem like anything out of the ordinary at the time, but when I looked back on it, it was fairly memorable. Getting a fishing hook stuck in my hand, feeding a crocodile, and Cam and Joe getting into a fierce argument certainly made it interesting.

"What are you wearing?" Leslie asked in surprise when she waltzed into the office at the Croc. I was having a cuppa with Stan. "Oh, and happy birthday!" she said with a grin.

"What's wrong with what I'm wearing?" I asked, standing and looking down at my new purchase.

"Nothing," she said. "It's cute. You're just a bit dressed up for fishing."

"It's my birthday," I said, suddenly self-conscious. "And it's only a sundress. What's the big deal?"

"No big deal," she insisted. "You just look different. I like it. You look hot. Doesn't she, Stan?"

"Very nice," he agreed.

"Come on then," Leslie said. "The boys are

113

waiting. And Beth."

We didn't usually see Joe or Beth on Sundays as they tended to spend their one mutual day off alone. An exception had been made for my birthday, and Mick had agreed we could take his boat out for a day on the water.

Cam let out a low whistle when he saw me. He was waiting on the road with Joe and Beth. Mick's boat was hitched up behind Joe's ute. "Looking good, birthday girl!"

"Thank you," I said, giving him a shy twirl.

"It suits you," Beth said with her usual warm smile. "Happy birthday!"

"Let's get going then," Joe said. He cast a cool glance in my direction as he wished me happy birthday.

We drove for a while, eventually pulling off the highway and onto a dirt track which took us further and further from civilisation. A kangaroo bounded nearby, stopping to look at us before hopping off again. The wildlife still amazed me.

Finally, we arrived at a little clearing, and Joe swung the ute around to manoeuvre the boat into the water.

"Why are you looking at me like that?" I asked Cam as we stood knee-deep in water to push the boat from the trailer.

"It's just weird seeing you look so girly," he said.

"So I usually look manly?"

"No," he said, chuckling. "You just look pretty today, that's all."

"Thank you," I said as Joe appeared and put a hand on my elbow.

114

"Stop yakking and get in the boat," he said. "I'd hate for you to end up as croc food on your birthday."

Leslie sat beside me in the front of the boat. "Any other day it would be fine, just not your birthday!"

I heard Beth laughing as Joe swept her from the shore to the boat in one fluid motion. "I don't know how anyone can put their feet in croc-infested water," she said. "All I can think of is all the newspaper articles about attacks. It makes me shudder just thinking about putting a toe in the water."

Cam looked at me and rolled his eyes. He glanced suspiciously at the water before dropping to his knees and screaming in a dramatic display of being dragged under. I had to laugh.

"It's all very funny until you actually lose a limb," Beth told him coolly.

When the boys were in the boat, Joe pulled sharply on the cord to bring the motor to life, and we puttered away down the river. The sky was the usual bright blue and the sun beat down. My sundress had seemed like a good idea in the shop. I'd felt like a change from the usual shorts and vest top. Maybe it was also because I knew Beth would spend the whole day with us. She always looked so sleek and elegant. With the heat and the dust, I never really felt fresh and clean. The little dress wasn't practical though. Sweat trickled down my back, and I shuffled to get comfy on the bench seat.

Sod it. Putting my beer aside, I pulled the dress over my head. My bikini was acceptable boat-wear.

"Birthday suit would be appropriate today, wouldn't it?" Cam said with a smirk.

"Dream on!" I said then sighed. "It's so bloody

hot already."

Cam helpfully reached into the water and swept an armful over me. He was intending to be annoying, but it was very refreshing.

"So what would you normally be doing on your birthday?" Leslie asked.

"I don't know." Birthdays were never really a big deal at home. "I usually hang out with my friend, Mel, but it's nothing special."

"Well today will be special," she said. "I will make sure of it!"

"This looks like a good spot," Joe said a little while later, slowing near a sandy shore. "Reckon we might find some barra round those rocks." Barramundi were the prized catch in the area. I looked at the rocks on the other side of the river, the water flowing faster as it diverted around them.

"Throw a line out there and see if you can catch us some dinner," Cam said, handing me a rod.

I moved to choose a lure and attach it to the line. "You always choose the pretty ones," Joe said, watching me.

"Makes sense, doesn't it?" I looked down at the glittery orange thing I'd use for bait. It had a feather too. "It's a *lure*. It needs to be attractive!"

"Ah," Cam said with a sigh. "So that's what you were thinking when you got dressed this morning? Now I get it. You can reel me in later!"

"You're closest, Leslie," I said, smirking.

She whacked him on the arm for me.

"Look out," I said, moving them aside to cast out. "And make sure you grab my camera when I catch a whopper!"

"You and your camera," Cam remarked. "How many films do you go through a week?"

"A few! They love me at the print shop." I enjoyed capturing all my crazy Kununurra moments. Thanks to Stan charging me less and less for my room every week, I could afford to splash out on camera film.

I'd been determined to spend the evening in the pub bragging about the size of my catch, but it wasn't to be. None of us had much luck. It was fun, nonetheless – fishing and chatting and drinking; it was all very chilled.

I'd just reeled in a little bream and was about to throw him back when Cam stopped me.

"What?" I asked, the slippery fish squirming in my hand.

"Look." Cam pointed down the river. "That looks like a hungry croc to me."

He was difficult to spot – completely still among fallen tree branches which were the exact same colour and texture as his rough skin. It gave me the creeps that he'd been there the whole time and we'd been completely oblivious. He was less than twenty feet from us.

"Get him on the nose and I'll buy you a beer tonight," Cam said, looking at the fish in my hand.

"Throw the fish to the croc?" I asked, sceptically.

"Yes!" Leslie agreed. "Do it!"

I looked at Joe, who said nothing but looked amused.

"Yes," Beth said, rolling her eyes. "Let's annoy the croc, that's sensible!"

"Quick," Leslie said, ignoring her and looking at

the fish in my hand. "The poor little thing's dying!" I shook my head as she realised the absurdity of her statement and fell about laughing.

"Please don't feed the crocodile," Beth said with a sigh.

Cam gave me a nudge and I threw the fish. It landed with a splash in the shallow water right by the crocodile's snout. As it wiggled to swim away, the croc twisted violently, thrashing in the water as it snapped up its prey.

"Think it might be time to leave," Joe said, pulling up the anchor and starting the engine. The croc went back to its motionless state, and a silly smile crept over my face.

"Not every birthday you feed a croc in the wild, is it?" Cam said excitedly.

"That was amazing," I said, feeling a rush of adrenalin.

"Shall we head back to town?" Beth suggested. She had her usual pleasant smile, but I had the distinct impression she wasn't amused.

"Okay," I said with a shrug. "I don't mind."

I moved to the cool box for more beers and didn't realise I'd blocked Joe's view of the river.

"Rocks!" Cam shouted. The boat swerved sharply and I lost my balance. I fell back onto the seat and then cried out as pain shot through my hand. The fishing hook stuck out through my palm, and I panicked at the sight of it. As I instinctively moved my hand close to my body, the taut line tugged the hook back, bringing a searing pain and a fresh shriek from me.

Joe was in front of me in an instant. His fingers

wrapped firmly around my wrist. "Don't move," he ordered, his voice raw and rough.

Tears filled my eyes, and I felt faint at the sight of the hook and the blood which began to seep around it.

Cam moved nearer. "Oh, shit." His pained expression did nothing to calm me.

"Hey," Joe said. "Look at me."

I swallowed as I met his gaze.

"Flesh wound," he said calmly. "Don't panic." He smiled, and his eyes sparkled beautifully.

"It hurts," I said, weakly.

"I can get it out. Just don't move." His gaze shifted to Leslie, who shot into action, bringing him a pair of pliers and a wad of tissues. "I have to cut the end off the hook," he told me gently. "It'll just hurt for a second, okay?"

"Okay," I said, keeping my eyes firmly on him and trying to absorb his sense of calm.

"Sorry," he said, wincing as he clipped the hook and pulled it through the skin.

All my muscles tensed with the pain, and it was an effort to stay still. Joe pushed the wad of tissues to the wound and closed my fist around it. He reached for my other hand, and I squeezed his fingers as I swallowed all the swear words I knew.

"Breathe," he said, his eyes meeting mine again. "You all right?"

"Yes," I said, wincing and taking a breath. "Thanks."

The boat bobbed. Beth had taken over and killed the motor. Her sympathetic smile reminded me I was still clinging to Joe's hand. I removed it slowly and Joe turned to Cam, the concern in his eyes suddenly replaced by anger.

"Great idea to leave tackle laying around, mate," he snapped, not moving from his spot crouched in front of me.

"Hey!" Cam shot at him. "Don't have a go at me. If you'd watch where you were going, people wouldn't be falling around the boat."

"I couldn't see. That was an accident. What are you doing leaving your rod lying around with a bloody great hook still on it? Do you ever think?"

"I *think* she's fine. Chill out, will you?"

"Don't tell me to chill out, you're lucky it wasn't worse."

I was about to jump in; I hated the tension. I'd never seen any animosity between Cam and Joe before and I didn't like it. Luckily, Leslie got between them.

"It could have been *way* worse," she said, looking at me. "Imagine if you'd landed on your arse. That'd be some birthday – Joe pulling a hook out of your backside!"

I smiled as Leslie sat beside me and patted my leg. Joe took one more look at my hand, removing the tissues and swapping them for a fresh wad. "The bleeding's stopping," he said. "But you need to get it looked at and properly dressed."

I nodded and he moved back to the tiller. The atmosphere was strained as we headed back the way we'd come. I was annoyed to have caused drama.

I'd expected it to be a nice quiet day on the boat.

Chapter 18

EVELYN – July 1994

Leslie came to the clinic with me, where a nice young doctor cleaned the wound and patched me up. She wasn't concerned and said it would heal fine in a week or so. I might have a little scar if I were lucky.

"Well, that ruined my birthday," I said to Leslie as we wandered back to the Croc.

"Why?" she said with a laugh. "Is that your drinking hand? We can still go to the Tav, can't we?"

"I guess so," I agreed. "I just feel bad that Cam and Joe argued."

"They'll get over it," she said. "They never really fall out about anything. No way they can stay angry at each other for long."

"I hope not. Will they still come out tonight?" They hadn't said much when they'd dropped us off at the health centre – just told me to call if I needed anything. Joe and Cam hadn't spoken the whole way back to town, and the atmosphere was horribly tense.

"I don't know. I don't really care either. We can go out without them for once. See if we can find some hot guys without them around cramping our style."

"Sounds good," I said. It didn't though. I wanted the boys to come out and celebrate my birthday, and I really hated to think they were arguing because of my clumsiness. Hopefully they'd be over it and come out later.

I tried my best to ignore their absence and have fun with Leslie in the pub. It was full of familiar faces, and people made a fuss of me, wishing me happy birthday and buying me drinks as I explained my bandaged hand repeatedly. I bumped into Johan, who I'd met on the farm, and spent some time chatting to him and laughing about the day I threw a sandwich at Len Jenkins.

All in all, it wasn't a bad evening, and I was wondering whether I might be able to catch Mel for a quick chat before bed. We always seemed to miss each other's calls with the time difference. It was frustrating; I was sure I'd feel better for a good natter with her. Plus, it was my birthday and there weren't many birthdays in my life that I hadn't spent with her. Not even talking to her would be really weird.

I decided I'd try to call her before bed and was just about to tell Leslie I was leaving when Joe and Cam walked in. The sight of them made me emotional; it hadn't seemed right that they weren't in the pub on my birthday. I flung my arms around Joe and squeezed him tight.

"All right," he said, laughing as he hugged me back.

"I thought you weren't coming," I said as I moved on to Cam, who lifted me off the floor when he squeezed me.

"We wouldn't miss birthday drinks, would we?"

"I can't really imagine you ever missing out on *any* drinks," Leslie said, appearing beside me.

"Sorry about the hook," Cam said sheepishly when Joe went to the bar.

"It's fine." I lowered my voice. "Sorry Joe yelled at you."

He rolled his eyes. "He's a right bloody drama queen that one! And I still reckon it was all his fault!"

"But you're friends again?"

"'Course!" he said. "It was only a bloody hook in yer hand anyway. You'll thank us for your scar before long. Just remember whose fault it was then, won't ya?"

"Here," Joe said, arriving with beers. "Stop yakking, start drinking!"

The boys were back to their usual banter as though nothing had happened. It was a great end to my birthday, and to make it even better, I managed to chat to Mel too. I told her all about my birthday, standing at the payphone outside the Tav after we'd been kicked out. I was very drunk and my friends stood around me singing "Happy Birthday" as I laughed down the phone with Mel.

Chapter 19

LIBBY – August 2017

I'd grown accustomed to hostel-living; people coming and going at all hours no longer disrupted my sleep. It didn't even register as odd when Yvonne nudged me awake the next morning. She was sitting on the edge of my bed, looking perfectly put together.

"Do you want to sail around the Whitsunday Islands on a yacht?" she asked eagerly.

I squinted and tried to get my eyes to focus. "That sounds expensive."

"Not really, it's a last-minute deal. Two days and two nights on a luxury yacht. It will be fantastic! Come on, let's go."

"Now?"

"Yes, hurry up!"

"What's the catch?" I eyed her suspiciously, but she just shrugged.

"It just seemed like such a great deal. There was a guy in the bar last night and they had four spots left and said we could take them for half price."

She gave me a smile that was part wince.

"You've already signed me up for this, haven't

you?"

"It just sounded so great. But Simon was worried about Andrew feeling like a spare wheel so we thought with the four of us . . ."

"Yvonne!" I complained. "Andrew would probably rather be left alone than get dragged on an awkward double date."

"It won't be awkward, I promise. Just say you'll come, otherwise I'll have to cancel it all."

"I don't know . . ."

"Come on. It'll be so much fun."

"I'm sure it will be, for you and lover boy. But what if Andrew doesn't want to be on a double date with me? Then I'm stuck on a boat—"

"It's a luxury yacht," she corrected me, her eyes dancing in excitement. "With an endless supply of champagne!"

I'd actually been looking into sailing trips and had decided it was just a little over my budget. Half-price tickets were hard to say no to. "When you put it like that . . ."

Yvonne clapped her hands together, delighted. "Quick then, the boys will be here to pick us up soon."

The thought of cruising around the many islands of the Whitsundays excited me more and more as I got organised. When I climbed into the jeep and Andrew didn't look like someone who was being forced to spend time with me, I decided I was in for a fun trip. Meeting Yvonne had been a stroke of luck.

It was a ten-minute drive to the impressive marina. Boat masts swayed in the breeze, tinkling gently. I breathed in the salty air and braced for the weight of my backpack as I hauled it onto my shoulder. It was surprisingly light.

"I can take that for you," Andrew offered, a hand already lifting my bag.

The feminist in me broiled. *I'm quite capable of carrying my own bag.* "It's okay. I ca—" I stopped and slipped my arm out of the strap. "Thanks." Apparently my poor aching muscles had over-ridden that little feminist voice in my head. *Well, he can carry it if he really wants to.*

Again, I felt scruffy in my shorts and T-shirt. Yvonne looked stunning in a white sundress and oversized sunglasses. Following Simon along one of many jetties, we stopped in front of an impressive white yacht and were greeted by four crew members, all dressed in tailored white shorts and polo shirts.

A quick tour had me coolly nodding my head in approval. Inwardly, I was awestruck. It was like something from a film, and I wanted to jump up and down and squeal with delight. Yvonne and I were sharing a room but it was a far cry from what I'd become used to over the past few weeks. The beds were deliciously soft, and the crisp white linens smelled wonderful. There was even a dressing table and mirror squeezed into the room; everything looked brand new and decadent.

The fresh fluffy towels were the ultimate luxury. The towel I'd been travelling with was old and worn to begin with and seemed to be constantly damp and musty.

When the boat pulled out of the marina, the four of us sat on sunloungers on the deck, sipping champagne and nibbling on appetisers. There were four other people on the yacht: two young couples. It seemed like a couples' cruise, and I felt slightly awkward.

"So is this it for two days?" I asked, ignoring my hesitations and focusing on the positives: I was on a luxury yacht, drinking champagne. "Just sitting around here, eating and drinking?" I clinked my champagne glass against Yvonne's.

"Not a bad way to spend a couple of days, is it?" Simon said.

"Not bad at all," I agreed, beaming.

We spent the day lazing in the sun and marvelling at the beautiful scenery as we cruised through the islands. The yacht's chef· brought us a tray of sandwiches for lunch, and we were introduced to the other couples, who were very pleasant but didn't seem interested in socialising.

It was fun getting to know the young crew and learning about sailing. We anchored in the afternoon and took time for a dip in the tranquil waters. It was sheer and utter bliss.

"Are you coming for a dip?" I shouted up to Andrew when I swam around the stern – I was catching all the nautical terms from the crew. He was leaning over the side, lost in thought. "The water's gorgeous."

As he climbed down the ladder into the water, I said, "I had you down as a perfect dive kind of person."

"I didn't want to embarrass you after your graceful entrance into the water."

"I've got that dive-bomb down to perfection," I said.

He smiled back at me. "It was quite impressive," he agreed before disappearing under the water. His features seemed softer when he reappeared, like the stress was being washed away. Closing his eyes, he floated on his back.

"I told you it's lovely, didn't I?"

"It's nice," he said, pausing before shifting his gaze to me. "I hope you don't think it's weird. I didn't know it was some sort of romantic cruise . . ."

"Me neither," I said quickly.

He gave me a funny look. "I just didn't want you to get the wrong idea."

My mouth twitched into an awkward smile. He clearly thought I was interested in him. What is it with good-looking people that they always assume everyone fancies them?

"I just heard yacht and champagne and didn't think anything more about it!" I said, my words coming fast. "Yvonne left out the other details. I'm sure it will be fun though."

"It's just that I'm not looking for any romance or anything."

Oh, my God, I've got the message, let's stop going on about it. Something odd came over me then: a confidence that came from him stating so bluntly that he wasn't interested in me. I could have some fun.

"You say that now," I told him with a smirk. "But you'll probably change your tune after a couple of days with me." I swam away from him, pulled myself back up the ladder and turned to see the perplexed look on his face.

I winked and walked away, amused by my self-confidence.

HANNAH ELLIS

Chapter 20

LIBBY – August 2017

"I can't figure Andrew out," I said to Yvonne as we got ready for a starlit dinner on the deck. "He told me he's not interested in any romance. That's a bit presumptuous, isn't it?"

"You have been flirting with him a lot! Maybe you're scaring him."

"I only started that when I realised how uncomfortable it makes him. I'm just having a bit of fun." And it was *so* much fun.

"Well, he just got dumped and came to Australia for a holiday to get over his ex, so that's probably why he's a bit awkward."

"Oh, that explains things," I said thoughtfully. Maybe I shouldn't tease him so much. But then again, I *really* was enjoying it.

Yvonne seemed amused as she carefully applied her make-up. Since my choice of outfits was limited, I'd opted for one of my two sundresses and had been ready and waiting for her for ages. I'd been drinking champagne on and off all day and was feeling giddy.

"Come on," I said, impatiently. "Let's go!"

With a final blot of her lipstick and a pout in the mirror, she stood and grinned.

Three small tables were set on deck. We joined Simon and Andrew at our table for four, which was elegantly decked out with white linens and tall candlesticks.

"Well, this is very romantic, isn't it?" I said to Andrew cheekily. "Don't get any ideas, will you?"

He shook his head and although he seemed amused, I decided I should tone down the teasing. I was probably walking a fine line between being funny and annoying.

"Look at that sky," Yvonne said, drawing the attention away from Andrew. "It's just stunning."

"Almost as stunning as you look tonight," Simon said, slipping his hand into Yvonne's.

Andrew and I made vomit noises that were so in sync it was like we'd rehearsed it. I looked at him in surprise before we both fell about laughing.

"Sorry, mate," Andrew said, slapping Simon on the shoulder. "That was cheesy!"

The food arrived, saving Simon from his embarrassment. It was divine: three delicious courses comprising succulent seafood and the most mouth-watering hot chocolate brownie I'd ever tasted.

Simon and Yvonne moved to look out over the water after dinner, leaving Andrew and me alone, candlelight flickering between us. It was such a romantic setting that it was hard not to think about Andrew in that way. I was tired, and my previous confidence vanished.

"I think I might turn in," I said, removing my napkin from my lap.

"Okay," he said, raising his eyebrows. "Are you okay?"

"Yes, fine," I said. "Just tired."

He stood when I did. "I'm sorry about earlier," he said, suddenly awkward. "I didn't mean to sound arrogant."

"It's okay." I moved past him and then stopped. "You did sound a bit arrogant . . ."

"I know," he said with a frown. "It wasn't anything personal, I'm just dealing with some stuff at the moment."

I smiled lightly and wished him goodnight. The last thing I needed was someone else's problems. I had enough issues of my own.

***

The next day was the same glorious weather and the same luxury of lying around the deck and being spoilt with delicious foods. We dropped anchor at a lovely little cove, swimming over to the beach for some sunbathing.

"One of the crew told me about a party tomorrow," Yvonne said as we soaked in the rays. "It's a full moon party on Magnetic Island. We could head up there tomorrow when we leave the boat."

She looked at me expectantly. She'd clearly already discussed it with Simon, and they'd no doubt need me to keep Andrew company. Andrew must have had the same thought and looked less than impressed with the idea.

"Sounds tacky," he said, lying back on the sand.

"Oh, it'll be so much fun," Yvonne insisted.

"You'll come won't you, Libby?"

"I guess so. I'm heading north anyway." Although at that point, the idea of finding my father seemed less and less appealing, so I could probably head in any direction.

"You'll enjoy it," Simon said to Andrew, with the implication that it wasn't really up for discussion.

"It might actually be fun," I said to Andrew when Yvonne and Simon moved back towards the water. When he didn't comment, I asked, "You really don't want to go?"

"It's not that," he said huffily. "I just thought I was coming over here to hang out with my brother . . ."

"And instead you're stuck with me," I said with a smirk. "That does seem really awful!"

He caught my eye and couldn't help but laugh himself. "I sound like a spoilt brat, don't I?"

"Yeah, you do!" I agreed. "I kind of get it: you came here to get over a breakup and thought your brother would be all attentive, but now he's found Yvonne and wants to spend all his time with her."

"Simon's got a big mouth," he remarked.

"What I don't understand is why you came all this way just to mope around? Why not have some fun?"

"I *am* having fun," he said.

"No, you're not. You're staring into space half the time, thinking about your ex. You're on this amazing trip in Australia. Enjoy it!"

"That's easy for you to say," he said, sitting up. "I feel like I'm surrounded by all these people who haven't got a care in the world and are only interested in getting drunk and hooking up with strangers. Sorry

I've got other stuff on my mind."

My forehead wrinkled as I frowned. "You split up with your girlfriend. I don't mean to be insensitive, but it's not really the end of the world."

"I don't expect you to understand—"

"Why?" I shot at him, annoyed. "You have no idea about my life."

"You came here on a gap year after uni to have a good time. And that's nice for you . . ."

My eyes bored into him and my words came out of nowhere. "Actually, I came here because my mum died and I wanted to find my father, who I've never met but who lives in some little town in the outback."

The corners of Andrew's mouth twitched before he laughed.

I kept staring at him. "It's not a joke," I said quietly as tears formed in my eyes. Standing, I headed to the water, intent on getting back to the boat as quickly as possible.

"You okay?" Simon called as I passed him and Yvonne.

I nodded and dived under the water.

The furious swim back to the boat was helpful in getting rid of my pent-up emotions. I sat up on deck, staring into space. Andrew's laughter had made me realise how ridiculous it all was. How ridiculous my life was at that moment. *I'm definitely not going to find Joe Sullivan. He'd probably just laugh at me too. What had I been thinking? How did I ever think this was a good idea?*

Andrew appeared a few minutes later, grabbing a towel to pat himself dry before perching on the next sunbed. "I'm sorry," he said. "You weren't joking, were you?"

I closed my eyes into the sun. "Just forget I said anything."

"I feel terrible."

"Don't feel terrible. It doesn't matter." I turned and squinted at him. "Please don't say anything to Simon and Yvonne. I don't want anyone to know."

"I won't say anything," he said, his eyes narrowed in concern. "Sorry about your mum."

"Thanks," I said, biting my lip as I turned away.

"You've never met your dad?"

"I *really* don't want to talk about it," I said, more harshly than I'd intended.

"Sorry. Do you want a drink?"

"No," I said, standing when I realised he wasn't going to leave.

In the cabin, I lay on the bed, enjoying the gentle sway of the boat. In an attempt to keep my mind occupied, I shot off a few messages to Heidi, telling her I was on a yacht for a few days, but not to worry, there was Wi-Fi on board so I'd still get all her messages. I sent an almost identical message to Aunt Mel. The time difference meant I hardly ever heard back from them immediately so my mind quickly drifted back to Andrew.

I couldn't believe I'd blurted everything out to him. It had been so easy keeping it to myself up until then. Now Andrew would feel sorry for me and ask me loads of questions. *That's ruined my time on the yacht.* It wasn't as though I could easily avoid him either.

"You okay?" Yvonne asked when she came and found me later. "You looked upset."

"Yeah, I'm fine thanks," I replied. I'd had a shower and put on fresh clothes for dinner. Things didn't seem so bad, and I decided I could handle Andrew for one last evening. I'd go back to travelling alone when we docked the following day. "I'm ready for some more delicious food. I'm just waiting for you."

"I just need a quick shower," she said. We exchanged a look; she needed more than the ten minutes it took me to get ready.

"I'll see you up on deck," I told her, leaving her to get ready in peace.

The sun was hanging low on the horizon, and it was peaceful looking out over the water. It was such a beautiful location. When I was handed a glass of champagne, everything seemed perfect. This is what I'd been in need of: a break from reality. That was all; finding my father would surely only cause me more stress, and right now all I wanted was to have some fun and enjoy this wonderful part of the world.

When Simon and Andrew appeared, I joined them at our table, ignoring the sympathetic smile Andrew flashed my way. Yvonne arrived soon after, and we slipped into another pleasant evening of eating, drinking and chatting.

"I asked the crew about that full moon party," Andrew said, once we'd finished dessert. "It actually sounds like it might be worth going to."

"I'm planning on staying on at Airlie Beach for a few more days," I told them. "I'd like to see a bit more of it before I move on."

"No," Yvonne cried. "You've got to come. It'll be so much fun!"

"Yeah," Andrew said. "You can't leave me alone with these lovebirds! Besides, what are you going to do in Airlie? Mope about on your own? I thought you were all about having a good time?"

I glared at him. *How utterly stupid of me to have said anything to him.* I reached for my drink to avoid having to reply.

"How often do you get to go to a full moon party?" Simon asked. "You don't want to miss that." Without making an excuse, he took Yvonne's hand and led her away to a quiet corner of the boat.

"They make me sick," Andrew said.

"No, they're cute. True love."

"He's always the same. When he falls for someone, he falls hard."

"You still feeling left out?" I asked, knocking back the last of my drink.

"No," he said with a crooked smile. "I've got you to keep me company, haven't I?"

"Not for long!"

It annoyed me that he knew my secret. He didn't say anything more on the subject, just stared at me with his silly smile until I gave in and laughed, pushing his face away when I couldn't stand him looking at me any longer.

Chapter 21

EVELYN – August 1994

I first met Kai in the kitchen at the Croc. He was sitting on the stainless-steel sideboard and held out a plate of sandwiches, telling me he'd made too many. I took one gratefully; I was always ravenous after work. He introduced himself and I reached to shake his hand.

"This is divine," I said, devouring the sandwich. "What's in here?"

"Pretty much one of everything that's in the fridge. Best way to make a sanger."

"You stealing food?" Admittedly, I did it occasionally, but only when I was really desperate. Generally I didn't approve of people who helped themselves to other people's food.

"No one will notice. I only took a bit from everyone." He laughed. "What are you, the fridge police?"

"It annoys me when people eat my food. I have to hide my chocolate in the fridge in the office. I want to get a little fridge for my room, but Stan says I'll raise his electricity bill too much."

"You been here a while then?" he asked.

"About four months. How long are you staying?"

He shrugged. "I'm on my way to Darwin, thought I'd stop here for a night. What is there to do around here?"

"I usually spend my afternoons at the pool."

"Ace! Mind if I join you?"

"You expect me to show you around now that you've fed me?"

"Yep," he said with a cheeky grin. He was pretty skinny and his dark hair was gelled into spikes, but he wasn't bad-looking, and there was something endearing about him. He had a positive energy and I decided I liked him immediately, which was rare for me with backpackers. At some point during my time in Kununurra I'd started to see backpackers differently. I thought I was above them.

"I'll get changed and see you in five minutes," I said to Kai.

Stan was loitering by the office when I came out of my room a few minutes later.

"You ever gonna put plants in those beds?" he asked.

My enthusiasm for gardening had waned when I started working at the hotel, and I hadn't done much of what I'd planned. To be honest, I hadn't had time: my social life had been better than I'd expected and my plans for the Croc had been put to one side.

"I'll get to it," I told him before turning to Kai. "Let's go."

"This place could be sweet as," he said as we headed to the road. "Needs a pool though. Who runs a hostel in this part of the world and doesn't have a pool?"

"A bar wouldn't go amiss either, would it?" I added.

Kai turned, walking backwards as he evaluated the grounds. "A few hammocks. Sunloungers around a pool." He raised a hand, planning exactly where everything would go. "A bar by the pool. It could be amazing."

"I've been saying this since I arrived. And the place looks way better than it did when I got here."

"Hey!" Joe's voice got my attention as we crossed the road. He was standing outside the shop.

The smile crept automatically over my face. "Hello!"

"Going anywhere nice?" he asked with a smirk.

"Thought I'd check out the pool." We'd had this conversation a hundred times.

"I hear it's a good place to spend an arvo."

"I'll let you know!" I said as I strutted past. "Fancy joining us?"

"I wish! Drinks after work?"

I nodded and turned away from him. A car horn got my attention and I waved at Cam as we passed the post office.

"Do you know everyone around here?" Kai asked.

"Not quite," I said, happily.

I called a greeting to Jack, the lifeguard, and then set up my towel in my usual shady spot in the corner. A few kids splashed with their parents in the toddler pool and an older guy swam laps, but otherwise the place was deserted.

"So what's in Darwin?" I asked Kai.

He smiled coyly. "A girl."

"I see."

"It'll sound crazy but I met her back home, in Broome. She was visiting a friend and I met her in a bar. This was about six months ago. We've been talking on the phone every day and I've been to visit her a couple of times. Then I just thought, why not go for it and move over there?"

"Yeah this is crazy. *You're* crazy."

He beamed at me. "I know! But . . ."

"Oh God. You love her?"

"Yes!"

"No, you don't," I protested. "You hardly know her."

"We talk on the phone all the time."

"She probably has a boyfriend already. You did tell her you're coming, didn't you?"

"Of course."

"And she was happy about this?"

"Yes." He hesitated slightly. "She's happy," he said, trying to be more convincing.

"Where you going to live?"

"Dunno yet," he said. "I'll figure it out when I get there."

"It's not going to work out," I told him, flatly. "Sorry to break this to you, but you will be passing through Kununurra on your way back to Broome within the month."

I couldn't bring him down from cloud nine – this boy was in love. "Make sure you give me your address so I can send you a wedding invite!" he said.

I shook my head. "When you're travelling back through here can you do me a favour and stay longer? You can help me with renovations at the Croc!"

"Not gonna happen," he said. "We swimming or what?"

***

Kai was great company. Following an afternoon at the pool, he managed to get Stan's barbecue working and served me up a decent steak with salad.

"I hope things don't work out with the Darwin girl," I said. "I could get used to having you around."

Cam arrived with Leslie and a case of beer. "This could get messy," Cam said, looking at the beer Kai had already brought. "You got the barbie going?"

"Kai did," I told him, nodding my head in his direction as way of introduction. He'd also dragged a couple of old wooden tables around which had previously lain weathered and abandoned behind the shed. There were a bunch of fold-up chairs in the shed too. It made a nice change to our usual picnic-blanket-on-the-grass arrangement.

Joe arrived soon after and left again to get sausages when he saw the barbecue was up and running. I sat beside him when he returned, stealing bites of his hot dog and listening to Kai retell the story of the Darwin girl.

"Someone tell him it's not going to work out," I said with a laugh.

"What?" Cam looked shocked. "He's packed up his life and is moving thousands of miles for her. That's true love!"

"True stupidity more like," I said.

Leslie's eyes widened, puppy-like. "I think it's romantic."

"Me too," Joe declared, nudging me. "It's just you who's cynical and miserable."

"Realistic more like."

"Speaking of romance," Leslie said to Joe. "Is Beth working again tonight?"

He shook his head as he swallowed the last of his hot dog. "She's on her way over."

It was an effort to keep my face from betraying my emotions. I really liked Beth, but I wished she wasn't coming. Then I was annoyed at myself for thinking that.

She swept in five minutes later, her smile as warm and beautiful and annoying as ever. Sitting beside Joe, she held his face as she kissed him. My stomach lurched, and I moved to join Kai by the barbecue.

"Vicky's driving me crazy," Beth said, referring to the owner of the beauty salon, whom she often complained about. "She's just got no vision. It's like she's scared of change. Such small-town mentality."

Joe laughed. "Maybe she should move to a small town . . . Oh, wait!"

Beth gave him a playful slap and then leaned closer into him. "I can't wait to have my own place. It would be so nice to be the boss."

I caught the look that passed between Cam and Leslie and wondered what it was about. Did Joe and Beth already have plans to leave Kununurra? I couldn't imagine Joe anywhere but here. And I couldn't imagine Kununurra without him.

I was deliberately slow getting through beers that evening. My emotions were all over the place, and I was sure that too much alcohol wouldn't work out well for me. Kai made no move to go to bed when the others left, and I accepted when he offered me another beer.

"What's with you and Joe?" he asked, cracking open his beer.

"What do you mean?"

"I was just surprised he had a girlfriend. I thought you and him might have had something going on."

My snort of laughter was forced and unconvincing. "No way. We're just friends."

"Well obviously, since he has a girlfriend!"

I sipped my beer and searched for a change of subject.

"This is why you're so cynical, isn't it? You love him!"

"Get lost," I said, forcing another laugh.

"Aww," he purred, wrinkling his nose. "That's so cute. I'm leaving tomorrow. You can tell me all about it."

"There's nothing to tell."

"What's his girlfriend like?"

I shrugged. "Beth's lovely. She's nice . . . and kind."

"But . . ."

"But nothing!" I said. "We're just not close. We've never really become friends. I'm not sure why."

His eyes sparkled in amusement as he looked at me, his head at an angle. "I think it's bloody obvious why!"

"Shut up," I said, giving him a playful shove. I wouldn't admit my feelings though. What would be the point?

"Are Leslie and Cam an item?" Kai asked.

"No." I raised my eyebrows. "You've not been distracted from Miss Darwin already, have you?"

Now it was his turn for the unconvincing laugh. "No. Of course not. This time tomorrow my new life begins!"

Chapter 22

EVELYN – August 1994

Kai was in the kitchen when I went for breakfast the next morning.

"Thought I was gonna miss you," he said with his infectious grin. "I'm gonna hit the road now."

He wrapped me in a bear hug and I squeezed him tightly, suddenly feeling in need of a hug. "Good luck with the girl," I said as we moved apart. "I hope you prove me wrong and it all works out."

"I'll send you a postcard and let you know how it goes," he said. "And let me know what happens with you and Joe!"

"Ha ha," I said dryly, in no mood to joke about him. "Drive safely!"

I smiled sadly as he left. I'd met so many people who were travelling through Kununurra but very few had made me feel connected to them in the way Kai had. I was sad to see him go.

As it turned out, I saw him again very soon.

"Decided to stay?" I asked ten minutes later when I set off for work and found him loitering by the payphone across the road. He looked confused.

"I just called to say I was setting off . . ."

"Uh oh! What did she say?"

"She forgot she was going away with the girls this weekend but she'll see me on Monday."

"Oh," I said. "That's . . ." I struggled for the right words.

"It's weird, isn't it?" He looked at me seriously, as though I held all the answers.

"A little bit," I agreed. You'd think she'd be waiting excitedly for him. At least, if she were even half as keen as Kai was.

He shook his head and the light came back to his eyes. "It's probably an honest mistake. And what's a couple more days?"

"You gonna stay for the weekend then?"

"I ought to get up to Darwin and start looking for a place to live."

"Friday's a great night in the Tav," I said, nodding in its direction.

"I guess I could stay one more night."

I flashed him a smile and carried on my way. "I'll see you this afternoon," I called behind me, my day seeming much better.

When I approached the hotel, I saw Joe sitting on the wall in front.

"Hey," I said casually, although my stomach seemed to think I'd taken a drop on a rollercoaster. "What you doing here?"

"Waiting for you," he said.

"Any particular reason?" It was strange for him to search me out, and I wasn't sure I was comfortable being alone with him.

He paused for a moment, staring into the distance.

"Beth wants to move to Sydney."

"Yeah, she seems pretty obsessed with that idea," I said, perching beside him on the wall.

He looked at me seriously. "She wants to go soon. She's just flown down for the weekend to start checking things out."

"That's sudden," I said. Although, maybe it wasn't. Perhaps it was just me who was only hearing about it now. "You didn't want to go with her?"

"Dad needs me at work," he said. It sounded like a well-rehearsed line.

"But she wants you to move with her?" I asked with a feeling of dread.

He nodded. "I don't know what to do."

"Well, what do you *want* to do?"

"I don't think I want to move to Sydney."

"So you'd try a long-distance relationship?"

He bit his lip and took a moment to answer. "I don't know. It all seems so complicated."

"You should probably be talking to Beth about this, not me." I stood up and moved towards the hotel.

"Sorry," he said. "We're friends though, right?"

Swallowing hard, I nodded.

"So, what do you think?" he asked.

"I don't think it's fair of you to ask," I said, taking a step back when he moved closer to me. I was about to walk away, then I turned back to him. "But I can't imagine you not being here."

***

Work was pleasantly uneventful, and I was amused to find Kai hard at work at the Croc when I arrived back.

149

HANNAH ELLIS

My flowerbed was finally getting its plants.

"Stan's not gonna pay you for that, you know?" I called.

He looked up from patting the soil down around the plants. "Thought I may as well make myself useful."

"I hope he at least gave you money for the plants?"

"He did!"

"You might get a beer if Stan's feeling generous."

"Sounds good. You off for your swim?"

"You know me so well," I said. "You coming?"

"I think I'll finish up here."

"Great! Now I'll have to help."

"I'll manage," he insisted.

I was happy to help though, and it was more fun working on it with someone else. We had a break when Stan brought us beers but quickly got back to work. Kai was even more enthusiastic about the place than I had been when I first arrived. The afternoon flew by, and we were busy sanding down the tables when Joe arrived. Kai was convinced the tables were good-quality wood and would come up nicely once they were sanded down and varnished. I wasn't quite so sure and was approaching exhaustion.

"Help me!" I said to Joe as I collapsed on my back on the grass nearby. "He's working me to the bone."

"No swimming today?" Joe asked.

"He wouldn't let me leave," I complained theatrically.

"Not true!" Kai said. "It would've been nice to get on with things without your constant chatter." He wandered away, muttering about beer.

"You okay?" I said when Joe sat next to me.

"I don't know. My head's a mess. I just wanna get drunk and forget about everything."

Kai's timing as he returned was perfect. "Cheers!" he said, passing out beers.

"You ready for a night at the Tav?" Joe said to Kai.

"I'm expecting great things!"

"Yeah," I said with a laugh. "Have as much fun as you can before you start your new life!"

"What *is* up with you?" Kai asked as I giggled away on the grass.

"Nothing!" My confused emotions had made me oddly hyper. "I just think it's going to be a fun night."

"But probably not so much fun when you have to get up for work in the morning," Joe remarked.

"I'll worry about that in the morning."

***

"You should forget about Miss Darwin and just stay here with us!" I said loudly to Kai at the end of a night filled with beer and laughter, dancing and joking. I suddenly loved my merry little gang so much and was compelled to tell them. Repeatedly.

The Tav had closed, and we were standing out on the road with a few other groups of people doing the same as us: trying to drag the night out just a little longer. "I don't want you to leave us, Kai," I went on. "I feel like you're family already. You need to stay with us!"

"Definitely stay," Cam said, pointing a finger at Kai and stumbling off the curb when he lost his balance.

I could feel my eyelids drooping, but I didn't want to go to bed. "I love you guys," I said again, leaning into Joe.

"You're so drunk," Joe said, laughing.

"I'm just a bit tipsy," I insisted. "Tiny bit! But I do actually love you all and this place. And everyone."

"How are you gonna get up for work tomorrow?" Kai asked.

"The question we ask most Fridays!" Leslie said.

"And I always manage it!" I said, slurring my words.

"C'mon," Kai said, taking my arm. "I'm going to do you a favour and take you to bed."

A leery cheer went up around our group.

"Told you we could get him to forget all about Darwin!" I called as Kai and I stumbled across the road, waving goodbye as we went.

"Don't go sneaking off tomorrow when I'm at work, will you?" I said to him when we reached my room. "Make sure you say goodbye."

"Promise," he said, heading off to his own room. "Good luck getting up in the morning!"

I fell onto my bed. "Night!" I mumbled to the gecko, who I could've sworn rolled his eyes at the state of me.

Chapter 23

EVELYN – August 1994

"Wakey-wakey!" The overly cheerful voice pulled me from my black hole of sleep the next morning. The banging on my door that went with it pained me so much that they might as well have been banging directly on my skull. "Come on! It's a beautiful day and I've brought you a present."

I groaned as I opened the door to be hit by the evil sunlight and ungodly heat. *Why do I have to work on Saturdays?* Retreating quickly, I fell back on my bed. Joe followed me in. "I brought coffee."

"I love you," I said, taking the mug from him.

"Still? Even in the sober light of day?"

I blinked him into focus and had the urge to kiss him. My cheeks flushed as thoughts of dragging him onto my bed filled my mind. He'd never been in my room before. He looked amazing, perched on the edge of my bed, his boyish smile making my head swim. *These sorts of thoughts will get me nowhere. He has a girlfriend.*

I smiled back at Joe. "I'm probably not sober yet, to be honest. How do you look so fresh?"

153

"I'm just better at drinking than you!"

"This is not fair. Do you want to do a job swap this morning?"

"You think you can do my job hungover?"

The thought was actually really nice. Mick would take good care of me, and it would be a piece of cake.

"Do you wanna do something this afternoon?" Joe asked. "Make it through work and I'll buy you a beer."

"Oh, please don't use that word around me," I said as nausea swept up from my stomach. I breathed deeply through my nose until it passed.

"Shall I round everyone up for a trip on the boat?" he suggested.

"Why not? I can sleep on the boat."

"Come in the shop after your shift?"

I stuck my bottom lip out. "I don't want to work. Why do I do this to myself?"

He grinned and left me alone with my coffee and a debilitating hangover. I wasn't sure I could dress myself, never mind spend several hours cleaning. I just prayed I didn't bump into any of the Kingstons. It was a struggle to deal with them at any time; with a hangover, they were impossible.

Unfortunately, I met Todd as soon as I reached the hotel – he was lingering in front of the door. I could've sworn he was waiting for me. I had a vague memory of seeing him the previous evening. "You look like death," he said.

"I feel like it."

"I saw you dancing in the Tav."

"I may have overdone it with the alcohol," I confessed.

"Get yourself back to bed," he said, suddenly sounding confident. There was an arrogance to his tone which didn't suit him. "I can find someone to cover your shift."

"I'll be fine," I said, but my stomach was churning and I wasn't sure I could manage to do my job at all.

"I insist."

"Really?"

"It's my hotel," he said. "If I say you can have a day off, you can have a day off."

"Yeah, but . . ." I was about to point out that it was actually Arthur's hotel, and he'd probably have something else to say about the matter. Since my hangover seemed to be getting steadily worse, however, I decided I should keep quiet and take him up on his offer.

"I'll get Tania to cover," he said. "You go and sleep it off."

I gave him a heartfelt "Thank you" and turned, thrilled to be able to sleep for the morning instead of cleaning up after strangers. I hadn't gone far when a thought occurred to me: Tania worked on my days off, but she worked at Walkabout Hostel on Saturdays so she wouldn't be able to take my shift. For a moment, I was torn between the idea of going back to bed and going back to make sure Todd didn't get into trouble on my account. Annoyingly, my conscience got the better of me and I turned back to the hotel. Todd was trying to be nice; I couldn't let him get into trouble because of me.

I was in the bar area when I heard raised voices coming from Arthur's office. Creeping nearer, I caught Todd's voice.

"What was I supposed to say? She's ill and can't work. It's not her fault. And it's the first time she's missed a day."

"You really believe she's crook?" Arthur shouted. "She probably just drank too much last night and thinks she can sweet talk her way round you."

"She's got food poisoning," Todd insisted. "Why are you making such a big deal about it?"

"Because you need to start acting like an employer around here instead of trying to make friends with the staff. You're an embarrassment." He paused. "Get Evelyn on the phone and tell her to be here in half an hour or she's fired."

"You can't fire her because she's crook," Todd said desperately. *Bloody hell, losing my job over a hangover is ridiculous.* It was tempting to reveal myself and tell them I'd be fine to work, but I had the feeling that might just make things worse.

"Well you can be the one to tell your mother she has to do the rooms today. Because there's no one else to do them."

"I'll do them," Todd said, only just loud enough for me to hear from my spot behind the door. "It's not a big deal."

"You're going to clean toilets?" Arthur asked, disbelievingly. "And you reckon you can run this place one day? You'll be the boss and you think it's okay for you to be cleaning toilets?"

I slipped quietly out of sight when I heard footsteps. The door flung open and Todd stalked out. He walked quickly across the courtyard, and I watched him go with mixed feelings. I pitied him; my dad had always been pretty detached and unfeeling, but at least I'd had my mum on my side. Todd had probably never known any affection from his family. My respect for him rose dramatically; he'd been kind to me even though he must have known it would cause him problems. Deciding it would hurt his pride if he knew I'd heard his confrontation with his dad, I slipped quietly out of the hotel.

A few hours of sleep did me the world of good and I felt much more human when I emerged from my room for the second time that day. Kai was standing in the middle of the lawn with a hosepipe in his hand. Turning, he sprayed water in my direction with a cheeky grin.

"Fancy coming out on Joe's boat with us?" I asked.

He glanced at his watch, frowning. "I should probably hit the road."

"Let's not pretend you're leaving today," I said, jovially.

"Fine," he said. "But I'm leaving before sun up tomorrow."

"Sure you are! I'll be back in five," I told him.

Joe was chatting to a customer about fishing tackle and gave me a quick nod when I walked into the shop. I browsed while I waited for him. Fishing was a serious business in Kununurra, and it was a good fifteen minutes before the guy left. By that time, I'd decided to try out a camping chair hidden away at the end of the shop and was nice and relaxed when Joe came back to find me.

"Sorry, I thought he'd never leave."

"That's okay. I'm comfy!"

"What happened? Shouldn't you still be at work?"

157

"I didn't manage to work today," I told him. "I'm going to have to tone down my Friday nights."

"You didn't lose your job, did you?"

"No," I said cautiously. *Hopefully not.*

"Dad should be here in an hour and I can leave then. Cam and Leslie are keen for a boat trip. Do you want to invite Kai?"

"I already did," I told him with a cheeky grin. A thought crossed my mind. "Would you mind if I invited Todd too?"

He looked surprised. "It's fine by me. The others might not thank you."

"It's *your* boat," I pointed out.

"It's my dad's, actually, but I see your point. Invite him if you want. I thought you weren't keen on him though?"

"I might have been too quick to judge him."

Joe looked curious as to my sudden change of heart but didn't question me further.

When I called Todd and asked him to join us, he seemed surprised but agreed, and he arrived at the boat ramp in Celebrity Tree Park just after me and Kai. The place always made me laugh; celebrities had supposedly planted the trees, but I'd wandered around reading all the plaques and only recognised a couple of names.

Leslie and Cam were helping Joe with the boat, and we waited by the water for them.

"Thanks for this morning," I said to Todd, casually. "I hope I didn't get you into trouble."

"Of course not," he said. "It wasn't a problem."

He blushed when I thanked him again. "I promise I won't make a habit of it."

158

"Good!" he said, managing a smile. "Here comes Joe."

It didn't take me long to regret inviting Todd. When Joe pushed the boat off the trailer into the water, Todd looked over at him. "I could've brought *my* boat," he said. "Will we all fit in that little thing?"

I cringed. Sometimes it was as if he were possessed by Arthur. The Kingstons all seemed to have the built-in desire to point out that they were better than everyone else. It made me want to shake Todd.

Everyone turned to look at him.

"We might be *one* person too many," Cam said pointedly.

"It's fine," Joe said. "It's nice and cosy!"

The day went on like that; Todd just didn't fit in, and I watched as my friends continually bit their tongues at his remarks. When Cam reeled in a huge barramundi, all Todd could do was tell us about the time he'd caught one way bigger. *A bigger fish, a better boat, we get it, Todd, you're a better person and we should all bow down to you.* I had to bite my own tongue at that point and remind myself of how he'd stuck up for me to his dad. He wasn't *all* bad. His comment went ignored; no one was willing to be brought down to his level. We revelled in Cam's fishing success and Todd slinked off to the back of the boat to put his line in the water.

I correctly predicted that I would get a talking to later about why on earth I'd invited Todd. Back on dry land, he left, saying he had to get to work, and the rest of us hung around, helping Joe with the boat and finishing off the beers.

"He's lucky I didn't throw him to the crocs," Cam remarked as Todd's car pulled away.

Leslie nodded along. "I'm always telling myself he's not such a bad guy . . . and then I spend more than five minutes with him and realise how wrong I am."

"Give him a break," Joe said. "He's battling some bad DNA. And if you grew up with those parents you'd be socially awkward too."

"Please don't invite him out again," Leslie pleaded with me.

"Okay, okay!" I laughed as they all glared at me. "He was nice to me at work today and I took pity on him, that's all. But I won't invite him again." I wobbled as I walked away from the water, the alcohol giving me a glow and making everything seem hilarious. "You need to get some better celebrities," I declared, looking round the park. "I only know Princess Anne and Rolf Harris. You should get someone better to come and plant you a tree!"

"Hey!" Joe said. "There are a lot of local celebrities. They're the best kind."

"Do you think I'd pass as a local celebrity?" I said, highly amused. "I could plant you a tree. We all know I'm good at gardening!"

"That'll be the day," Cam said, slinging an arm around my shoulders. "We'll know things have *really* gone wrong when your name's on a plaque here."

"I might be a big celebrity one day," I insisted. "Then you'll be begging me to plant you a tree!"

***

The following weeks were strange ones. Beth arrived back from Sydney and made the official announcement that she and Joe would be moving down there. Plans weren't final but she was adamant that they'd move by the new year, if not before. I desperately hoped it wouldn't be before then. I wanted him around as long as possible.

Joe didn't speak to me about it, but there was a heaviness to him that I'd never known before. His smile didn't reach his eyes any more, and he seemed to struggle to focus on anything; he was always lost in thought. Occasionally, I felt sorry for him, but mostly I was angry with him. He should have had more of a backbone and told Beth how he really felt instead of just going along with her plans.

At work, I made a concerted effort to talk to Todd. Sometimes he could be sweet. Most of the time, I wondered why I even bothered. The arrogance that was the Kingston family trait was hard to overlook. Eventually, I decided we were destined to be acquaintances rather than friends; he was such hard work.

I did have one new friend though: Kai. He didn't leave Kununurra, and I was so glad. He was such a positive addition to our group. It felt like we'd always been friends. It turned out the girl in Darwin wasn't as keen as he was; she worried that things were moving too fast and she was too young for such a big commitment. Kai kept talking about going back to Broome, but I knew he wouldn't. He was like me; he fitted right into life in Kununurra and had no real desire to leave. Plus, Stan had agreed to employ him at the Croc.

Chapter 24

LIBBY – August 2017

We took a Greyhound bus north and I absorbed local knowledge from the friendly driver. Fields of sugar cane lined the road, and we caught glimpses of the snaking rivers which made up the Burdekin region. We covered three hundred kilometres in less than four hours. The huge distances we were covering along the coastline amazed me. The country was vast, and I struggled to get my head around the amount of space; it just seemed to stretch on forever.

At Townsville, we waited to board the ferry to Magnetic Island. When I saw how many others were going the same way, I was glad Simon had called ahead to reserve rooms at a hostel.

Andrew had been suspiciously quiet on the bus ride, and I was waiting for him to try to talk to me. I had the feeling he was dying to ask questions.

"Stop giving me weird looks," I finally said when we sat alone on the ferry. Simon and Yvonne had gone to find drinks. "What do you want to know?"

"I don't want to pry if you don't want to talk about it."

"Just ask, will you?"

"Fine. So your dad lives in Australia?" I nodded. "And you've never met him?"

"Nope."

"And what does he think about you coming to visit?"

I shifted in my seat. "He doesn't know. I don't even know if he knows I exist."

"Wow!" he said. "That's . . ."

"Crazy, isn't it? I don't even know if I can go through with it. He lives in this little town called Kununurra. I looked it up – it's the middle of nowhere: crocodile country."

"So your dad's some Crocodile Dundee type?"

"I have no idea. I've been having such a great time over the past few weeks, I'm not sure I want to ruin it by finding out I'm the daughter of an alcoholic or a druggy or something." I paused. "I don't know anything about him. He might not live there any more. Or he might be a crazy recluse living in a hut in the outback!"

Andrew's warm smile put me at ease. Initially I'd been annoyed at myself for blurting it all out to him, but it suddenly felt good to talk about it.

"You won't know unless you find out. He might be a nice guy."

"But even if he's the nicest guy in the world, how's he going to react when I turn up out of the blue and tell him I'm his daughter?"

Andrew's eyes lingered on mine. "But you came all the way out here. Don't back out now."

I shook my head. "I don't know what to do. I'm scared of what I'll find if I go looking for him."

He gave my hand a quick squeeze and then thankfully dropped the subject.

The boat trip was short and we were on the island before I knew it. Mokes – small open-topped cars – were the popular form of transport on the island . After a short wait to rent one, we got on our way, driving the dusty island roads to find our accommodation at the Koala Village.

"I quite like this place," Yvonne remarked early in the evening as she lazed in a hammock in front of our bungalow. We were sharing with two other girls. Simon and Andrew were in another bungalow nearby. It was one of the nicer places I'd stayed, with a pool beside the bar and bungalows scattered around, each containing two dorm rooms. The grounds were immaculately kept and hammocks were plentiful. It was also conveniently located close to Horseshoe Bay – the site of the full moon party.

We'd had a dip in the pool when we arrived and then left the boys to get changed for the party. Yvonne insisted on getting a bottle of wine for us to drink while we got ready, but so far we'd just been trying to master the art of drinking cheap wine from plastic cups while swinging in hammocks. There was a lot of giggling. Yvonne seemed tipsy already.

"You look nice," Andrew said, when we finally met at the bar.

"Thank you," I said, doing a quick twirl in my sundress. "I think you could've chosen a better adjective than nice, but I suppose I'll take the compliment anyway!"

"Lovely?" he said, standing and falling into step beside me to follow Simon and Yvonne over to the beach.

"It would have been better. Bit late now though."

"Is Yvonne drunk?" Andrew asked as we watched her stumble along in front of us, laughing hysterically as she went.

"Yeah," I said, smiling. It was entertaining to see her so uninhibited.

We joined a line of partygoers who ambled along the road from the Koala Village to the beach at Horseshoe Bay. Others arrived from further afield in mokes. The atmosphere was jovial even before we reached the beach. Bottles of beer and cheap wine were passed between complete strangers. Rows of mokes were parked up along the road, and I slipped off my shoes as we moved onto the sand. The full moon hung low over the water, bright and magical. Barbecue smoke wafted around, and the smell of sausages made my mouth water.

We hadn't eaten properly all day and joined the line for burgers and hotdogs before heading to the bar, where we all opted for the full moon special. It was an unnatural neon blue cocktail, syrupy and sweet. I sucked it through the straw with a grimace as we wandered, eventually stopping beside one of several bonfires which flickered along the beach.

Simon and Yvonne whispered and giggled, and I could see why Andrew was a bit put out – Simon had definitely prioritised Yvonne over him. Luckily, Andrew seemed to have cheered up about the situation.

"You know, you should really make sure you enjoy your trip," I said to Andrew, who looked at me, confused. "I mean, don't waste it worrying about your ex. Have fun!" He looked amused, and it dawned on me that I was a bit tipsy. "Pretend you haven't got a care in the world and go a bit crazy."

His smirk was very cute. "I'm not taking advice from you," he said.

"Why not? I give great advice!"

"Because you came all the way out here looking for someone and now you're going to back out because you're nervous."

"I have every reason to be nervous," I told him.

"And I have every reason to mope around being miserable!"

I smiled at his logic. Yvonne suddenly loomed over me, insisting I dance with her.

"I'll be back," I said to Andrew. "Try and have fun while I'm gone!"

In one area of the beach, a crowd of people danced, flinging themselves around, barefoot and joyful. Music drifted from speakers dotted around, and I was happy bopping away in the sea of strangers. The wine had gone to my head and when Yvonne set off back to the boys, I went in search of water.

The beach was busy and I meandered between sweaty bodies as I tried to find my little group. All the fires looked the same, and I had no idea where exactly I'd left them. Admitting that I'd lost them, I sat halfway up a sand dune and observed the action on the beach. Everyone was having such a great time, and it really was a beautiful setting for a party.

I was just starting to think about walking back to the hostel when Andrew appeared in front of me.

"There you are!" he said, cheerfully. "How am I supposed to have fun when I spend the whole evening looking for you?"

"I looked everywhere for you," I said as he plonked himself beside me. "Where are Simon and Yvonne?"

"They called it a night. Yvonne could hardly walk!" He gave me a funny look. "Where are your shoes?"

"Oh God!" I looked down. "Where *are* my shoes? Stop laughing!" I snapped. "We have to go and look for my shoes!" When he showed no sign of moving, I took his hand and pulled him up.

"I'm supposed to be having fun, not searching for shoes," he said.

"You can have all the fun you want after we find my shoes."

"Okay, where did you leave them?"

"With you! By one of the fires . . ."

"Here," Andrew said, when we reached the nearest bonfire.

"They're not mine," I told him, looking at the strappy sandals he was holding up. He dropped them back where he found them and moved on to the next pair of abandoned sandals. The beach was full of them and by about the tenth pair, we found it quite hysterical.

"They're nice though," Andrew said, scrutinising his latest find – cute little kitten heels. "Just take them."

"I can't take someone else's shoes!"

"Why not? Someone else probably took yours."

Taking a break from the shoe hunt, we sat beside a bonfire with a group of strangers. A couple of people strummed guitars and others sang along with the well-known tunes.

"I'm going to find more beers," Andrew said.

"I can't move," I told him. The stars were mesmerising as I lay back on the sand.

"Stay there. I'll be right back."

"Don't lose me again," I said.

"Just don't move."

As the music and hum of people buzzed around me, my eyelids drooped and I fought to keep my eyes open.

I'll wait for Andrew to get back and then I'm going to bed.

Chapter 25

LIBBY – August 2017

The sand had turned cool when I woke, and I was grateful for the hoodie draped over me. It carried Andrew's scent and I could hear his voice nearby, light and joking. His talk of surfing mingled with someone else's laughter. My eyes blinked open to find the flames of the bonfire dancing before me.

"How was the nap?" Andrew asked.

Sitting up, I ran my hands through my tangled, sand-filled hair. Embarrassment was a vague idea until the remaining alcohol in my blood kept me from caring. The crowds had thinned on the beach, and only a handful of people were left around the fire.

"What time is it?" I asked groggily.

He pulled his phone from his pocket and lit up the screen. "Just after two. Do you want to head back?"

With a nod, I stood up, pulling Andrew's hoodie on as I did so. He didn't comment.

"Thanks for staying with me," I said as we walked. I'd always felt safe when I was travelling, but it occurred to me that passing out drunk on a beach surrounded by strangers probably wasn't very

171

sensible. Having Andrew beside me made it seem okay.

We walked in silence until we reached the road, where the loose gravel reminded me of my missing shoes. Cursing mildly, I hopped from foot to foot. Andrew strode on, not even attempting to hide his amusement.

"Wait!" I tried to catch up with him but my feet wouldn't comply. Every step brought pain, and I only managed to stumble along for a few steps. Andrew came back to me.

"You've already got my hoodie, don't ask for my shoes as well."

"If you gave me *one* we could hop back together!"

He turned his back to me, and I took it as an invitation for a piggyback.

Ten minutes later he set me down on the soft grass at the Koala Village. I'd expected to have to creep around as others slept on, but it turned out that the party had moved from the beach to the Koala Village. Andrew escorted me past the revellers by the pool and back to bungalow number seven, where we found another party in full swing. The hammocks were all inhabited and people lazed around on the grass while music blared with an obnoxious thumping bass. Through the open door, I could see people sitting on the beds, mine included. It was disheartening; all I needed was sleep, but it seemed like an unlikely prospect.

"I think I'll have a wander," I told Andrew. "See if I can find a free hammock to sleep in."

"This place is crazy," he said as we walked around the complex. Groups of people were scattered around the place, and it seemed like anyone who wanted to get any sleep was doomed.

"Aha!" I said a little while later, excited to find an empty hammock in a lonely corner.

"Are you seriously going to sleep there?" Andrew asked.

"My bed is taken!" I flopped ungracefully into the hammock and wriggled to get my balance right. "And this is really comfy."

"I'm not sure it's safe to sleep out here."

"I'll be okay. Everyone's so friendly."

"I was thinking more about the wildlife." He glanced around, nervously. "There's about ten thousand species of things that can kill you around here."

"Ten thousand?" I asked, amused.

"Approximately!"

"I'm sure I'll survive. You don't need to babysit me!"

"Not sure I can really sleep in my bed either with all that racket going on."

"You'll have to find your own hammock then," I said. "I'm not shari—" The screech that cut me off was loud, wild and far too close. Jumping out of the hammock, I was behind Andrew in a shot and clinging to his arm. "What on earth?" I said, looking up at the source of the noise.

"Bats," Andrew said. "One of the few things around here which won't kill you!"

"Bats?" It was too loud for bats.

"Yeah. Fruit bats are really loud. And really big."

Rustling overhead drew my attention and the screech came again. Two huge black creatures flapped their massive wings, fighting and shrieking before taking off, causing a breeze as they left.

"Oh my God! They're huge."

"Yep," Andrew agreed.

"What are you doing?" I asked when he manoeuvred himself easily into the hammock.

"I found myself a hammock, like you suggested."

"But that's mine."

Light from the nearby path bounced off his eyes, glimmering as he grinned mischievously. "You got out."

I glared for a moment. Then I walked purposefully over to the hammock and took hold of it with both hands, giving it a quick, forceful tug. Andrew flailed before tumbling out. Smugly, I reclaimed the hammock.

"You got out!" I said innocently when he brushed himself off and stood looking down at me. The hammock wobbled when he climbed in next to me, and I turned my nose up at having his feet beside my head. "You better not snore," I said.

"You actually think you can sleep in this?"

"Why not?"

"Well, it's pretty wobbly for one thing." He rocked the hammock to make his point. "And did I mention the wildlife?"

"You're a bit of a scaredy cat, aren't you?"

"I'm not the one who jumped a mile at a little bat."

I gave him a quick kick before I closed my eyes. "Goodnight."

The murmur of voices and hum of music drifted in waves on the warm night air. Suddenly revived, I opened my eyes and gazed through the branches to the sparkling sky. The haze of the Milky Way was visible directly overhead.

Andrew's voice broke the silence, smooth and serious. "I really think you should go and find your father."

"I'm starting to regret telling you about him," I said.

"How about we make a deal?" he said. I eyed him suspiciously. "I'll relax and forget about my ex, and you'll go and find your dad, like you intended . . ."

"It seems like you get the better end of the deal!"

"Maybe! But it's good for us both. We'll both make the most of our time in Australia."

He went quiet and I was glad he didn't push me any further on the subject. When he closed his eyes, I found myself studying his face. He looked so peaceful. His hair was ruffled, his skin had a deep tan and there was a day's worth of stubble along his jaw.

The air was still, and it was absolutely silent when my eyelids finally grew heavier. I was aware of Andrew's body next to mine as I felt myself slipping into sleep.

HANNAH ELLIS

Chapter 26

EVELYN – October 1994

Six months had flown by and any ideas about travelling the rest of Australia had disappeared. I was completely and utterly at home in Kununurra. I enjoyed my routine of working in the mornings, eating a late lunch with Kai at the Croc and then spending a couple of hours at the pool.

Once or twice, it occurred to me that my time in Australia was limited and there was still so much more I could see. Leaving Kununurra was never a serious consideration though.

"Hi!" I called to Joe as I approached the Croc one Saturday in October. It was a relief to finish work, and I was looking forward to an afternoon with my little gang. Kai had finally decided to go back to Broome for a visit, and it was strange not having him around the place.

"How was work?" Joe asked, seeming distracted as he opened the door to his pickup.

"I survived!" I said. "What are we doing this afternoon?"

"Beth's got one of those social nights at the salon

tonight so she got the day off. I'm heading over to see her now. Leslie got called into work. I'm not sure what Cam's up to."

I'd assumed we'd be going out on the boat or driving out to one of the springs. My disappointment must have been written all over my face, but I did my best to hide it. "Are you still going to the movie tonight?" I asked hopefully. The drive-in movie theatre had flyers up all around town advertising the showing of *Muriel's Wedding*. Everyone was talking about it.

"I'll probably give it a miss," he said. He wasn't his usual cheerful self. "Leslie and Cam are definitely going though."

"Okay," I said, feeling my mood take an abrupt nosedive. I was irrationally disappointed by the change to the Saturday afternoon routine. "Have fun with Beth!"

"You okay?" Joe asked when I didn't move from the spot.

"Yeah," I said automatically. I couldn't say anything else; Joe and I never talked about anything serious. I wasn't okay though. "You?" I asked.

He leaned on the car door and seemed like he was about to say something. I waited while his gaze drifted away from me. He looked tired. "I'm fine," he said, his eyes finally meeting mine and lingering for a moment too long. "I better go."

I didn't move until his ute was out of sight. Then I stomped into the Croc feeling like I might explode. I had the rest of the day to kill and was filled with a rage which had taken me by surprise. Grabbing a shovel from the shed, I went to work on an empty flowerbed – one of the only empty ones since Kai had started working at the Croc. I attacked the hard soil, attempting to turn it over and pulling out weeds as I went.

"What are you doing?" Stan called.

"I'm gardening," I shouted at him.

"Okay," he said, taken aback.

"I'm going to turn the soil over and then go and buy plants!"

"Why are you shouting?" he asked calmly, keeping his distance from me. I was wobbling precariously on the line between sane and crazy.

"I don't know," I yelled. "I can't help it. You'll need to give me money for plants . . . Arrrgggghhhh!"

"What?" Stan asked when I dropped the shovel and moved at lightning speed across the lawn.

"There's a bloody snake," I told him, still shouting and jumping around erratically now as well.

"Where?"

"By the bush over there," I said, pointing. "I hate snakes. I hate this place!"

He edged closer. "It's just a blue-tongue."

"It moved like a snake," I insisted. "And it's really big."

"Definitely a lizard," he told me.

"I just can't do this!" I screamed, not even sure what I was referring to. "I've had enough."

"Okay," Stan said slowly. "Let's stop shouting."

I inhaled deeply and nodded, feeling like a complete idiot. "Sorry."

"No worries. Come with me, we'll have a drink."

In the office neither of us said anything for a few minutes, but the beer Stan gave me calmed me down and I felt much saner again, though slightly embarrassed by my outburst.

"What's going on then?" Stan finally asked.

"I don't know," I said miserably.

"You don't want to talk about it you mean?"

"I really don't know," I said again. Actually, I *did* know. I just didn't want to admit it to anyone, including myself.

He opened a drawer and pulled out a deck of playing cards. "You play poker?"

I shook my head.

"Kids," he said, tutting as he shuffled the deck. "What do they teach you these days?"

"You gonna teach me?" I asked.

"Seems like it."

By the end of the afternoon, I was a pro. Stan roped in a couple of guys who were staying at the Croc – farm workers who were in town for the weekend – and we whiled away a good few hours.

"You off to see this film everyone's on about?" Stan asked when we packed up the cards. The other fellas had gone over to the Tav for the evening.

"No," I said, feeling the anger seeping back.

"Why not?"

"I don't feel like it, I'm gonna get some food and go to bed. Hopefully tomorrow's a better day."

"It's humid today," he said. "The heat does funny things to people."

I left him to rustle up some dinner and was just tidying up when a figure appeared in the kitchen doorway.

"You ready?" Joe asked.

"For what?"

"Movie night, of course. Cam was picking Leslie up so I said I'd swing by for you and meet them there."

"I thought you weren't going?"

"Changed my mind," he said quietly.

"I wasn't planning on going," I told him.

"Since when? Cam said you were coming."

"I've got some stuff to do."

He tilted his head to one side. "I brought loads of snacks. You need to help me eat them."

"It's a shame Beth can't go," I said, closing a cupboard with more force than I'd intended.

"Yeah." He shifted his weight and glared at me. "You coming or not?"

I held his gaze, trying to decide. My emotions were a jumble when I walked past him in the direction of my room. I didn't know what to do. Of course I wanted to go to the movie with him, but spending time with Joe felt increasingly like tormenting myself.

"Please come," he said when I reached my door.

That's all it took. I was powerless to refuse.

***

The Picture Gardens were just outside town. Rows of pickups were lined up haphazardly at the back half of the field, while closer to the screen, rows of assorted seating were set up – mostly camping chairs and deck chairs. When we pulled up beside them, Leslie and Cam were seated atop an assortment of cushions and blankets in the back of Cam's ute, with the truck-bed facing the screen.

Joe's ute was set up similarly, and I felt awkward

as I sat beside him in the back. I wondered if Beth knew he was with me. On the occasions she came out with us, she was kind and chatted to me, but sometimes I had the feeling it was all fake, like she felt she had to make an effort but secretly would rather I wasn't there.

Silence fell when the big screen lit up. The air was warm and stars were visible overhead. True to his word, Joe had snacks and passed me things at intervals over the course of the film. I struggled to concentrate, and kept quiet when Joe leaned over to make the occasional comment about the film. It was coming to the end when my skin began to tickle. I'd got used to the flies and mosquitoes, but this felt different. I swiped at my cheek but felt nothing. The tickling continued and my hands moved frequently to my face. Joe leaned over and ran a finger down my cheek.

"What is it?" I asked.

His eyes sparkled in the dim light. "Nothing that'll hurt you."

I rubbed my face with both hands, making him laugh.

As soon as the credits rolled up, Joe took my hand and helped me down from the truck-bed. When he opened the passenger door I moved inside, puzzled as he sat beside me and switched the light on before pulling the rear-view mirror towards me.

"Oh my God!" I said, taking in my reflection. My face was streaked with black, and I vaguely resembled a chimney sweep. "What is that?"

Joe's face was the same: smeared with black.

"They're burning sugar cane," he told me. "It's

the ash. Winds must have changed direction."

"How weird," I said, looking at my reflection once more and attempting to rub away the soot.

When I turned to Joe he reached for my cheek, sending my heart into overdrive. "It's our snow." Our eyes locked and the air around us was charged. "Black snow."

"What did you think?" Cam asked, peering in the window. "All right, wasn't it?"

"I loved it!" Leslie announced, arriving at the opposite window.

I smiled back at her. My heart was racing and I felt like I'd been caught out.

"Shall we head to the Tav?" Cam asked.

"I'm gonna head home," I said. "I'm done in."

"Well that's very boring," he replied. "What about you, Joe?"

"I'll see you there," he said.

We drove back in silence and said a quick, curt goodbye outside the Croc. Tears stung my eyes as I crawled into bed, and I had to push thoughts of Joe from my mind, reminding myself of Beth and their perfect relationship.

Chapter 27

LIBBY – August 2017

With a jolt, the hammock moved and I was awake again. I'd barely had five minutes' sleep. Andrew was standing next to me.

"Do you want to go back to the beach?" he asked. I squinted up at him, confused. He took my hand and pulled me up. "Every night I tell myself I'll get up to watch the sunrise. And so far, I've not managed it. Now's my chance!"

"Okay," I said, stretching and blinking away sleep.

To avoid Andrew having to carry me, I slipped into my room to get my tattered trainers. There was someone in my bed, and the remnants of a wild night were scattered around the floor. We walked in silence to the beach and arrived just as the first glimpse of sunlight arrived on the horizon. I followed Andrew to a spot on top of a low sand dune and automatically sat close to him. When he put an arm around my shoulder, I leaned into him like it was the most natural thing in the world.

Neither of us said a word. We just sat for half an

hour in awe of the changing colours of the sky. Waves rolled gently onto the shore, creating a perfect lullaby as the sun gave us the most breathtaking of shows. The rich reds and golds seeped into the bright blue sky and shimmered elegantly on the surface of the water. *I should get up for this every morning.* It was perfect.

When the sun had fully risen and the sky settled back into its stunning bright blue, Andrew pulled me up. My legs moved automatically until Andrew stopped me, tugging on my hand until I'd turned to face him, dazed and confused.

My insides fluttered at the look in his eyes, and when he moved to kiss me, my heart rate increased dramatically. He'd taken me by surprise, but kissing him felt so natural, and I didn't want it to stop.

"I'll bet we can find your shoes now," he said when he finally moved his lips from mine. A clean-up crew had arrived on the beach and Andrew was right; in the blinding light of day, my sandals were easy to find, scattered with many others in the soft sand.

Walking back to the Koala Village, a hangover niggled at my head and my stomach. The magic of night-time had disappeared, leaving me feeling washed out. I was in desperate need of a long sleep and a good wash. When Andrew left me back at my quiet bungalow, I returned his hoodie, ignoring him when he insisted I could give it to him later. He kissed me again, making my insides flutter.

"I had a fun night," he said, pulling away. "And I definitely wasn't moping." I knew what he was going to say next. "I took your advice. You should take mine."

"I'll think about it," I said, smiling as I moved zombie-like inside, happy to find my bed had been vacated. The room smelled sweaty and foul but I didn't care; I flopped into bed and passed out.

At lunchtime, I showered for too long, only dragging myself out from the blissful spray when someone banged at the door and demanded I hurry up. Thoughts of my father swirled in my head, and I found myself unable to focus on anything else. I'd come all this way and I should find out. I should do what Mum wanted and find Joe Sullivan.

By the time I reached the bar area and picked at what was left of the continental breakfast, it was clear in my head what I needed to do. And I wanted to get on with it. It felt like I was being physically pushed; I needed to go and find Joe Sullivan, and I needed to do it immediately.

Yvonne hadn't been in our bungalow when I'd gone to bed – I assumed she was with Simon somewhere. When she didn't reply to my messages, I guessed they were still asleep. I hung around for a while, hoping to catch one of them; I couldn't even remember which bungalow the boys were staying in. Deciding that if I waited I'd chicken out, I fetched my backpack and hitched a ride to the harbour with my roommates. I felt slightly uneasy at not saying goodbye to Andrew but sent a message to Yvonne, telling her I'd hit the road and not to worry when she couldn't find me.

With a sense of purpose I hadn't felt since leaving the UK, I boarded the boat back to Townsville and from there found my way to a bus which would take me the 350 kilometres to Cairns. I managed to spend a night in Cairns without speaking to anyone except the girl on reception at the hostel.

I lay awake for most of that night. The flights were booked so I couldn't back out, but to say I was apprehensive was an understatement. In the early hours, just as I felt myself falling asleep, an image of Andrew swinging in the hammock and grinning at me entered my head. Reaching for my phone, I thought of sending him a message before realising I didn't have his number. I'd have to ask Yvonne for it. She'd messaged me to say she had an awful hangover and couldn't believe I'd left without saying goodbye.

I'd also had a message from Uncle Rob telling me to call home, an email from Aunt Mel, giving me the rundown of her week, and the usual mundane messages from Heidi telling me exciting news like what she'd had to eat for lunch.

Thoughts of Andrew lingered. After pouring my heart out to him, I felt connected to him, and I was annoyed with myself for leaving in such a hurry.

Chapter 28

EVELYN – December 1994

The Christmas of 1994 was the first Christmas I'd spent away from home. I'd been invited to spend the day with Joe's family at his parents' house. He had ignored my concerns that I'd be gatecrashing a family event and insisted that I should come. Stan would be there too and Leslie – and Beth, of course. Cam was with family, and Kai had gone back to spend a couple of weeks in Broome.

Stan and I had breakfast together on Christmas morning. It was the first time I'd been inside his little cottage, which was hidden away at the far end of the grounds of the Croc. It was a cosy little place, and it was the first time I'd seen evidence of his late wife. There were pictures of both of them around the house, and her impression was left all around in the furnishings and ornaments. Stan clearly hadn't made many changes to the place. He poured tea from a teapot with a delicate floral pattern and served up bacon and eggs. It was a quiet breakfast but I was content. As a gift, I'd bought him a huge corkboard. I wanted him to hang it in his office and pin photos to it. A photo guest book, always on display. He liked the idea.

When I unwrapped his gift to me, I had to laugh. A photo album. He wanted me to fill it with photos of my time in Kununurra. He'd already added the first few photos for me. I promised to fill it with memories and treasure it forever.

"It was that or a hedge trimmer," he said, "but I thought you'd struggle to get that on the plane."

"You're talking a lot about me leaving," I said. "Looking forward to getting rid of me, are you?"

He shook his head. "I'm actually very glad you came along when you did."

Reaching over, I gave him a kiss on the cheek. "We better get going. You need a drink, you're getting all soppy on me!"

We drove to Mick and Claire's house and the day was instantly rowdier. It was a stunning house in a wonderful setting. The lawn was perfectly kept and rolled at a gentle incline down to the river, which glistened below. There was a hot tub on the deck and a long sheet of thin plastic had been set up on the slope of the lawn with a hosepipe to create a makeshift water slide for the kids – although when I arrived, Joe was shoving a squealing Leslie down it while her young niece and nephew looked on in great amusement.

"Happy Christmas!" Mick called when he caught sight of me and Stan.

There was a round of hugs and greetings, the excitement of the whole Sullivan clan rubbing off on me.

"Hope you've got your bathers," Joe said,

wrapping me in a great big hug.

I pulled my T-shirt off my shoulder to reveal my bikini strap. "I'm all ready!"

"Great!" Leslie said. "You've got to have a go on the slide."

Her brother-in-law sprayed me with a water gun in lieu of a greeting, and I moved to the deck to undress and join in with the water fun. It was a good half an hour before I noticed Beth at all. She must have been inside the house and I'd been having too much fun running around the garden like a big kid.

I hadn't seen much of Beth recently but there was a new awkwardness to our exchanges. All she seemed to talk about was her Sydney plans. It was the last thing I wanted to hear about, since I was trying to pretend it wasn't happening. Our interactions had become increasingly stilted and polite.

She kissed my cheek as she wished me merry Christmas.

"Happy Christmas!" I replied, before we descended into an awkward silence.

"Is it strange not being with your family at Christmas?" she asked.

"Not really," I said. "It doesn't feel like Christmas to me. I'm used to it being freezing cold." I paused, but then felt the need to fill the silence. "Leslie and Joe feel like family anyway," I said without thinking.

She smiled politely, but it hardly hid her true feelings. I felt uncomfortable around her, and I always seemed to blurt out inappropriate comments when I was tense.

Joe arrived on the deck, dripping wet and laughing. "Come and join the fun," he said, looking at us both and wrapping an arm around Beth's waist. When she leaned in to kiss him passionately, he looked surprised.

Claire was in the kitchen when I slipped inside, feeling like I'd been punched in the stomach. "Do you need any help?" I asked.

"Yes!" she said. "The meat just needs to go out to Mick . . ." She handed me a big platter.

"Wow!" I looked at the array of salads and dips to go with the barbecue. "This all looks delicious."

"Not quite like your English Christmas, is it?"

"Not at all!" I said. "I love it. Thanks for inviting me."

"It's nice to have you. Nobody else is offering to help! Besides, Joe and Leslie never stop talking about you – it would be weird if you weren't here."

I smiled and took the meat outside. Beth had managed to peel herself off Joe and people were sitting around on the deck, chatting and drinking while the kids carried on playing on the water slide. After handing the meat over, I sat with Leslie, who squeezed my hand. "I'm so glad you're here!" she said.

"Me too," I told her.

Joe smiled at me as he moved to help Mick with the barbecue, and I found myself annoyed with him. He shouldn't be so friendly; if he didn't flash me the smiles and the winks, my life would be so much easier. He made everything so confusing.

Christmas at the Sullivans' was exactly as Christmas should be. It was all about spending time with loved ones and having fun. The air was filled with laughter and barbecue smoke, and everyone seemed to be enjoying themselves. Gifts were exchanged, and I was surprised when I was inundated with presents too. Even Leslie's sister had bought me something: a cute little manicure set. Joe and Beth gave me a book by a local author – fiction set in the Kimberley region, full of places I would recognise. Leslie gave me a Kununurra souvenir shot glass and from Mick and Claire I got a stubby cooler with the slogan *I survived the outback!*

Sadly, I realised that most of my gifts had a similar theme; they were souvenirs, things to remind me of my time here once I'd left. My flight was booked and I only had a couple of months remaining. The thought made me feel sick. Then I remembered Joe's impending move to Sydney, and my heart sank even further.

Joe beamed when he opened the key ring I'd bought for him; the fob was a blue pickup like his, and he seemed really pleased with it.

We were lazing around late in the afternoon when I suddenly felt the urge to go back to the Croc. Beth was cuddled up with Joe on the porch swing, and I was filled with jealousy that I couldn't ignore.

When I took a bunch of dirty dishes into the kitchen, Joe followed me in. "You having a good time?" he asked.

"Yeah, lovely. I'll probably head off soon though. Give you a bit of a break from me."

He gave me a puzzled look. "Don't be daft."

"You probably want some time just with family," I said, turning to load the dishwasher.

"You *are* family. It's Christmas, you can't go and sit alone in your room."

"Leave her," Beth said gently, appearing quietly beside Joe. "If she wants to leave, she can. She's not a prisoner!" Her voice was light and jokey. She was always graceful and would never be rude, but I could tell she would be happier if I left.

"Cam's coming over later," Joe told me. "At least wait and see Cam."

I agreed with a nod and exchanged another polite smile with Beth. Secretly, I think she wanted to kill me, though I wasn't sure what I'd done to annoy her.

"We have to head over to my place soon anyway," she said, her hand delicately placed on Joe's neck.

"Not yet," he said, looking at the kitchen clock in surprise.

"We agreed," Beth said, almost but not quite letting her emotions run away. "Half the day with your parents, half with mine. Like always."

"I know," he said. "Let's just stay a bit longer though. Cam's not even here yet."

Feeling uncomfortable, I slipped past them and back outside. I didn't move far from the door but lingered in a pathetic attempt to eavesdrop. I could only pick out odd words, as their exchange was fast and quiet. They weren't the sort of people to air their dirty laundry in public; there wouldn't be a big scene, but they were obviously deep in an argument. I got the feeling it ran deeper than just their plans for Christmas.

By the time they re-joined the party, I'd slipped back into the garden. Beth was her usual composed self as she said goodbye to everyone, but her eyes were red and it was clear she'd been crying. Joe stood by his ute waiting for her and shouted that he'd be back in a while before they drove away.

I was happy to see Cam and his family turn up only a few minutes later. They had spent their Christmas Day on the river. Three boats pulled up to the riverbank and the rowdy occupants announced their arrival with whoops and cheers and a few of them singing "We Wish you a Merry Christmas" at the top of their lungs.

"How's my favourite British chick?" Cam asked, giving me a hug. "Having a good Christmas?"

"Yeah," I said, my thoughts still lingering on Joe and Beth and wondering what had happened. "It's been really good."

"It's about to get better," he said. "I'm teaching you to water-ski!"

I frowned. "I saw a croc down there earlier."

"You better learn to stay up on your feet then," he said with a grin. Then he turned to shout, "Evelyn's first attempt at waterskiing coming up! Someone get a camera and everyone gather round for a laugh!"

"Thanks!" I said, following him to the boat.

It was so much fun. To everyone's delight, it took me a while to get the hang of it, and there were a few hilarious false starts which saw me nose-diving into the water. Then I got a feel for it and managed to get up out of the water. Cam steered the boat down the river, picking up speed as we left the house behind. He glanced back occasionally and shouted encouragement.

"Let's turn around and show them what a pro you are," he said after a while. We headed back and a cheer arose as we passed the house with me standing relatively confidently on the skis. Joe had returned and I caught his eye. I was having such a great time and laughed loudly before we left everyone behind again. On my next drive by, I got a bit cocky and lifted an arm to wave. *Disaster*. I let the rope go as I lost my balance and crashed spectacularly into the water. Below the surface, I spent a moment upside down and confused before hitting the air again, coughing and spluttering. Joe was at the riverbank and crouched to my level.

"You okay?"

"Think so," I said, choking and reaching for his hand. "I lost the skis somewhere."

"Don't worry about it. Cam'll get them. You scared me for a minute. Thought I was gonna have to brave the crocs and jump in after you!"

He pulled me out in one movement and I stumbled on my jelly legs, falling into him. "You okay?" he asked again.

"What happened?" Cam shouted, turning the boat around. "You think you're the queen, giving everyone the royal wave?"

"I thought I was getting good," I said, laughing.

Chapter 29

EVELYN – December 1994

From the deck, Joe and I had a perfect view of the river and watched as everyone took turns on the water skis. Of course, they were all pros, and Cam particularly showed off with a few tricks, waving wildly at me while he was at it.

"You did well for your first attempt," Joe said.

"I'm not sure about that, but I had fun," I told him. "Is Christmas always like this here?"

"Yes. It's always the same."

"I love it," I said.

He tipped his bottle to his lips. "Me too."

"You excited about your move?" I asked, feeling like we'd been ignoring the elephant in the room for long enough.

He inhaled deeply. "I'm not sure excited is the right word."

"But you're really leaving?" I asked sadly. It shouldn't matter; I'd be leaving soon too.

"It seems like it," he said. "We found a place to live. It's only small, but it'll do to start with."

I ignored the twisting feeling in my gut. "Is Beth

okay?" I asked. "She seemed upset . . ."

He shrugged and stood up, stretching. "Women!" he said, with a grin that annoyed me. *Why won't you just talk to me? Tell me how you really feel. Tell me everything.*

"I'm going to find out when we're having dessert," he said, walking away.

"There's dessert?" I shouted after him. I was still full from lunch.

"Oh yes!" he said with a twinkle in his eyes.

The selection of desserts was certainly impressive. Everyone had contributed something, and I was overwhelmed by the choice. My mouth was watering as I stood taking it all in.

"Don't start with the chocolate cake," Leslie warned me. "You'll never manage anything else if you start with that. The trick is to take small pieces. And take your time."

"Slow and steady wins the dessert race," Cam said. "And Leslie takes it very seriously!" The pair of them were very giggly as we ate, exchanging looks and grinning at each other. I couldn't decide if they were drunk or flirting.

I'd just put my plate in the kitchen when Mick wandered in behind me. "Sure you can't manage a bit more?" he asked.

"No chance," I said. "I'm so full, it's painful."

"The profiteroles are really good. Did you try one?"

"No," I said as he draped an arm around my shoulders. I was slightly stunned when he pulled me towards the table full of desserts. "I'm definitely full." My voice was light as I tried to discreetly move away from him.

"They're only small," he said.

I gasped when the chocolate and cream-covered pastry landed in the middle of my face with a thud. A squeak escaped me as I sputtered and wiped at my face. Mick moved away from me, chuckling. "Sorry! I couldn't resist!"

My eyes followed him as he walked outside, laughing as he went. Joe was standing in the doorway.

"Your dad just . . ." I stopped, not quite able to put the sentence together. *Your dad just hit me in the face with a profiterole.* It was far too ridiculous to say out loud. I wiped cream from my eyelashes. "I'm covered!"

"He does that sometimes," Joe said with a grin. "Here." he reached for my cheek. "Actually, you might just need to go and stick your head under the hose."

"Don't laugh at me," I said, taking a slice of chocolate cake and slamming it into his own face.

"Hey!" he said, laughing and wiping at his face. "That's not allowed."

"Well no one told me the rules of your little food-in-the-face game!" I said, pouting as I walked outside.

"Sorry, Evelyn," Claire said. "We should have warned you."

I walked past everyone with a face covered in chocolate and cream. "That would've been nice!"

"It was good to relax while we ate this year," Leslie remarked happily. "We knew he'd go for you. He likes an unsuspecting victim."

Mick was looking highly amused by his childish antics. "It's not Christmas unless someone has food in their face, is it?"

I'd just finished hosing myself off when Stan announced he was leaving to go and check on things at the Croc.

"I'll come with you," I said. The sun was setting and the atmosphere was winding down.

"No," Stan said. "You stay and have fun. You don't want to spend your evening at the Croc."

"I don't mind," I said.

"Stay," Leslie said. "Someone will drop you back later."

I wasn't sure who was going to be sober enough to drive, given how much alcohol had been consumed throughout the day. And no one seemed to be slowing down. But I stayed anyway and settled into a relaxed evening of drinking and watching the beautiful sunset over the water.

"Come and sit with me a minute," Cam said with a flick of his head as I walked past him later. His family had left with the boats a while earlier, and the kids had been taken home to bed. Numbers were dwindling and the mood was mellow.

"What?" I asked, slowing beside him.

He patted his knee. "Sit with me for a minute."

The others were chatting and paying no attention. "What's up?" I asked, ignoring his instructions.

"It's Christmas. Just pretend I'm Santa and take a seat."

"You're being creepy," I said. "Slow down on the beers."

I was about to walk away when his face fell serious. "Please. Just for a minute. I want to test something. I promise not to grope you."

"What's going on?" I asked, sinking slowly onto his lap.

He pulled me closer to him. "I just want to conduct a little experiment."

"You're being very weird."

A frown fell over his face. "As I suspected, she's not the slightest bit bothered."

"Who?"

"Leslie," he said, his gaze returning to me. "Not even a hint of jealousy."

"You like Leslie?" I asked, with an arm around his strong shoulders. She was deep in conversation with Mick and didn't even seem to register me sitting with Cam.

"Yeah," he said, suddenly shy. "Don't mention it, will you? I don't want things to get weird."

"But if you tell h—"

"We've been friends for a long time. If she felt anything else it would've been obvious by now, wouldn't it?"

He was right; if Leslie felt more for him, everyone would know about it.

Cam leaned closer to me. "There's only one person who looks uncomfortable with this situation and it's not Leslie."

My eyes scanned around until they landed on Joe. He leaned against the post at the corner of the deck, looking intently at me. His forced smile made my heart race. When he turned away, I stood up, uncomfortable with my own feelings. Sure that I'd had enough, I put my beer down and tried to ignore my heart rate, which had taken a sharp increase. The sadness which seeped into my bones was overwhelming and hard to ignore.

"You okay?" Claire asked when I wandered into the kitchen, my eyes full of tears.

"Can I ask you a huge favour?" I said, trying hard not to let the tears spill over. "Could I use your phone?"

"Of course you can!"

"It's long-distance," I said, sniffing. "I'll give you the money."

"Don't worry about that," she said, her eyes full of sympathy. "I should have offered earlier. Of course you'd want to call home. I wasn't thinking."

"I'll be quick," I said.

"Take your time. Use the phone in our bedroom and you won't be disturbed."

I thanked her and made my way to the back of the house. My intention had been to call home from the office at the Croc when I got back there. With the time difference, the later I called the better, but I had a sudden urge to speak to Mel.

She answered quickly, and my tears spilled over at the sound of her voice. "Hi!" I said.

"Oh my God! Happy Christmas! How are you?"

"I'm okay," I said. "I miss you."

"I wish you were here. How's Christmas over there?"

"It's really good," I told her, unable to hide the overwhelming sadness that had taken hold of me.

"What's wrong? Are you having a terrible time? Are you homesick? You can come home, you know?"

"It's not that," I said. "I'm fine. I've just been drinking all day and hearing your voice has made me emotional."

"You'll be back before we know it and we can have some wild nights out. I can't wait! Did you get my parcel?"

"Not yet. Things always take forever to get here. It'll turn up soon, I'm sure."

"What did you do today?"

"I went waterskiing," I said with a laugh. "I completely embarrassed myself and nearly drowned! It's so hot here, you wouldn't believe."

"That's crazy. It's thick snow here."

I heard the doorbell ring in the background and the bustle of noise and people. "I have to go," she said. "I'm sorry."

"It's fine, I shouldn't be on the phone long anyway. Tell Rob I said hi."

"I will. Talk soon. Merry Christmas!"

I put the phone down with a heavy heart. A night out with Mel would be lovely. Part of me knew it would always be bittersweet; a night out with Mel would mean I was back in the UK and far from everything that had become so dear to me in Kununurra.

I opened the bedroom door to find Joe in the hallway. "You made me jump," I told him.

"Sorry," he said. "Is everything okay?"

I wiped at my cheeks. "Yeah. I'm fine."

"Homesick?" he asked with a look of concern. "It must be hard to be away from your family at Christmas?"

Not homesick. I've just had such an amazing day that every Christmas from now on will be a disappointment. I smiled at Joe when he raised his eyebrows. *Next Christmas I won't be here. Next*

Christmas I won't be with you. And even the thought of it is painful.

"Maybe a bit homesick," I said.

The truth was, I'd never felt so at home in my life.

Chapter 30

EVELYN – December 1994

As I expected, no one was sober enough to drive, so at Claire and Mick's insistence, I stayed the night at their place along with Leslie, Cam and Joe. It ended up being a fairly early night; it had been a long day, and I was exhausted. Leslie and I shared the guest room and I woke early to her gentle snoring. On my way to the kitchen, I found Joe asleep on the couch in the living room. One arm was thrown up over his head while the other rested across his chest. He didn't stir, and I watched him for too long – until my heart threatened to explode and my emotions bundled together into one big ball of sadness, sitting right on my chest.

The house was quiet and everyone slept on when I walked through the front door and down the driveway with tears falling down my face. It was quite a trek, but I walked the whole way back to the Croc to shower and change before I made my way to the hotel.

"You're off today, aren't you?" Todd asked. He was sitting at the reception desk and looked bored.

"Yeah," I said, shocked that I'd managed a smile. It betrayed the tumult of emotions which raged inside me. I'd decided that work might be a good distraction. "I'm kind of skint and wondered if I could pick up some more shifts."

"Haven't you spent the last month complaining you wanted time off over Christmas and New Year?"

I grimaced. "I should have checked my bank balance first!"

He shook his head, probably adding scatterbrain to his mental list of my vices. "You'll have to ask Dad."

Arthur gave me a similar shake of the head and told me I'd have to talk to Tania; he didn't care who took the shifts, as long as one of us was there. One phone call later and I had a full week of shifts and a very happy Tania.

I hadn't even left a note when I left Mick and Claire's house that morning, so I wasn't surprised when Cam appeared, wandering the hotel corridor looking for me.

"What happened?" he asked. "I thought you were coming out on the boat with us today? Everyone's been looking for you."

"Sorry," I said, pushing my trolley full of mini-toiletries, toilet rolls and towels down the hall. "I should have called. I got roped into working."

He looked at me sternly. "Todd said you volunteered."

"I'm skint," I said, ignoring the fact I'd been caught in a lie. "And I felt bad that I'd bullied Tania into taking so many shifts this week."

"What's really going on?"

I parked the trolley at the next room on my list

and resisted the urge to break down and cry. "I need the money," I said, my voice cold and flat. "I'll be on the road again soon and I'll need money."

Cam's piercing stare made me uncomfortable, and I stepped into the hotel room to get away from him. "Have fun on the boat," I said, hoping he'd leave me alone.

"He loves you, you know?"

My resolve to keep myself together very nearly crumbled.

"Please leave," I said. "If I'm caught chatting, I'll be in trouble. I've got loads to do."

"Okay," he said, lingering in the doorway. "But if it's any consolation, I think he's an idiot. He's letting Beth walk all over him."

When I finally brought myself to look up, Cam was gone. I went into autopilot, making beds and cleaning bathrooms, gently straightening out personal possessions. It went too fast, and at the end of my shift I wondered how to kill the hours until bedtime. Lying on my bed staring at the ceiling didn't make time go fast, but I didn't want to see anyone so I was reluctant to venture out. Eventually, I sat up and started writing a letter to Mel. It started mundane, telling her what I'd been doing in a fairly detached way. Then I started to tell her about Beth and Joe, and my emotions soon poured out onto the page with heart-wrenching honesty. My hand struggled to keep up as the pent-up feelings rushed out of me. I growled as my biro gave out, the nib ripping into the paper as I scribbled, frantic to encourage ink to appear.

Even the pen was against me, and I flung it across the room before scrunching up the sheets of paper.

My head dropped to the table and I sobbed at the unfairness of it all. It crossed my mind to pack my bags and leave Kununurra right there and then. Maybe I'd just stayed too long. Maybe the heat was getting to me.

My mind wouldn't budge from the thought of Joe leaving. The idea of him not being around was more than I could bear. If only I could reset my emotions.

As illogical as it seemed, I decided that the best plan was to avoid him. I could probably carry on and pretend everything was fine, if only I didn't have to see him.

It soon became clear that my plan wouldn't be so easy to put into action. Joe was standing in the doorway to Bushcamp when I left for work the next morning.

"Hey!" he called.

I waved with as much enthusiasm as I could muster. "Morning!"

"How you doing?"

"Fine," I said, quickening my step. "Late for work!"

"You missed a good day yesterday."

I smiled wanly. "I've got to run. Catch you later!"

***

Leslie was sitting at the bar when I finished my shift. I couldn't even escape my friends at work. "Where've you been hiding?" she asked.

"I saw you two days ago!"

"You avoiding all of us or just Joe?" she asked,

sucking her Coke through a straw and not looking at me.

I silently cursed Cam and his big mouth. "Just Joe," I confessed.

"Good. Wanna come to mine for a movie afternoon?" I hesitated as she slurped the last of her drink. "I promise you won't see Joe. We don't even have to mention his name."

"Okay," I agreed, glad I didn't have to miss out on seeing my friends.

It was impossible to avoid seeing Joe completely, but for the week after Christmas, I managed to only see him in passing. My liver had a well-earned rest.

Leslie promised to call on me on New Year's Eve to escort me to the Tav. I think she was worried I would skip out on the festivities if she didn't come and frogmarch me over there. Much as I didn't feel like socialising, I also had no desire to sit on my own feeling sorry for myself. I'd just slipped into my dress when the knock came at the door.

"You're early," I said as I opened it. "Oh, hi." I was surprised to see Beth standing in the doorway.

"Could we talk?" she said, not bothering with her usual polite smile.

"Yes." I held the door open wide. "Do you want a drink or anything?" I asked nervously.

She shook her head and took a seat on the end of my bed. "I'm sorry I was always cold towards you," she said, her frankness catching me off guard and causing me to do a goldfish act with my mouth opening and closing as I searched for a response.

"I like you, actually," she said sadly before looking me right in the eye. "I just never liked the way Joe looked at you."

I sat beside her on the bed, shaking my head and spluttering unintelligibly. "I never . . . we never . . ."

"It's okay," she said, finally taking pity on me with a sad smile. "I'm not accusing you of anything. But please don't pretend you don't have feelings for him."

I wanted to protest and convince her of my innocence, but her big eyes pleaded with me for honesty and I couldn't think of a good reason to lie to her – or myself.

"I do have feelings for him," I said. "But he loves you. He's going to Sydney with you." I smiled in some attempt at a pretence of being happy for them.

"No, he's not," she said.

My heart quickened. "What?"

"Joe belongs here." She shook her head and let out a strange laugh. "He's going to work in Bushcamp forever. His life will always be much the same as it is now. He'll work, he'll fish, he'll drink . . ." She paused. "He'll get married and have a couple of kids. And he'll be blissfully happy! That's Joe." She choked on a sob and I reached for her hand. "I wanted him to be someone else. To be ambitious and want the things I want. But forcing him to move and follow my dreams is just cruel."

"He's not going to leave?" I asked tearfully.

"When I told him to stay, he looked like a prisoner who'd been told they could go free." She stood then, clearly not wanting to linger in my company for longer than necessary.

I nodded when she said goodbye, unable to form any words.

As I watched her leave, I wondered at how hard it must have been for her to talk to me. She could have just left and not said anything to me. It was easy to see why Joe loved her. *She's so bloody perfect.*

Chapter 31

EVELYN – December 1994

I was still processing the visit from Beth when Leslie waltzed in, all dressed up for the big New Year's Eve party.

"It's official," she said, excitedly. "Joe and Beth have split up!"

"I heard."

"You don't seem very excited?"

"I'm not sure what to think. Beth just came to talk to me. I feel really weird."

"What's to feel weird about? Now you and Joe can get together! I'm excited, even if you're not."

"I don't even know if he *wants* to be with me," I said, standing and moving to the door. I didn't dare hope that something might happen between me and Joe, but it was such a relief that he wasn't leaving Kununurra. "Come on. I really need a drink."

The Tav was heaving and Leslie and I fought our way to the bar before moving outside where there was slightly more space. Joe and Cam were deep in conversation, sitting opposite each other on a long table. They shuffled along when they saw us.

"Where've you been hiding all week?" Joe asked while Cam and Leslie slipped into their own conversation.

"Working, mostly," I said. "And helping Stan out a bit."

"I thought you were avoiding me?" His voice was calm but the statement came out as a question.

My shoulders rose and my head bobbed in a gesture that meant absolutely nothing. At this point, it seemed obvious to everyone that I was avoiding Joe, and I suspected everyone knew the reason why. Joe must've known too.

"You're not working tomorrow, are you?" Cam asked.

"No, I intend to sleep all day!" I said.

"Great," he said, grinning mischievously. "So we can party all night!"

"Let's do shots," Leslie said, standing and nudging Cam to go to the bar with her.

I waited for Joe to say something about Beth and about his cancelled move to Sydney. When he kept quiet, I tried to help the conversation along. "Everything okay with Beth?"

"Fine," he said, lifting his glass to his lips. My eyebrows knitted together when I looked at him. "I guess you heard we split up," he said finally.

"Yeah," I said. "Sorry."

"I'm not going to Sydney," he added with a shrug before changing the subject. "You must be glad of a day off tomorrow after all your shifts this week?"

My mind struggled to keep up. Was that really all he was going to say on the subject? I had no idea where I stood if Beth was out of the picture, but I'd at least expected him to talk to me about it. Did he think it was none of my business? Did he think I wouldn't care? Maybe he really didn't have any idea why I'd been avoiding him.

"That's all you're going to say?" I asked, my annoyance clear. "You split up and now you're staying? End of conversation?"

He looked confused. "What am I supposed to say?"

"Nothing," I said angrily, deciding I couldn't be bothered explaining things. Cam and Leslie were heading back over. "Nothing at all!"

I reached for the sticky green liquid as soon as it was on the table and knocked it back.

"Cheers, then!" Cam said, looking at me with a raised eyebrow.

"Cheers," I said, slamming the glass down. The great thing about living in a small town was there were always people I knew in the pub. Scanning the crowd, my eyes landed on one of the lifeguards from the pool. I raised my hand to wave. "I'm just going to say hi to Craig," I said, taking my beer with me.

The next few hours were spent flitting around the crowd, chatting with everyone and anyone: whatever it took to stay away from Joe. The trouble was, the more I drank, the more I could feel his eyes on me, and when I glanced his way, our eyes would lock and my stomach would do acrobatics.

I joined Leslie on the dance floor for a while, and it wasn't until I was on my way back from the toilets late in the evening that I finally came face to face with Joe. He was waiting for me and I couldn't escape.

"Can we talk?" he asked. Before I could answer,

he took my hand and pulled me towards the front door. The feel of his hand in mine was all I could concentrate on as we bumped our way through the crowd.

"Please stop avoiding me," he said out on the road. "It's driving me crazy. It's New Year's Eve and I just want to spend the evening with you."

My resolve crumbled at his proximity. I just wanted to spend the evening with him too. I wanted everyone else to disappear and it just be the two of us.

"I couldn't stand to see you with Beth any more," I confessed. "And I couldn't stand the thought of you leaving. That's why I spent all week avoiding you. I'd just had enough of it. Then Beth turned up and told me that you'd split up and I thought . . . I don't know what I thought but . . . I just don't know what to think."

"I'm sorry," he said, both his hands in mine. "I just had such a crap week and my head is all over the place . . ."

"I understand that you and Beth breaking up can't have been easy," I began, trying not to let my emotions get the better of me.

"It's not that," he said. "Breaking up with Beth was a relief. It was not seeing you that was hard. I didn't know if I'd done something to upset you?"

"No." I sniffed. "I just thought that if I stayed away from you then maybe I could get over you."

"Don't do that," he said, a smile spreading over his face. "Please don't do that!"

"Okay," I agreed, my whole body tingling as he moved closer to me.

"There you are!" Leslie shouted as the door

crashed open. "It's almost midnight! Come on!"

We followed her inside, hand in hand. I would never have imagined that 1994 could end quite so happily. Standing in the busy courtyard as the countdown was shouted around us, I gazed into Joe's eyes. He didn't bother waiting until midnight to kiss me, and it was so intense that I was barely aware of the noise all around us. When our lips finally moved apart, I laughed at the confetti scattering around us and my heart swelled even more when I caught sight of Cam and Leslie kissing in the corner.

1995 was off to a good start.

Chapter 32

LIBBY – August 2017

From Cairns, I got a flight to Darwin and then had a three-hour wait for my next flight. It was an hour's flight from Darwin to Kununurra. I jerked out of my daydream and peered through the window as I felt the plane begin its descent. The dusty red landscape stretched out below, and I had to strain my eyes to find any sign of civilisation. The town of Kununurra was visible beside the winding river. Mum had been here, I thought to myself, suddenly overwhelmed by emotions.

I wasn't prepared for the stifling heat of the outback. Walking down the steps of the small aircraft, I was enveloped by the hot, humid air and fought the urge to run back on board and beg the pilot to turn around and take me back. If I retraced my path, I could be back in the Koala Village in twenty-four hours. I imagined finding Andrew, Simon and Yvonne sitting by the pool, laughing and drinking cold beers. I'd pull up a chair and blush under Andrew's gaze.

But no, I was here, in the little outback town I'd

set out to find all those weeks ago. I walked across the tarmac, which felt soft underfoot as though it were melting in the heat. My bag was delivered to the baggage reclaim area and I followed the exit signs through the small but modern air-conditioned airport and out onto the road, where the heat engulfed me once more. For the first time since I arrived in Australia, I didn't know what to do. Previously, I'd been surrounded by other backpackers, and at every bus station there'd been rows of transport to take us to the various hostels. Here, people walked to their cars in the small car park and I was left alone. I knew there was at least one hostel in the town but I cursed myself for not calling ahead. They would probably have collected me from the airport. I'd got so used to everything just falling into place that it hadn't even occurred to me. After a few minutes, I ventured back into the airport and took a seat on a bench. It was quiet and cool in the airport. The hum of a water filter in a fish tank caught my attention, and I spent ten minutes watching the large fish swim hypnotically around.

Rummaging in my backpack, my hand finally landed on Mum's old photo album, and I flicked through the familiar photos. It felt like looking at a film set that was somewhere just on the other side of those doors. I was so close to the action. Mum had been here, twenty-two years before, and she'd carried the memories with her like secret treasures. This place had such an impact on her life – not just because it was the place where I was conceived. There was more to it than that, I was sure. What was it about this place that made her whisper about it on her deathbed? I needed to find out.

The girl at the cafe was the only person I could find when I looked around. I asked her if she knew how I could find a taxi into town, and she cheerfully told me she'd give me a ride when she finished in half an hour. She sold me a Bundaberg Ginger Beer and I returned to my spot near the fish tank to wait for her.

"There are usually more backpackers around," she said as I stepped into her car. She was called Michelle and was cheerful and chatty. "Most come in on the morning flight though. Or drive into town. Usually on the way to Darwin or Broome, but some stick around for the fruit-picking."

I nodded along as she pulled out of the car park and onto the wide, deserted road. It felt so strange to finally be here, and I tried to concentrate on Michelle's constant chatter as we drove, vaguely answering her questions about where I'd been and how long I intended to stay in Kununurra – and in Australia. All I wanted to do was stare out of the window and take it all in.

"That's Lake Kununurra," she told me, pointing as we reached the edge of the town. She beeped the car horn and waved madly when she saw a friend in a passing car, then we drove through quiet rows of wooden houses before coming to the heart of the little town. Michelle pointed out the shops, the pub, a public swimming pool, the post office, the petrol station. She pointed down the road and told me proudly of the town's hotel; apparently she worked at the bar there sometimes.

"And here's the Kununurra Croc. Kai owns it – he's a good 'un. If he's full there's another backpackers' across town. The Croc's the best though."

"Thanks for the lift," I called as I got out of the car.

"I'll probably see you around. I'm usually in the pub on Friday nights."

"I'll look out for you," I said before she pulled away, leaving me outside the Kununurra Croc Backpacker Resort. The sign looked new, and from the outside the place looked modern and even a bit fancy. I hoped it was within my price range. Walking through the lush green gardens, I saw a pool with a bar beside it. Next to the bar was a covered area providing shade for a barbecue and a few rows of long trestle tables with matching wooden benches. I dropped my backpack in the shade, unable to carry it any longer. The heat was draining my energy at an alarming rate. A couple of people were in the pool and a few more sat at the bar.

"Checking in?" the guy behind the bar called over to me.

I nodded and he moved towards me, plucking my backpack off the ground as he introduced himself as Kai and motioned for me to follow him. "It's really nice here," I said, following him past the pool area to the long two-storey building beyond it.

"Thanks!" he said, looking pleased with himself. "Once upon a time it was a complete dump. I've done a lot of work on the place over the years." He dropped my bag and opened a door on the ground floor. I followed him into the small office and accepted gratefully when he offered me a bottle of water.

"What sort of room are you after?" he asked.

"Dorm or private?" He gestured to the wall behind him where a price list hung. I was happy to find that the rates were pretty standard. I'd definitely paid more at places which weren't as nice. Hopefully the rooms were as pleasant as the rest of the place.

"Four-person female dorm, please."

"Good choice," he said, tapping on the computer. He handed me a form which I filled in with my details.

"I'm not sure how long I'll stay," I told him when I came to that part of the form. "Probably just a few days."

"That's okay. Leave me your passport as a deposit and pay when you leave."

When I handed the form back, my eyes scanned the room. I was drawn to a corkboard full of photos. My breath caught in my throat and I moved closer, unable to believe my eyes. Mum was grinning at me from one of the photographs. She was sitting at a wooden table with Joe Sullivan laughing beside her.

"It's hard to believe it's the same place, isn't it?"

"What?" I said, snapping out of my trance. My eyes had filled with tears and I kept them fixed on the wall.

Kai tapped the photograph. "This was taken out there. The table is even the same."

"Really? This is here?"

"I told you it was a dump. I had the tables and benches restored. They'll last forever, those beauties!"

"When was the photo taken?" I asked, finally looking up at him.

"When I first arrived. Back when I was young and crazy! This guy, Joe, ended up being my best mate.

He and his wife, Cassie, own the camping shop across the road. Lovely couple."

Looking at Kai, I realised I recognised him from Mum's photos. I snatched my attention back to the picture on the wall, debating whether to tell him that the girl was my mother. "What about her?" I asked, intrigued as to what he might tell me. If he even remembered her.

"She was a character. A real livewire. She was backpacking – came for a week and stayed for the best part of a year! It's a funny place. People tend to either love it or hate it. That girl fell in love with the place." He smiled fondly and moved away. I didn't want the conversation to end.

"What happened to her?"

He looked at me seriously. "She left. Went back to England, I guess. I'm not really sure."

For a moment, I wanted to tell him. He looked like he'd be interested; as though he'd like to know what became of her. And he could tell me more about Joe. It was a shock to hear that he was definitely still in town. And working right across the road. *And he has a wife.*

"Here's your key," Kai said, handing it to me. I'd hesitated too long and I couldn't find the right words. At least I knew it wasn't going to be difficult to track Joe down. I followed Kai outside, and he opened the door to the next room to show me the communal kitchen. "You're in room fourteen. It's just up the stairs."

The room was clean and airy. I switched the button on the air con and waited. It was blissfully cool in minutes and I lay back on my bed. *What am I doing here?* Everything suddenly felt very real. It had seemed like a great adventure but actually being there felt wrong. Some things should be left alone. I shouldn't be digging around in my mother's past. If she'd wanted me to know my father, she would have done something about it long ago, not just while she was delirious on her deathbed. *Why on earth did she do that? I was quite happy, why did she put the ideas in my head?* She had made me curious about him when I'd never been curious before. *But I can fulfil my curiosity without anyone knowing why I'm here. If I just meet him, that will be enough. I don't need him to know who I am. I just want to see him once.*

I knew I wanted more than that though. I wanted to know more about the year my mum spent here. And what happened? Why didn't she keep in touch with Joe or any of her friends? I needed to find out, and I could only do that by talking to Joe Sullivan and telling him exactly who I was. At least I knew where to look for him. He had a wife called Cassie – and Kai had already told me where to find them.

In an instant, I was off the bed and shoving my bulky backpack into a locker. My feet moved quickly and I was out the door and down the stairs before I knew it. It felt like I didn't even take a breath until I was standing outside the camping shop just across the street. The shop window was filled with an array of camping equipment. Everything was squeezed in haphazardly and hastily cut-out signs announced the prices in black marker.

I only hesitated for a moment before pushing open the door.

Chapter 33

EVELYN – January 1995

After the New Year's party, Joe left me at my door with a kiss that left me wanting more. There were times when I wished he wasn't quite such a gentleman. When he didn't get in touch the following day, it took a lot of self-control not to search him out. I was dying to see him, but I wanted *him* to be the one to initiate something. I wanted *him* to ask me on a date. With a huge effort, I ignored the voice in my head that told me he probably wasn't over Beth. Thankfully, Kai arrived back to keep me occupied with more renovations at the Croc.

A few days passed without seeing Joe, and it was a relief to confide in Leslie when I saw her.

"They've been together years!" she said. We were sitting at one of the many tables in the newly refurbished barbecue area at the Croc. "He's probably just taking a bit of time to process things. It'd actually be a bit weird if he split up with Beth one day and jumped into a relationship with you the next."

"The trouble is, he didn't split up with Beth. It was all her idea, wasn't it? If she hadn't ended it they'd still be together. He'd be in Sydney with her."

"No," she said, wrinkling her nose. "It was a mutual decision. He never wanted to go to Sydney. Everyone knew that. He loves you. Just give him some time."

"That's the problem," I said. "I don't have much time."

"Sounds like you're dying!" Cam remarked, joining us with a sausage sandwich.

"You have to come and get them," Kai called. "There's no table service!"

A few others were sitting around too: guinea pigs in Kai's trial run for his big sausage sizzle the following week. He'd finally managed to get Stan to agree to a barbecue evening, and Kai was taking it all very seriously. He was determined to make a good profit to prove his worth.

It had been four days since New Year's Eve and I missed Joe. Seeing the adoration in Cam's eyes every time he glanced at Leslie wasn't helping me either. She seemed to have gone cold on him again since the party. I'd hardly had time to talk to her alone, but from the short conversation we'd had, I gathered her sudden affection for him had been induced by alcohol and the excitement of a new year. Hopefully the same wasn't true of Joe.

I was starting to think that romance was cursed in this town. It was tempting to shout at Leslie and point out what she was missing. Cam was a lovely guy; they'd be so cute together. I held my tongue and listened to them chat. Maybe Joe would turn up, I thought, looking towards the gates. Not seeing him was driving me mad. I looked for him everywhere.

When he didn't show up, I turned in and had yet another early night.

***

"What's up?" Todd asked when I walked into work the next morning. My degrading uniform annoyed me more on that day than it ever had.

"Why do I have to dress like this?" I snapped at him. "It's ridiculous and inappropriate. I think I should report it to someone."

"I don't know," he said, clearly taken aback by my outburst. "Ask my dad. It's not like I have a say in anything around here."

"Well maybe you should, Todd!" I shouted when he went to walk away. He turned and looked at me, perplexed. "You're the heir to this place, aren't you? One day it will all be yours! Why don't you act like it?"

He stood taller and his nostrils flared. "You try standing up to him. Do you think I haven't tried? He won't listen to anyone else's opinion, and he acts like everyone around him is stupid."

I'd said too much. Taking my mood out on Todd had been unfair. My emotions were taking over and rational thought had gone out of the window. "Fine!" I said, cockily. "I'll show you how it's done. Come on."

I marched past Todd and didn't slow down until we reached Arthur's office. My knuckles rapped hard against the door, and I glared at Todd before following instructions to go in.

"What?" Arthur asked, jerking his head up from

229

his paperwork, looking thoroughly annoyed by the interruption.

I'm going to lose my job today. I felt the anger course through my body. It was more about Joe than the uniform, but I had to direct my feelings somewhere, and I knew I was about to fire it all directly at Arthur. May as well go out with a bang, I decided, pulling myself to my full height and looking down on Arthur.

"This," I said, pulling on the tight, low-cut nylon top, "is unacceptable. Absolutely unacceptable. The skirt is way too short, the material is awful. It's like a French maid outfit and I cannot work like this any more!" Arthur leaned back in his chair, his expression blank as he absorbed my barrage. Once I got going, I couldn't seem to stop. "I don't see any of the men around here wearing skimpy little outfits. It's degrading and sexist. I don't know how you get away with it, and I fully intend to get on the phone to . . . to . . . someone official and make a formal complaint. Morally, this is wrong and I can't condone it any longer." I inhaled triumphantly and folded my arms across my chest, immediately unfolding them when I realised I was pushing my cleavage up to an indecent level.

Arthur's face crumpled and he erupted with laughter. I'd heard Arthur shout and swear at his staff. I'd watched as he humiliated people and fired them on the spot. But I had never seen anything as disturbing as Arthur laughing. I took a step back. *What the heck?*

"Really?" he said, as the laughter subsided. "You don't like the uniform?"

I tried my best not to let him rattle me. "That's

230

what I just said, isn't it?"

"And yet you've been wearing it for how many months without complaint?"

I searched for words but ended up mumbling unintelligibly.

"Pathetic!" Arthur said, his voice loud and overbearing. "Bloody kids today have no convictions. You think it's degrading? But it takes you almost a year to say anything? What is wrong with you?" He waved a hand. "Get out of my sight."

"No," I said, realising he was right; it *was* pathetic that I hadn't stood up for myself and I was determined not to back down now. "Not until you agree to change the uniform."

He leaned forward, speaking slowly. "Get back to work, Evelyn."

For the briefest of moments, I caught a look pass across his face and realised he was enjoying this far too much.

I held his gaze, shaking my head slowly.

When he brought his fist heavily down on the desk, I jumped but still refused to leave the office.

"Fine," he said, returning to his paperwork. "Go and see Mick at Bushcamp. He has a catalogue for work wear. Pick out something appropriate and come and show me tomorrow. You'll have to put in the order, I don't have time for it."

"Okay," I said, my voice weak and disbelieving. "I'll do that. I was thinking of tailored shorts and a shirt. Something smart bu—"

"Evelyn!" Arthur cut me off without looking up. "I don't care. Get your work done and then go and see Mick. And get out of here before I change my mind."

I should have just left at that point, but I thought I'd see if I could push my luck a bit further. "I've also had this great idea about putting some photos up around the bar area . . . pictures of the locals . . . make it a bit of a feature somehow—"

"Get out!" he growled.

"Yes. Okay," I said quickly, scurrying for the door. *One thing at a time.*

I stared at Todd when he closed the door behind us. "What just happened?" I asked as adrenalin pumped through my body.

"You better get to work," he said with a look of annoyance.

"I can't believe that just happened." My hands clapped together and I jumped up and down. "That was amazing."

"It's just a uniform," he said curtly. "It needed updating. Of course he would agree to that."

Ignoring Todd's prickly tone, I flung my arms around him and squeezed him tight.

He pushed me away. "Get off me! You've got work to do. Get on with it, will you?" He sounded scarily like his dad, but he couldn't bring me down from my high. I moved through the hotel with a spring in my step. My morning was spent on cloud nine and I'd never cleaned the rooms so quickly. With everything done, I left work early and hurried to pay Mick a visit.

It had hardly even crossed my mind that this would mean seeing Joe. After days of trying to think of excuses to see him, I waltzed into the shop without a thought. Seeing him stacking shelves halfway up a ladder floored me, and I stood for a moment, watching him with a huge grin on my face.

"You look like the cat who got the cream," Mick said, taking me by surprise when he walked quietly out of the back room. Hopefully I managed to snatch my eyes from Joe before he realised I'd been staring at him.

"I hear you have a catalogue of work wear," I said to Mick with a coy smile.

His eyebrows knotted together and he looked cheerfully puzzled. "I do."

"I'd like to have a look please. And tomorrow I'll be putting in an order for new uniforms for the cleaning staff at the hotel!"

"Well, well, well!" Mick chuckled. "I can hardly believe it. How the bloody hell did you pull that off?"

"Sometimes, Mick," I said, mock-seriously, "you just have to stand up for your convictions and demand change."

"Good on ya," he said. "I'm proud of you!"

"*I'm* proud of me!" I squealed, turning to Joe. "You should have seen me. I went all crazy and shouted at him, and when he told me to get out of his office, I held my ground and refused to move. It was incredible!"

His face shone with a lazy smile and his beautiful eyes lingered on mine in a way that made my palms sweat and my heart race. I turned away quickly, my thoughts drifting somewhere inappropriate with Mick in the room.

"You have to help me," I said, laughing as I fought to keep my thoughts on track. "I have to show Arthur what I've chosen tomorrow and get him to okay my choice." Mick slapped a glossy brochure on

233

the counter. "I'm thinking knee-length shorts and either a polo-neck T-shirt or a shirt. What do you think?"

"Joe will help you find something that Arthur won't be able to refuse," Mick said, moving to the ladder where Joe had been working and leaving us to it. The next hour was spent bumping shoulders with Joe while we pored over the brochure. Conversation wandered from the uniforms, and we ended up laughing about Arthur and his grumpy ways.

"I should probably get going," I said eventually. "Time for my swim!"

"I missed you," Joe whispered.

"It seemed like you were avoiding me this time," I said.

"Sorry. I had stuff to deal with."

"Beth?"

He nodded. "It's all sorted out now. She's gone to Sydney and I'm free and single. I just needed some time to get my head straight."

We stood close together and I longed to kiss him. "I understand," I said. "We should celebrate."

"As soon as I finish here," he said, glancing at his watch.

He looked at me questioningly when the mischievous grin spread across my face. "Mick, you can manage without Joe for the rest of the afternoon, can't you?"

"He's spent the last hour giggling with you, I think he should get on with some work now."

"Oh, but he's been so helpful," I said fluttering my eyelashes. "And tomorrow I'll be putting in a big order. It's all thanks to him, really."

"Don't start giving me the big eyes, young lady. I'm immune to that sort of thing."

"If I can get round Arthur, I can get round anyone!"

Joe chuckled. "Nice try. Drinks later?" he suggested.

"Oh bugger off, the pair of you!" Mick called as he moved to the back of the shop.

We hurried out the door before he had time to change his mind.

Chapter 34

LIBBY – August 2017

A bell tinkled above the door and my eyes darted around the badly organised shop. The room was long and dotted with tents and outdoor furniture. Plastic foliage mingled with the items for sale, giving the place a jungle feel. Boxes were strewn around the floor: some empty, some half-unpacked. The till sat on a counter ahead of me and a cordless phone wobbled slightly beside it as though it had just been deposited there. There was a wall behind the counter filled with cowboy hats. Now *they* were well organised. Each hat had an equal amount of shelf space, and they all sat at the exact same angle.

I reached for a rich brown hat and was surprised by the softness. My fingers brushed the fabric and a voice broke the silence.

"Hi!"

I jumped, snatching my hand back.

The woman smiled broadly at me and bent down behind the counter again before reappearing and wiping her brow with the back of her hand. "I just got new stock in," she said. "It's not normally so chaotic!

Interested in an Akubra?"

"A what?"

"Akubra." She picked up the hat I'd been admiring. "That's a nice one," she said, placing it on my head and wiggling it before scanning the shelf and reaching for another and trying that one on for size. "That's a better fit," she said proudly, turning me to a mirror which hung further down the wall.

"Huh! I like it," I said, surprised.

"You look like a local," she told me.

"I bet you say that to all the tourists."

She winked. "You got me! Suits you though."

I removed the hat and winced as I caught sight of the price. "It's not really what I came in for."

"What can I help you with then?" she asked, straightening the hat on the shelf.

The silence stretched a moment too long while I toyed with what to tell her. "I was just browsing really," I finally muttered.

"Did you just get to town?" she asked, moving back behind the counter.

"Yeah."

"I'm Cassie," she told me cheerfully. "If you need to know anything about this crazy town, just ask. I know it all."

"Thank you. I'll just have a look around, if that's okay."

"Be my guest," she said. "Shout if you need anything."

Wandering aimlessly through the shop, I tried to make myself inconspicuous while stealing glances at Cassie now and again, eager to know what sort of woman Joe had married. More clues as to the sort of person my father was. I stared at random pieces of camping equipment as though I might actually be interested in buying something. At the far end of the shop, I stopped among a gathering of small tents and watched Cassie from afar. She opened up box after box, occasionally taking out items and placing them on the counter in front of her.

"Hello!"

"Oh my God!" I shrieked, looking down into the eyes of the little blonde-haired girl who sat cross-legged in a tent, a picture book in her hand and a water bottle beside her. "Where did you come from?"

She looked puzzled. "I was here all the time," she said. "Watching you."

"Well that's creepy," I muttered under my breath. "Are you supposed to be sitting in a tent?"

She screwed up her face as though it were a difficult question. "I'm supposed to be with my childminder in the afternoons. But she drinks too much so Mum said I'd have to hang out here until she figures something else out."

"Oh," I whispered. "I see."

"I was just reading books. Mum's busy today so she can't play."

I nodded, unsure what to say. Her eyes stayed fixed on me as I casually moved away. My heart raced as a thought occurred to me, and I turned back to study her. "Cassie's your mum?" I asked, drawing near to her.

She nodded and regarded me with big eyes.

"And Joe's your dad . . ." I whispered, thinking aloud.

"You know my dad?" she asked.

"No," I said quickly. "I just heard his name."

"What's *your* name?"

"Libby," I told her.

"I'm Ruby," she said. "You wanna play with me?"

She had the most enchanting smile. I crouched to her level and our eyes locked. Her hair dropped halfway down her back and curled at the ends. Mine had been the same when I was her age. Her blue eyes sparkled. Surely the same shade as mine. I bit my lip. This girl was my little sister. Half-sister, anyway.

"You're not bothering the customers are you, Ruby?" Cassie's voice startled me and I stood up quickly.

"No, just chatting," Ruby said.

"Childcare round here is a nightmare," Cassie said, smiling at me. "We've had a few problems with the childminder so Ruby's been spending the afternoons with me in the shop until we sort something else out."

I nodded dumbly, hardly able to drag my eyes away from Ruby. "I better go," I said, suddenly feeling the need to bolt. The myriad things in the shop created a maze, and I couldn't get to the door fast enough.

The bell tinkled over the shop door before I got to it. "Mum!" the skinny girl called as she charged in. "Mrs Mitchell is being such a cow. I wanted to go to the Swim Beach with Sarah and Jade but the witch gave us a ton of homework. Can I just not do it?" She slowed when she saw me. "Sorry," she said sheepishly. "Hi."

"Hi," I said. Stopping in my tracks, I watched as she perched on the stool behind the counter. *I have*

240

two sisters.

My eyes scanned her quickly. I wanted to search for traces of myself just as I had done Ruby. This girl had beautiful olive skin and dark features like her mum. Her glossy brown hair was scraped back into a ponytail but showed no signs of being frizzy like mine. She was nothing like me. There was something rebellious about her too. Her baby-blue polo shirt was adorned with the school crest. It clung to her frame and stopped just above a short black skirt. It didn't look as though it was standard school uniform. My eyes stopped at her feet. She had bright pink toenails and no shoes. I glanced away when she caught me looking.

"Are you sure I can't tempt you to an Akubra?" Cassie asked.

I dithered, not sure what to do with myself but not wanting to leave.

"You should get one," Ruby said, suddenly beside me.

"A brown one would suit you," the older girl said. I caught the wink she shot at Cassie.

"Try one," Ruby said, pulling at my arm.

"Okay." I followed her back to the wall of hats and smiled when Ruby tried one on. It was far too big but she pushed it back on her head and grinned up at me.

"How long are you in town for?" the other girl asked.

"I'm not sure." I took a beige hat and tried it on, moving along to check it out in the mirror.

"The rodeo is in town next week," she told me. "If you're here for that, you'll definitely need an

Akubra."

"A rodeo?" A real live rodeo?

She nodded and flashed a cheeky smile. "Cowboys!"

"That sounds like fun." I checked my reflection again before placing the hat back in its place.

"Skye's on commission," Cassie told me.

"Three more Akubras and I can afford an iPhone."

"So there's no rodeo?"

"There *is* a rodeo," Cassie said. "But there's no law about headwear."

"No written law," Skye chipped in. "But seriously, who goes to the rodeo without an Akubra?"

"Get on with your homework," Cassie said. "Leave the customer to browse."

"I better go," I said. "But maybe I'll come back for a hat if I'm still here for the rodeo."

"Stay for the rodeo," Ruby said while she escorted me to the door. "It's fun."

"Thanks for the tip." My eyes lingered on her for a moment before I stepped out onto the street and breathed in the hot, humid air. *Will I ever get used to that? It's stifling.*

On the street, I took a minute to pull myself together. *I have a whole family hidden away in this strange little town. Now I just need to meet my dad.*

Chapter 35

EVELYN – January 1995

It was a strange week and by the end of it I was ready to shake Joe. Or maybe just give up on him and leave. I'd seen a lot of him and that in itself was great. But – bar a bit of flirting – things were no different between us than they'd always been. That's not entirely true; we were awkward around each other. Joe seemed uncomfortable around me and was constantly inviting the rest of the gang to hang out with us. I was starting to think that we'd gone too far into the friendship zone and that was all we were destined to be.

I kicked up dust beside the road as I waited for the gang to arrive. They were late, and I was tempted to give up and go back to bed. It was Sunday and we were supposed to be going out to Middle Springs. I'd done my best to wake Kai, but he said he was too hungover to move. In fairness, the previous night had been a big one and I wasn't feeling too great myself. Going back to bed wouldn't be so bad.

"Sorry," Joe shouted as he pulled up. "I can't get Cam to move from his bed and Leslie's in a weird mood, she's not coming. Where's Kai?"

"Hungover," I told him with a raised eyebrow. "I guess I could have stayed in bed after all."

He looked thoughtful as he leaned on the steering wheel. "Shall we wait and go another day?" he said after a moment.

"Okay," I said flatly. *Why is he avoiding being alone with me? Does he think I'm going to try and jump him with no one else around?* I probably would, to be honest, but what's the problem with that? "I'll talk to you later," I said grumpily, turning to go back inside.

"Evelyn," he called. "We could still go, if you want?" I turned and saw the uncertainty in his eyes, as though he thought I might say no. He covered it quickly with his boyish smile. "It'll probably be pretty boring just with me . . ."

I opened the door and flung my bag into the footwell. "It will be very boring!" I said. "But I can probably endure it."

As we drove out of town, I was filled with nervous excitement. A whole day with Joe to myself was like a dream come true. I just hoped he'd kiss me again soon or I might go crazy. He'd seemed so keen at the New Year's party. Perhaps I should just take the initiative.

The half-hour drive went by quickly. The radio wafted out mellow tunes and Joe pointed out places we passed and talked about the wildlife. After almost a year, I could still find things I'd not seen before or never heard of.

Occasionally, Joe would fall into an anecdote about times he'd spent at the springs and waterfalls. He spoke a lot about his family, which always included Leslie.

We arrived to find Middle Springs deserted. The water was inviting and I immediately stripped down to my bikini.

"I need to cool off," I told Joe, who was reaching for the picnic things from the back.

The water was blissfully cool and I swam out to the middle to float on my back. I watched a water monitor swim nearby and kept an eye to make sure it kept its distance. They were harmless big lizards, but nonetheless I didn't want it to get too close. It seemed he felt the same way and swam away from me.

"Are you coming in?" I shouted to Joe. He was standing by the ute, watching me. My heart quickened when he pulled his T-shirt over his head. He walked in until he was up to his waist, then dived and disappeared under the water. When he resurfaced, he shook his wet hair and grinned at me. He'd gone quiet and it unnerved me. *Why are things so awkward between us?*

"It's a shame the others couldn't come," he said, swimming closer to me. "I've enough food and beer for five!"

"I will do my best to help you out with that problem," I said.

"You're a great friend! I can always rely on you."

We fell into silence again. *Is he still thinking about Beth?* Maybe it was just too soon. Maybe we needed other people to act as a buffer. I had a feeling the whole day was going to be a disaster.

"I think I need a drink," I said. *Beer might help.* My thoughts and feelings were suddenly out of control; a beer might relax me. At least I might not be so self-conscious after a beer or two.

Joe followed me out of the water and we lay towels on the rough ground. I swigged the beer too fast, and Joe gave me an odd look. Like he could suddenly read my mind and knew how uncomfortable I felt.

"Aren't you having one?" I asked.

"Better not," he said. "Driving . . ."

"Doesn't usually stop you having the odd one or two," I remarked.

He lay back on the towel. "Maybe later."

By the second beer, I was completely relaxed and all my worries faded to nothing. In fact, for some reason, I suddenly thought it would be a good idea to talk about Beth. I wanted some reassurance that he was over her.

"Have you heard from Beth since she left?" I asked.

I regretted asking immediately. His frown told me this wasn't a great topic. "I've spoken to her on the phone a few times," he said.

Why not just stab me in the heart? "Really?" I asked, my tone just slightly too high-pitched.

"It's hard to just cut all connections."

Somehow, I made a nod look angry. *He's talking to his ex more than he's talking to me.* I still couldn't shake the feeling that the breakup was entirely Beth's idea.

"Do you still love her?"

There was a pause and I wished I hadn't asked. "I'm worried that the breakup was all her idea," I said quickly, "and if it were up to you, you'd still be together."

He looked me in the eyes. "Things weren't right between us for a long time, and I should've broken things off with her a long time ago." He moved his hand to mine. "I want to be with you."

It was what I needed to hear and it should have put my mind at rest, but I still felt something wasn't right. Joe leaned in to kiss me but there was no passion. He seemed so hesitant and unsure.

"You hungry?" he asked.

I shrugged and he jumped up to set up a picnic. Later, when he fell asleep on the picnic blanket, I paddled my feet in the shallow water and took in the peaceful surroundings. It hurt that he couldn't tell me he didn't still love Beth. Perhaps it was irrelevant anyway; my time in Australia would soon come to an end, and what would that mean for me and Joe?

It was the first time in a while that I'd thought about my return to the UK. I felt so at home in Kununurra and I had such great friends. It was strange to think of leaving and probably never returning. I could come back though, I told myself, because suddenly it seemed unfathomable that I could leave this place – these people – and never return.

"What are you thinking about?" Joe said, breaking my thoughts. I'd been holding my breath and I inhaled sharply. "Are you okay?"

I turned away from him, needing a second to compose myself. "I'm fine," I said. "I love it here."

"It's one of my favourite places," he said.

My eyes were damp but I didn't care, and I gave up trying to hide it as I turned back to him. "Tell me about your other favourite places." I thought he was going to change the subject or fob me off with some random story, but he held my gaze and looked serious.

"Can you play pool?" he asked with an intensity the question didn't deserve.

"I'm not bad," I said, hesitantly. "Why?"

He stood, shaking out his towel. "I want to take you somewhere. Come on."

"Now?"

"You up for a drive?"

I helped pack up the picnic things. "Where are we going?" I asked when we were back on the road.

"You'll see," he said.

We drove back to the Victoria Highway and then headed west, away from Kununurra. Twenty minutes later, wafts of dust billowed up as Joe pulled the ute in front of an old wooden structure. A couple of other cars stood outside of the Old Victoria Pit Stop. It looked like a saloon bar from an old western, and I expected tumbleweed to roll by at any moment.

"It looks like something from a horror film," I said.

"Yeah, it's pretty dodgy," Joe agreed. "But you asked about my favourite places."

"This place?"

"My dad brought me here when I turned fifteen. We played pool and drank some beers. I thought it was so cool! We still come out here sometimes, just the two of us. I've never brought anyone else."

I peered out to get another look at the place. It really did look dilapidated and scary. "I guess we should check it out then," I said. "It might be fun to beat you at pool."

He laughed as we headed for the door. "Dream

on!"

"You should be scared," I warned as he held the door open for me. The few patrons turned to look at us when we walked in, along with the barman, whose expression softened when he saw Joe. He raised a hand and Joe shouted politely for a beer and a Coke. Joe led me to a pool table and the balls clattered as he set up the table.

I thanked the barman when he brought the drinks and then turned to Joe. "Have you turned teetotal and forgotten to tell me?" I asked.

"It might not be a bad idea. My liver would probably appreciate the break." I looked at him, searching for the real reason he wasn't drinking. "It's a long drive back. I better not."

"Come on then," I said. "I'll let you break . . ."

"You can't break?" he asked, chalking his cue.

"Not very well," I admitted.

He won the first game but I insisted I was just rusty. I managed not to embarrass myself so that was something.

When the barman looked our way, I ordered another beer and then racked up the balls for another game. "I was only warming up," I said to Joe.

"Are you one of those people who gets better the more they drink?"

"Possibly," I said, laughing. I took a long swig of beer and then moved to take my shot.

Joe grinned. "You really can't break!"

"I never could."

"Do you want me to teach you?"

"Nope," I said. "Take your shot and don't be patronising. I'll still beat you!"

Later, when I sank the black ball to win the game, I threw my arms up in delight. People around us turned to look as I danced around the table.

"I was always gonna let you win the second game," Joe said, his eyes sparkling in amusement.

"Let me win? Pff! Best of three?"

"Let's just call it even and hit the road."

"Okay," I agreed. The thought of the day coming to an end was disappointing, but I was glad he'd brought me to play pool. I was reassured by the fact that he'd wanted to take me somewhere special to him and that it was a place he'd never brought Beth.

"Where are you taking me next?" I asked cheekily as we walked outside. The alcohol buzzed in my system, and I felt like trying my luck.

"I reckon it's time to get back to town." He paused for a moment. "But I guess we could always check out the action in the Tav."

"You finally gonna have a drink with me?" I asked.

"Maybe," he said with a wink.

Chapter 36

LIBBY – August 2017

My mind was elsewhere, lost in a daydream, when I walked back to the Kununurra Croc and meandered slowly through the peaceful gardens. The pool was empty and only a handful of people sat at the tables beside the bar. I nodded a greeting at no one in particular and took a seat at the bar. When Kai appeared, I ordered a beer and drank it too fast. *I have two sisters.* I'd never really contemplated having siblings, but I found myself liking the idea.

"You okay?" Kai asked, snapping me back to my surroundings.

I held up the empty beer bottle. "Can I get another?"

He nodded but when the beer bottle arrived on the bar, he placed a large glass of water beside it too. "Make sure you drink enough water," Kai said amiably. "The heat catches people out."

I was dying to ask him about my mum, but it was hard to know how to bring it up. "Thanks," I said and he left me alone.

Anger washed through me about halfway through

the second beer. I raged at my mum in my head. *Why on earth didn't you talk to me sooner? Why did you leave me to figure all this out alone?* As always, any anger I felt was quickly replaced by sadness. My eyes welled up and my hand moved to my neck in search of the comfort of my necklace. Panic hit me as I groped at my collarbone. *Where is it?* Glancing down, I pulled at my T-shirt, hoping to find it nestled in my clothing. *No, no, no. Where is it?*

With urgency, I hopped off the stool and retraced my steps through the garden. It couldn't have been gone long or I'd have noticed. I scanned the ground and then moved up to my room, even unpacking my entire backpack to look for it.

"Are you sure you're okay?" Kai asked when I returned to the bar, scanning the ground where I'd been sitting.

"I've lost my necklace," I said frantically, groping at my neck again to check it was really gone.

"It won't be far away," he said, kindly. "I can help you look."

When there was no sign of it, I rushed back to Bushcamp, scanning the ground as I went. Cassie and the girls helped me look, but it wasn't there. *When did I last have it?* I couldn't remember.

My heart raced as I hurried back to the Croc. Kai looked sympathetic and suggested looking in his office. He headed away from me and I moved over to look around the long wooden tables. *I can't have lost it.* My heart was beating so fast and a wave of nausea washed through me.

"I can't believe I lost it," I said quietly when I walked into Kai's office to find him peering under the desk.

"Well, there's no sign of it in here . . ."

I parked myself in front of the photo of Mum and couldn't stop the tears falling down my face. I reached a hand to the photo as I sobbed.

"Hey," Kai said soothingly. "It's not the end of the world. It'll probably still turn up."

"That's my mum," I spluttered through my tears.

"What?" He looked confused, and my body heaved with sobs.

"She gave me the necklace." His hand on my arm led me to a chair, and I sank down into it, sniffing loudly as I tried to catch my breath.

"You're Evelyn's kid?" he asked.

When I nodded, his eyes grew wider. He moved to pass me a box of tissues from his desk.

"You remember her name?" I asked, once I'd composed myself slightly.

"Of course."

"It was so long ago – I didn't know if I'd find anyone who'd remember her."

"Some people leave an impression," he said wistfully. "Evelyn was the first friend I made here. She stayed in the room next to me. I can't believe you're her kid. Jeez, I must be really old!"

I managed a smile and took a deep breath, embarrassed by my outburst. "She loved this place," I said, unsettled by the sudden silence. "She wanted me to come and explore it."

He paused, looking at me intensely. I knew what he wanted to ask. He opened and closed his mouth before he finally spoke. "She couldn't come?" His eyes searched mine for answers.

253

I shook my head sadly. "Cancer," I said. "A year ago."

He looked genuinely upset and somehow it made me feel better. "I'm very sorry to hear that," he whispered, giving my hand a squeeze. "Evelyn was a good 'un." He paused as he moved away from me and lingered by the photo on the wall. "You've probably heard all about me," he said finally, a silly grin on his face.

"She didn't tell me much. But I've seen photos of you," I added, feeling bad for him.

He flashed me a sorrowful smile. "I suppose she told you all about Joe?"

Unsure how to answer, I stared at Kai for a moment, trying desperately to read him. *Does he know that Joe's my dad?*

"She wanted me to find him," I said.

"That's no surprise. They were thick as thieves. Like two pieces of a puzzle. He was a mess when she took off. I thought he'd never get over it." He moved towards the door and I followed, hoping he wasn't about to clam up on me. "He got over her eventually. He finally met Cassie and things fell into place for him." I returned to my place at the bar and waited while Kai served more drinks. "You got brothers and sisters?" he asked.

An image of the girls in the shop popped into my head. Ruby and Skye: my little half-sisters. I chewed on my lip and shook my head.

"Funny," he said. "I always thought Evelyn would have a whole bunch of kids."

"It was just me and Mum," I said.

"Dad not on the scene?" he asked.

I stared at him. "No."
Not yet.

Chapter 37

EVELYN – January 1995

The drive home went too fast and we were back in familiar territory before I knew it. Joe glanced at me and I smiled back at him.

"Let's make one last stop," he said, pulling off the main road. The sun was just setting and the light was fading when I followed Joe out of the ute.

"Where are you taking me now?" I asked when he led me away from the road and into the shadow of the rock formations ahead.

"You've been here all this time and you've never been to Kelly's Knob?" He tutted his disapproval and strode ahead. It had been suggested a few times at the end of a night's drinking that we head up to Kelly's Knob. It was a lookout point over the town, and somehow I'd never actually made it out here.

"Wait," I called, hurrying to catch him. "I can hardly see where I'm going." The path curved around and ascended steeply.

"There's a rail here," he told me as we reached steps. I gripped it tightly and when Joe reached his hand back to me, I took that too. I was out of breath when we finally reached the top.

"It's incredible," I said, looking out over Kununurra. A final strip of sunlight glowed along the horizon and lights flickered on across the town. Joe settled himself on a bench nearby, and I looked at him seriously. "This is *my* favourite place," I told him.

Darkness was spreading around us, and I could only just make out the smile that crept across his face. It was true though. At that moment in time, it was my favourite place in the whole world, and there was nowhere I'd rather have been.

"How are we gonna get down from here in the dark?" I asked. "It was hard enough coming up, and at least there was a bit of light then."

"I'll help you," he said, reaching his arm along the back of the bench, which I took as an invitation to sit with him. I leaned my head on his shoulder and he pulled his arm tighter around me. I wanted to commit every detail of the moment to memory to keep with me forever: the way our legs touched and the feel of his chest against me; the weight of his arm and the scent of him which filled my nostrils. A hint of stubble grazed my forehead when he moved.

"I wanted to ask you something," he said quietly. "I've been trying to find the right moment but I'm scared of the answer . . ."

"What?" I said, sitting up straighter.

He turned towards me. "What's your plan?"

My mind couldn't quite process the question. "What do you mean?"

"I mean are you going to go back home in a couple of months and leave me with a broken heart?"

The fact I could affect his heart so much that I'd

be able to break it gave me butterflies. "I don't have a plan," I said slowly. "This place feels like home. I hate the thought of leaving."

He reached for my hand and pulled me towards him. "I don't want you to leave."

"I've been avoiding thinking about it," I said. "But you're right, I need to make a plan." He was so close I could feel his breath on my cheek. "I hate the thought of leaving you," I whispered.

His hand rested on my hip when he kissed me, slowly at first and then with an urgency that I returned as I moved my arms around his neck and pushed my fingers into his hair. I was breathless when he finally pulled away, resting his forehead against mine. He gave me another quick peck before pulling me to my feet. "Let's go and get a drink."

It was almost impossible to see the path, but Joe guided me expertly as though he'd done it a thousand times. I wondered briefly if he came here with Beth and then quickly pushed the thought from my mind. The fact that he still spoke to her often had thrown me, and I was trying desperately not to make too much of it. I really needed to stop thinking about her.

Back at the road there was a faint glow from nearby streetlights. Joe unhooked the tailgate and we climbed into the back of the ute. "I'm glad the others couldn't make it today," I said as Joe passed me a beer.

He sat beside me and slipped his hand into mine. "Me too. We never seem to get rid of them."

"I thought you were avoiding being alone with me . . ."

"Maybe I was," he said with a small smile. "I

259

don't know. I was worried that you were going to leave soon, and I didn't want us to start something and then you leave."

Panic hit me in the chest with full force. "So if I'd have said I was leaving in a couple of months, you wouldn't want anything to do with me?"

"It's not like that," he said quickly. "I just wondered if it would be better if we stayed friends. Instead of complicating things."

I pulled my hand from his as the future of our relationship became very clear to me. Or *lack* of a future. "Joe," I said, breathlessly. "I want to stay. But that doesn't mean that I *will* stay. It's not that simple."

"Why isn't it? You can extend your visa for another year and after that we figure something else out."

"I can't extend my visa." This is why I hadn't made a plan; why I'd avoided thinking about what I would do when my year came to an end. Because I knew all along: I had no choice but to leave. "There's no way for me to stay here, legally."

"But you just said you wanted to make a plan and stay here. This is your home."

"It's not though. Not really. I won't have any choice but to leave the country."

His head landed against the back of the ute with a thud. "There must be some way," he said angrily.

I buried my head in my hands. "I don't know if there is."

He swore mildly and swigged at his beer.

"So we're back to being just friends then, are we?" I snapped.

"No," he said, firmly. "We need to figure out how

you can stay."

"But what if I can't stay?"

"I don't know! I don't know what you want me to say."

I jumped down from the back of the ute. "Just take me home."

"Shouldn't we talk about this?"

"There's nothing to talk about!" Every ounce of rational thinking left my body, and my brain went to mush. I knew that whatever I said would be irrational ramblings. Because I *would* have to leave. Joe was right; there was no point in us being in a relationship when I was going to leave.

"Evelyn!" he called, following me.

"There's nothing to say," I told him again. "I'm going to have to leave the country, and you don't want to be in a relationship that has an expiry date. So let's just not see each other at all."

"Now you're being crazy," he said.

He was right, of course – I *was* being crazy; there was no denying it. I *felt* crazy. "I don't want to just be friends," I said, suddenly tearful. "I can't do this. It would be better, wouldn't it? If we just stayed out of each other's way." *I could leave sooner than planned – that would make things easier. Dragging things out will be far too painful.*

He pushed his head back into the driver's seat, and when he didn't say anything it angered me even more. "I don't know what to do," he said finally. The engine roared to life and he manoeuvred the ute back onto the road and headed for town.

Five minutes later, he pulled up outside the Croc. I was seething with anger and jumped out of the ute before Joe could get a word in.

"Whoa! What's the rush?" Kai asked when I bumped into him in my haste to get to my room, where I could have a breakdown in private. "You coming to the Tav? I'm heading over to meet Leslie and Cam."

"Not tonight," I said frostily.

"You got something better to do?"

I laughed, taking myself by surprise. Kai gave me a strange look. "You okay?"

"Absolutely fine!" I said with an undercurrent of sarcasm. "I'll get changed and see you over there." Kai had a point; I had nothing better to do, and crying on my own all evening wasn't going to do me any good.

At the Tav, I found Leslie sandwiched between Cam and Kai in the quietest corner of the room. "You're a sorry sight," I said, looking sternly at Leslie. "Let's go and dance."

"It's way too hot out there," Cam grumbled.

"It's way too boring in here," I argued.

Kai shook his head and moved over to make space for me. "Get a beer and sit down, will ya?"

"I've had enough beer for one day," I told him. "And I really want to dance! Come on. You have to dance with me." I knew Leslie wouldn't take much persuading, and the boys would follow her anywhere.

The courtyard was hot and humid, the heat hanging like a cloud around the sweaty bodies.

"What's going on?" Leslie shouted over the din of live music when I pulled her onto the small dance floor. "Were you out with Joe all day?"

"Yeah," I said. "I don't want to talk about him

though. I just want to dance."

"Did you have an argument?" she asked, persistent as ever.

"I told him I don't want to see him again."

She laughed. "You'd better close your eyes then."

I glanced round and caught sight of Joe making his way in our direction.

"I'm going to get another drink," Leslie said.

"Don't leave me," I protested, but she was already walking away. I turned from Joe and danced alone, smiling at the familiar faces on the dance floor.

"Hey!" Joe shouted at me.

"What?"

"Talk to me."

"I thought we were going to avoid each other," I shouted.

"I never agreed to that," he replied. "Let's go somewhere and talk!"

When I ignored him, he pulled me close to him and swayed to the music.

His body against mine made me want to sob at the injustice of it all. *Why do I have to leave?*

"I'm going to have to leave in two months," I told him sadly.

"Then we better make the most of those two months, hadn't we?"

My heart raced and I leaned closer, hugging him to me.

"You do want to be with me, don't you?" he asked, looking confused.

"Yes," I said slowly.

"You don't look happy."

I took a step back and looked into his big blue

eyes. "It's just that until today, I've managed not to think too much about leaving."

His face fell serious. "Don't worry about it yet. Maybe there's another way for you to get a visa. Or I could move to England!"

He wrapped his arms tighter around me and I laughed. "You'd freeze!"

Chapter 38

LIBBY – August 2017

Sleep didn't come easily. I tossed and turned as my mind whirled like a cyclone, picking up thoughts and whizzing them around before discarding them and moving on to something else. Grieving was supposed to get easier with time, but suddenly I missed my mum so fiercely that I struggled to breathe. Part of me wanted to gather every tiny detail of her life, and part of me wanted to leave it all and get on with my own life. Mostly, I wanted to find out this story from *her*. I should have asked her years ago, when I had the chance. It never occurred to me that time would run out for us.

When I finally dragged myself from my bed and ventured out of my room, I saw the door to the office open. A selection of postcards were displayed on a stand outside, and I picked out a few to send home. I'd probably get back before they arrived but it was nice to send proper mail for a change from all the messages and emails.

"Morning!" I said to Kai, who had his feet up on the desk and a cup of coffee in his hand.

"G'day!" he said cheerfully.

My eyes automatically moved to the photo on the wall.

"You can have it, if you want," Kai said, swinging his feet down and sitting up in the chair.

"Thanks. I think I'll leave it where it is though." I held out the postcards and pulled a crumpled note from my pocket but Kai waved it away.

"I was thinking," he said. "I should show you around. Show you where your mum used to hang out. I was trying to think of which springs we used to go to. Definitely Middle Springs and maybe Blackrock. We used to take a boat out on Lake Kununurra. I can definitely organise a few trips."

I nodded from the chair opposite. *A tour guide would be welcome.*

"We didn't have a pool here back then so she used to swim in the public pool a lot. Evelyn helped me do this place up when I first arrived. She was close to the owner, Stan – he was a character too. He sold the place to me for next to nothing when he retired. Not that he ever really retired. He was always around here, grumbling about something or other. He passed away a few years back," he told me sadly, pausing before he went on.

"What else can I tell you . . . she worked in the hotel, you should check that out. There are old photos up over there too."

"She worked in a hotel?" I asked, my mouth twitching into a smile. My mind raced to the day I told Mum I'd got a summer job in a hotel and how much she'd laughed. At the time I'd been affronted, sure she was making fun of my choices. She'd sworn she wasn't, eventually keeping a straight face and telling me she was glad I'd found a job. Her smirk had lingered though, and it had angered me. Maybe the smirk wasn't to do with me after all. Perhaps she'd just been remembering?

"Joe can fill you in more than I can," Kai said.

"I guess I should meet him . . ."

"Oh, you've got to meet Joe. I can't wait to tell him Evelyn's kid's in town. He won't believe it!" He looked thoughtful. "I'm all tied up today so I won't be much of a chaperone, I'm afraid."

"It's fine," I said quickly. "You don't need to go out of your way. I only wanted to have a look at the town – see it for myself after Mum'd talked about it. I think I'll just have a stroll around today, maybe take a look at the hotel."

"Take your togs, there's a nice pool by the bar. That's where the old photos are. Definitely check it out. And ask for Todd – he's the owner since his dad died. He knew Evelyn. He might have some stories for you."

"Todd? Okay, I will. Thanks."

Laughter-lines appeared when Kai smiled, and his eyes twinkled. I was self-conscious as I got up to leave. "Sorry," he said. "You just look like her. You've brought about a million memories to the surface. The good old days!"

***

The unimaginatively named Kununurra Hotel was only a ten-minute walk, but I was drenched in sweat and panting like a dog when I got there.

267

HANNAH ELLIS

"Hey!" A familiar face greeted me when I walked into the fancy bar area. It was Michelle, the girl who'd driven me from the airport.

"Hi!" I said. "Thanks again for the lift yesterday."

"No worries," she said. "Water?"

"Yes, please!" I returned her smile and leaned on the bar. "How do you survive in this heat?"

"Heat?" she said. "Highs of thirty-four today, pff. This is nothing!"

"Well I'm melting."

"I can see that!"

Hastily, I drank the cold water and asked for a refill. I searched the walls when Michelle took my glass, but there was no sign of photos as Kai had promised. The place was classy. Everything about it screamed luxury, and I felt suddenly out of place in my scruffy shorts and vest top.

"Did you get a room at the Croc?" Michelle asked, passing me more water.

"Yes. Kai's nice."

"Yep, he's as sound as they come. And the Croc's a good place to stay."

"It seems like it," I agreed, looking around some more. "If you work here, you must know the owner? Todd?"

She rolled her eyes. "Sure do. He's a slave driver!"

"Really?"

"Ah, he's okay. Most of the time! He's my dad. You after a job or something?"

"No. I just . . . I'm doing some research . . . on the town. Kai said I should talk to Todd."

"Cool! He's around somewhere. I'll find him."

She bounced away and I watched as she almost collided with a middle-aged guy coming the other way. "There you are." She turned back to me. "Found him!"

"Will you ever learn to watch where you're going?" he asked, continuing past Michelle and behind the bar. "I thought you'd gone to work already."

"Just stopped to serve a customer," she told him sweetly, looking over at me. "This is my friend, Libby. I gave her a ride from the airport, I told you, remember?"

"Hi," he said, giving me a curt nod. "Is Kevin not here yet?" he asked Michelle.

"I've not seen him."

"I'm paying him," he grumbled. "Why can't he get here on time?"

"Sack him?" Michelle suggested.

He raised an eyebrow. "You wanna take his shifts?"

"Don't sack him. Please don't sack him!" Todd's lips twitched into a reluctant smile, and I could see where Michelle got hers. "I gotta go, Daddy Dearest! Libby wants to ask you some questions about the town. Be nice, won't you?"

He looked at me properly, his eyebrows slightly furrowed. "I take it you're Evelyn's kid?" he said once Michelle had skipped away. "Kai told me you were coming."

"Yeah," I said, unnerved by him; he made me uncomfortable somehow. "Kai said Mum used to work here. He thought you might have some old photos . . ."

269

He stared at me for a moment and then moved away abruptly. When he reached for a bottle of gin on the shelf behind him, I was tempted to bolt. His cold manner was disconcerting.

"There she is," he said quietly. The photo caught my eye then, stuck to the wall where the gin had been. I moved to get a closer look. She was laughing into the camera with an awful French maid outfit on. The lump in my throat was hard to swallow. I leaned further over the bar, squinting.

When Todd pointed up, I tilted my head and laughed at the array of photos stuck on the ceiling above the bar. They were full of people I didn't recognise and occasionally a familiar face. A younger version of Todd looked down on me with, presumably, a tiny Michelle in his arms. He smiled shyly into the lens.

"Come here," Todd said, and I walked around the bar, occasionally glancing up at the photo ceiling. He replaced the gin and pulled another bottle down to reveal yet another picture. No one I recognised but they were standing behind the bar I was standing at, pulling a pint. When Todd gave me the nod, I peeked behind another bottle, and then another. There were photos hidden behind every one. After a while, I came across another of Mum. She was sitting on a boat, a fishing rod in one hand and a beer bottle in the other. She looked so happy.

"She went fishing?" I asked as a memory popped into my head. A little scar on her hand that she told me came from a fishing accident when she was young.

"She loved it," he said with a nod. "I'm sorry to

270

hear she passed away."

I was glad Kai had warned him. Awkwardly explaining things to everyone would be exhausting.

"The hidden photos were her idea," he said. "My dad was running the place back then and Evelyn tried to persuade him to have a photo wall but he wouldn't hear of it. Said it would lower the tone. After she left, I started to find photos hidden around the place. It became a tradition: anyone who worked here would hide a photo somewhere when they left. Then the locals joined in the game. There are so many photos around here you wouldn't believe. Under chairs, tables – look anywhere, you'll find photos."

The smile didn't leave my face as I moved away from him and ducked my head under a table. He was right: there were photos taped underneath. Next, I upturned a stool at the bar and found another.

"That's so cool!" I said, looking up at Todd, who was watching me intently.

"I'm glad you came," he said, his features softening. "I always thought Evelyn would come back someday. She should've stayed in touch."

"I'm not sure why she didn't," I said. "I never heard anything about this place until she was dying . . ." I took a breath. "Then suddenly she's telling me to go and find Joe Sullivan in some crazy outback town that no one's ever heard of."

"Did you find Joe?" he asked.

"Not yet," I said.

"So you're staying at the Croc?" Todd didn't wait for an answer. "I hope Kai is looking after you well."

"I can't complain."

"There's always this place if you're sick of

slumming it."

I snorted, taken aback. "Sorry, it's just that I'm on a budget."

"I wasn't going to charge you."

My eyebrows shot together and I felt uncomfortable again. "Thanks, but I like it at the Croc."

"You're your mother's daughter," he muttered, only just loud enough for me to hear. "I'm not sure what else I can tell you, really. Joe and Leslie knew Evelyn best, and Cam, but he moved away."

I hovered while he walked the length of the bar, straightening things out.

"Joe's next on my list of people to talk to. I'm surprised to find so many people who remember her. I just wanted to look around, really – see the places she went and where she lived."

Todd leaned on the bar, his face scrunched up, saying nothing and giving me the creeps.

"Thanks for showing me the photos," I said.

"No worries. Come back if I can help with anything else."

Chapter 39

LIBBY – August 2017

My encounter with Todd left me unnerved. It seemed like there was probably a lot he could tell me about my mum's time in Kununurra, but I had the feeling that whatever he had to tell, I didn't want to hear. Mum'd told me to find Joe. Maybe there was a reason that she hadn't told me any more. *I should talk to Joe.*

As I passed the camping shop, I was drawn to it and fought the urge to go in. Cassie and the girls had been so warm and friendly. I would love to spend more time with them. Although, what I wanted more than anything was a refreshing dip in a pool.

Back at the Croc, a few people sat around the pool and bar area. Kai was nowhere to be seen, and a tall lanky guy had taken over bar duties.

"Hi!" a blonde girl said when I spread my towel on the sunbed next to hers.

"Hi." I smiled at her.

"Just arrived?"

"Yesterday."

"What do you think so far?" the stocky guy next to her asked.

"I think it's hot!"

"Crazy hot," the girl replied. "I'm Sylvie."

"Libby," I told her. "Where are you from?"

"Sweden."

I looked over at the guy. "Jakob from Germany!" he said proudly.

"Your English is very good," I said to both of them.

"English is easy," Jakob declared.

"I think so!" I said. My language abilities were embarrassing.

"Swimming?" Sylvie asked, standing. I followed, and my enthusiastic dive-bomb into the pool covered Jakob in water. He chuckled and came to join us.

We chatted as we swam; Sylvie explained how she'd been travelling with a friend but they'd gone their separate ways a few weeks back. She'd arrived in Kununurra a few days before and was intrigued by the place. She wasn't sure how long she'd stay. Jakob had been here for three months. He'd just finished his stint of fruit-picking and told us stories about how awful the first weeks on the farm had been, until he got used to the work and the heat.

The three of us spent the rest of the day by the pool. I found them both to be easy company, and I managed to relax and stop myself from thinking about the reason I was in Kununurra. At least until late in the afternoon, when I caught sight of a woman looking at me from the bar. She was older and didn't look like a backpacker.

Tom and Sylvie were splashing around in the pool when she wandered over to me. "Libby?" she asked, perching on the chair next to me. Her intense stare unsettled me until she broke into a wide smile. "I'm sorry, Kai told me about you. I was just curious."

"You knew my mum?" I asked. "I think I've seen photos of you."

"Yeah. We were friends." She extended her hand. "I'm Leslie."

"Nice to meet you."

Kai wandered past, weighed down with shopping bags. "See you've met the old ball and chain!"

I looked back to Leslie. "You guys are married?"

"Fifteen years," Kai called. "Expecting my medal in the post any day now!"

Leslie rolled her eyes as though it wasn't the first time she'd heard that joke. Kai joined us a moment later, draping an arm around Leslie and kissing her cheek. "She's all right, really," he told me with a wink.

"It's me who deserves the medal!" Leslie said. "Haven't you got work to do?"

"Yes!" he replied, standing. He lingered for a moment. "She looks like Evelyn, doesn't she?"

"It's such a blast from the past," Leslie said, beaming at me. "I had so much fun with Evelyn. I was gutted when she left."

"I didn't know if anyone would remember her."

Leslie looked at me kindly. "I was sorry to hear . . ."

"Thank you," I said quickly, shifting my gaze as I felt my chin start to quiver and I fought off tears.

"I'll see you later," Leslie said, squeezing my hand briefly. "Don't miss out on the sausage sizzle tonight, will you? It's the highlight of the week around here."

It took a moment to get my emotions under control.

***

Kai fired the barbecue up early in the evening, and the smell of food cooking moved us over to him.

"How was your day?" Kai asked.

"Fine," I replied. "I went to the hotel."

"Did you meet Todd?"

"Yes," I said hesitantly. "He's a little . . ." I searched for the right word.

"Jeez, did you catch him in a bad mood? He can be a grumpy bugger sometimes."

"He wasn't particularly friendly."

"Ignore him," Kai said. "He's mellowed over the years, but he's still moodier than any woman I've ever known." He winked at me before his face fell serious. "I thought he'd have been interested to meet you though. He knew Evelyn well."

I shrugged. "He showed me the photos."

"They're pretty cool, hey?" he said as he started throwing sausages on the grill. "You hungry?"

"Starving!"

"Great, I've too many snags as always." I looked blankly at him. "Sausages," he explained with a grin. "I tried calling Joe but I couldn't get hold of him. I usually catch him for a beer sometime over the weekend. Maybe he'll call in here later."

My appetite disappeared. The thought that he might just turn up at any time made me nervous. My evening was ruined after that; I had a bite to eat and took my time drinking a beer, but I felt suddenly nervous about meeting Joe. *What if he was as cold as Todd had been? What if he doesn't want to know me?* I'd be no worse off, I told myself. I'd always been fine without a dad before. What difference would it really make?

I found myself smiling inanely at Jakob, who was telling a joke. Reaching for my necklace, only to be reminded of its absence, made my stomach lurch. At the next lull in the conversation I said goodnight and headed to bed.

HANNAH ELLIS

Chapter 40

LIBBY – August 2017

The next day I had breakfast with Jakob and Sylvie. Jakob had bought a car when he'd arrived in Australia, with the intention of staying for two years and selling it again before he left. After breakfast, the three of us climbed into the old banger and Jakob took us for a drive. We ended up at the Swim Beach – a stretch of sand along the edge of Lake Kununurra which proclaimed to be crocodile-controlled, whatever that meant. An image of uniformed crocodiles wandering around on their hind legs, policing the area, came to mind. It was quickly replaced by more serious images when I cooled off in the water with Jakob and Sylvie. It was only a quick dip for me and then I retraced my steps out of the water.

"Where are you going?" Jakob asked.

"To sunbathe," I replied, moving quickly to get out of the murky water and away from whatever sharp-toothed dangers lurked below.

The afternoon was pleasant; Jakob was well-prepared and set up sun umbrellas to provide protection from the scorching sun. We played cards and chatted amiably. When the heat overwhelmed me, I'd manage a quick dip to cool off but couldn't relax enough in the water to swim far out into the lake. They teased me about my anxiety but I didn't really care. I wasn't losing a limb.

As the afternoon went on, Jakob became increasingly excited about an evening in Kelly's Tavern – or the Tav, as he called it. Apparently, it was the social event of the week. In such a sleepy town, I wasn't holding out much hope for a wild night.

He was right though; the Tav was *definitely* the place to be in Kununurra on a Friday night.

"Where did everyone come from?" I shouted over the din. It was a shock to cross the threshold into the Tav and find a barrage of people blocking the way to the bar. Every inch of floor space was taken up by people, and there was a constant buzz of conversation in the air.

"I thought you might be surprised!" he said, leaning close to me. "It's Friday . . . workers come into town from the farms and stations. During the week, this place is dead, but at the weekend it comes alive!" He could say that again.

I scanned the room, wondering if Joe might be there. The crowd was mixed with a range of ages, but none of the faces looked familiar. It didn't matter that the image I had of Joe was from twenty-something years ago. I was convinced I'd know him if I saw him.

Once we'd fought our way to the bar, Jakob led us to a side door and out to a large courtyard area. The heat hit me again as we stepped away from the air-conditioning. Outside, the music was "drunken karaoke", and my eyes followed the noise to a small stage in the corner. There was a sound system set up next to flashing disco lights and a drunk girl propping herself up against a microphone stand and wailing something incoherent into it. No one was paying any attention.

Various groups of people sat around on an assortment of mismatched garden furniture, and scattered people were standing. It was a much younger crowd than inside. Everyone was casually dressed, mainly in shorts and T-shirts.

Jakob spotted friends and they shuffled down to make room for us on the picnic bench. I vaguely recognised them from the Croc.

"You're Libby, right?" a guy with a London accent asked.

I nodded.

"Kai from the hostel was looking for you earlier. Did he find you?"

"I've not seen him today," I said.

"Is he after you or what? He's a bit old for you, isn't he?"

"It's not like that," I told him. "He's a friend. He's been helping with some research I'm doing."

"Well you should watch him," he went on. "We've seen some dodgy guys running hostels while we've been travelling." The girl opposite nodded her head as though they'd already discussed this.

"Kai's a good guy," Jakob said. "I've been here a while. He's not dodgy."

I took a sip of my beer and turned away from the couple, wondering why Kai was looking for me.

"What research are you doing?" Sylvie asked.

I gulped down more beer, stalling for time as I decided how much to say. "My mum was here when she was my age," I said, deciding to stick to the truth. Not everything, of course. "She wanted me to see if there was anyone still living here who she'd been friends with."

"Wow," Jakob said. "That's interesting. Have you found anyone?"

"Kai!" I replied. "He remembers her. He's tracking down other people for me."

"That sounds like so much fun," Sylvie remarked. "It's like a treasure hunt!"

"Kind of." *I'm just not sure what it's going to lead me to. I need to drink more.*

"Anyone need another drink?" I asked, standing and polishing off the first beer.

Sylvie shook her head and Jakob laughed. "You English girls always drink so much. Go on then, I'll try and keep up!"

I don't always drink so much, I thought as I made my way through the throng. Just when there's a chance I might bump into my long-lost father at any moment.

The heat made me a lightweight, my body absorbing the alcohol at lightning speed. The more I drank, the easier it went down. By the fourth beer I was leaning over the line between tipsy and drunk. The positive was that all fear of running into Joe had vanished. The negative was that karaoke was starting to look like a fantastic idea. I was the life and soul and had everyone around me laughing.

"We should all do karaoke!" I said, loudly. "Who's in?"

"No way," Sylvie said. "It's so embarrassing."

"That's because you're drinking water!" I said. "Let's do shots . . ."

There was a cheer from people at the other side of me, who'd previously dragged me into a conversation about dangerous wildlife, one of them claiming he knew a guy who'd been bitten by a croc. It had made me think of Andrew and his paranoia about the Australian wildlife. I'd decided to message him earlier but had put the phone away when I realised I didn't have his number nor any way to contact him. I fired off a message to Yvonne, telling her to get his number for me, but I didn't get a reply. It was probably for the best.

"Okay," Jakob said. He'd been keeping up with me on the beers. It seemed to be a point of pride. "I'll get shots!"

"I'll help," I said, stumbling as I stood.

I had an alcohol glow and was smiling to myself when I heard my name called. Looking along the bar, I saw Kai waving furiously and beckoning me over. "Back in a minute," I told Jakob.

I didn't register the guy next to Kai until I reached them. Even then, I didn't make the connection. I wobbled as I greeted Kai with a hug, leaning into him heavily.

"Did you remember what I said about water?" he asked, keeping a hold of my arm until I was steady again.

"I might have just drunk beer instead," I told him, giving him my crazy eyes and laughing.

He shook his head but smiled warmly. "This is Joe," he said. "I was just telling him about you."

283

I looked at the guy perched on the barstool. My eyes refused to focus and I blinked hard. It certainly wasn't the reunion I'd planned. I wasn't sure what I had expected but meeting my father for the first time when I was drunk and swaying wasn't it. *Must sober up and be cool.*

"Hi," I said, offering my hand. He hesitated, staring at me.

"Can you believe Libby is Evelyn's daughter?" Kai said. "Crazy, isn't it?"

He finally took my hand, shaking it briefly in an awkward gesture. "Crazy," he muttered. "Looks like you're having fun. I hear Kai's been looking after you?"

"Yeah," I said. My head was spinning, and I cursed myself for drinking too much. I didn't know what to say to him.

"I'm too old for this place," he said, slapping Kai on the shoulder as he stood.

"You're pretty old!" Kai quipped. Joe didn't seem to hear.

"Great to meet you, Libby," Joe said, giving me a cursory glance.

I opened my mouth to say something but my brain wouldn't work, and he was already halfway across the room anyway.

Without thinking, I followed his path.

He was climbing into his shiny blue pickup when I reached him. "Hey," I called, making him turn to look at me. "I wanted to talk to you about my mum. She wanted me to find you . . ."

We were stuck in a deadlock then, looking at each other and saying nothing. I couldn't find the words, but I didn't want him to leave. I had questions; I just couldn't quite remember what they were. I took a deep breath and tried to get my thoughts in order. *What happened with you and my mum? Why didn't I hear about you before? Didn't you want to know me? Did you even know about me?*

"She's really dead?" he asked, taking me by surprise.

I nodded and blinked away tears. He didn't hide the tears that formed in his eyes. A moment later, he hopped into his pickup and screeched out of the car park. He came to an abrupt stop on the road and leaned out of the window. "You're staying in town for a while?" he asked. I nodded dumbly. "You should drink some water."

"Okay," I whispered as he pulled away down the road.

HANNAH ELLIS

Chapter 41

EVELYN – February 1995

The weeks before I left Kununurra went by in a blur. Thoughts of leaving niggled constantly, tainting the good times and making me increasingly anxious. Subconsciously, I think I'd been worrying about it for a long time. Maybe since I'd first met Joe. But now it bubbled to the surface and I knew I couldn't ignore it any more. I was going to have to leave. If only I'd stuck it out on the farm, I'd have been able to extend my visa. It was too late now though. In a month, I'd have to leave and say goodbye to Joe. Possibly forever. It seemed impossible. And unbearable.

The heat had been building steadily, and during the first week in February the humidity rose to sauna-like levels. It was like a fog in the air, threatening to suffocate. I'd always felt fairly immune to the heat, but I was starting to feel like it might make me insane. There were always rumours about the heat making people go crazy and I started to see why. Everywhere, people talked about rain. There'd been showers throughout January but only ever a sprinkling that did nothing to bring the temperature down. It was as though Mother Nature were teasing us. The wet season was late this year and heavy rain was expected any day. I never thought I'd be excited about the prospect of rain.

My afternoons at the pool were replaced by trips to anywhere with air-conditioning. Some afternoons I sat in Stan's office, chatting and playing poker with him and Kai. Other days I hung out in the Tav or even the supermarket, the freezer section being a favourite spot.

It was Monday afternoon and I'd finished work and was almost back at the Croc when a huge raindrop splattered in front of me. Then came another and another. The heavens opened and I ran to get to shelter before I was washed away. At my room, I stood with the door open, looking out at the deluge. Within minutes, the water was flowing off the roof like a waterfall. Joe jogged up the path with a huge grin on his face. He stopped in the middle of the lawn and spread his arms out beside him.

"What are you doing?" he shouted over the noise of the violent downpour. "Get out here!"

"Are you mad?" I shouted back, laughing. He turned in a circle, looking up and opening his mouth like a kid. He shook his head like a dog after a swim and then pushed his soaking hair off his face.

"Come out and play," he called. "You're missing all the fun!"

I ran at full pelt, stopping directly in front of him. "This place is crazy! You stay inside when the sun's out and go outside when it rains. I'm used to the opposite!"

"This is proper rain. I bet it puts your English

drizzle to shame."

"It does," I said, the familiar feeling of dread creeping over me at the mention of home. "I don't want to leave," I shouted. The rain seemed to come down even harder and the roar almost drowned my words out completely.

He pushed a dripping lock of hair off my face. "You don't have to."

"What?" I asked, sure I must have misheard him.

"I don't want you to leave either. You can stay."

We'd been avoiding the subject and this felt like a bad time to have brought it up. "I can't stay though. My visa's going to run out. I can't get another one."

"I've looked into it," he said. When he paused, panic washed over me. *Oh my God. He's going to propose.* It was exactly the sort of thing Joe would do. It's not like the thought hadn't crossed my mind, but I'd dismissed it as insane in a second.

"I spoke to Arthur," Joe continued. "He agreed to sponsor your visa. You'll have to keep working for him, but that would be okay, wouldn't it?"

The rain stopped suddenly. Like someone had turned off the tap. I looked up, unable to believe that the rain could stop so abruptly. Everything fell silent.

"What do you think? You'd be okay working for Arthur? I think you'd have to go back to England for a while until the visa's approved, but it would just be for a month or two."

My work uniform was dripping wet and my hair clung around my face. "I don't think it's that simple," I said. I'd looked into every possibility myself, of course. "I have to have a skill that's needed here."

"Arthur can claim that he needs you."

"But I don't do anything that someone else couldn't do. Anyone could do the job at the hotel."

"It's very difficult for Arthur to keep staff in this part of Australia," he said with a sly smile. "He has records that show no one's stayed in that job for more than a few months for the last twenty years. You've lasted longer than anyone."

"The only reason people don't stay is because Arthur's a grumpy old bugger!"

"It doesn't matter," Joe insisted. "I've spoken to people at the Department of Immigration and to people at the local government department. If you want to stay, we can figure it out. You can stay!"

I was at a loss for words and I wasn't sure I could let myself believe what he was telling me. *Could I really stay?* "You did all that for me?" I asked.

He nodded and I wrapped my arms around his neck and hugged him tightly. I moved my lips to his and we stood together, dripping wet and full of hope. Suddenly my future looked so much brighter.

"Get a room, will ya!" Kai shouted. I looked up and blushed. "You guys going to Cam's place tonight?" he asked.

"Yeah," I called.

"I have to get dry and get back to work," Joe said, turning to leave us. "I'll see you at Cam's."

The rain had created a buzz in the town and the mood was electric as I sat in Cam's apartment eating pizza and drinking beers. The thought that I might be able to stay had given me a lift, and I was excited to find out if I really could get a visa extension. I hardly dared hope that it could be true. I snuggled into Joe on the couch while Cam entertained us with his story

290

about driving through flooded roads to get back into town.

"Okay," Kai said when Cam took a break to drink his beer. "I have some good news."

"What?" I asked.

"We might be getting a pool at the Croc!"

"No way!" Cam said.

"Seriously," Kai said, excitedly. "I've been looking into it and got some quotes . . ."

"And Stan agreed to it?" Leslie asked.

"Well not yet," he admitted as the rest of us groaned.

"So it's not happening at all?" Cam said.

"It definitely *will* happen," Kai was adamant. "Stan had that look in his eye – you know, when he's saying no but you can see that he actually thinks it's a good idea?"

"But he *did* say no?" I asked, laughing. I loved Kai's enthusiasm for the Croc.

"What else you got planned for the Croc then?" Joe asked Kai, who happily launched into his favourite topic.

Over the next couple of hours, we drank and chatted and laughed like we had done so many times before. The evening passed too quickly and before I knew it, Kai was complaining about having to be up early for work. "C'mon," he said, looking at me. "You'd better see me safely home."

Joe ushered me to the door while Leslie negotiated with Cam to sleep on his couch. He'd give her his bed without a doubt.

"You wanna stay at my place?" Joe whispered, taking me by surprise. Physically, we'd been taking things pretty slow, and even though Joe'd made a few comments about us spending more time alone, I hadn't really been expecting it that evening.

"Yes," I said without hesitation. I definitely wanted to stay with him.

"I'll walk Evelyn home later," Joe said to Kai as he stumbled through the doorway.

Kai laughed. "Yeah right! Have fun! See you tomorrow," he called as he set off alone.

I thought about that moment a million times over the years. Had I known that I wouldn't see Kai again, I would have hugged him so tightly he'd have complained he couldn't breathe. I had no idea though, so I just watched him go and returned my attention to Joe, smiling at what was to come.

"Goodnight!" I called to Cam and Leslie.

Leslie had been such a brilliant friend, and I didn't even say goodbye, just a measly goodnight.

I was so blissfully ignorant of what lay ahead. The events of the following hours changed my life completely. But at that moment, I had no idea. All I knew was that I was in love with Joe Sullivan.

Chapter 42

LIBBY – August 2017

I'd been wondering whether or not food was a good idea when a shadow fell over me. Joe stood beside me. I hadn't expected to see him again so soon but was happy that he'd come looking for me. My anxiety at meeting him had been banished to the back of my mind, mainly because all I could think about was my hangover.

"How're you feeling?"

"Like death," I told him, my sunglasses not doing nearly enough to tone down the brightness.

"You didn't take the advice about the water then?"

"I'm not great at taking advice." I paused. "I'm not great at much, really."

"Wow." He pulled up a seat beside me. "That *is* a good hangover! Your mum was always pretty cheerful with a hangover."

My mouth twitched into a half-smile, which faded quickly. "Shame I don't take after her in that respect." The silence that surrounded us was awkward. "She wanted me to find you."

"Why?" His expression was blank until I lifted my

sunglasses to meet his gaze. "Sorry," he said. "I just don't really understand. Why did she never come back herself?"

I still had no idea if she'd told him about me. If he didn't know I was his daughter, it would explain his confusion. My brain struggled to function properly, and I struggled for something to say.

"I think she was sad she didn't get to come back here. Maybe she thought she would, one day. Then she ran out of time."

His eyes glazed over and he looked thoughtful for a moment. "So what happens now? She wanted you to find me. But then what?"

"She didn't say." When Joe stood up, I panicked, worried that he'd walk away and I'd have come all this way just to have these snippets of conversations with him. An image of Mum flashed into my head. The day she'd spoken to me about Joe. "She wanted me to tell you she was sorry," I blurted out.

I'd expected questions. *What was she sorry for?*

"I've gotta run," he said after a moment. "We're off out on the boat. You wanna come? Cassie and the girls are waiting in the car. I heard you already met them . . ."

"Yeah. In the shop."

"So, you coming?"

"I'll grab my things," I said.

*   *   *

Ruby squealed when I opened the car door five minutes later. "Sit next to me. Sit next to me!"

"Nice to see you again," Cassie said, twisting in the front seat as I climbed in between the girls. "I hear you're not feeling great?"

"I've found the worse place in the world to be hungover," I said bluntly.

There were chuckles from the front as we pulled away. We drove out of town, towing the boat behind us and turning into Celebrity Tree Park and the boat ramp, which dropped into Lily Creek Lagoon. The girls were great tour guides, pointing everything out for me.

"Lots of famous people planted the trees," Ruby informed me as we stood watching Joe expertly reverse the car to drop the boat into the water.

I looked around at the pristine park with its neat arrangement of trees spread around. "Really? There were celebrities here?"

"Baz Luhrmann," Skye said proudly. "I'm not sure you'll have heard of any of the others."

***

An hour later, I had a beer in one hand and a fishing rod in the other. I'd been bullied into the beer by Cassie. It was the last thing I wanted but she was right: my hangover was gone within a few sips. The boat bobbed serenely and the girls were in the water for a quick dip with Cassie.

"I've got something!" The line tugged and I gripped the rod, setting my beer down as a rush of adrenalin pumped through me. "What do I do?"

"Reel it in?" Joe suggested with a smirk.

I wound the handle furiously.

"Slow down," he said, moving over to me. "Pull the rod up and then reel as you lower it."

"I don't know how," I said, not sure why I was panicking so much. "Help!"

He put a hand over mine to lower the rod. "You've got it. Now reel."

"I'm trying," I snapped at him. "Can't you do it?"

"It's your fish," he said, backing away.

I kept reeling the line in and moving the rod up and down. Joe stayed quiet, chuckling occasionally as I flailed over my first fishing experience.

"There it is!" I said as the fish floundered and splashed at the surface. I was surprised at its size. It had felt heavy on the line but it was decidedly small.

Joe stepped in and took the fish in his hand. "You did it."

"I caught a fish," I said proudly.

The girls cheered from the sandy bank at the shore.

"Get a photo," Cassie shouted.

Reluctantly, I took the little guppy when Joe handed it to me. He pulled his phone from his pocket, snapping a photo of me holding it at arm's length before he took hold of the fish again. In one fluid motion, he unhooked it and then put it back into the water.

"Not quite dinner, but not a bad effort," he said.

I hadn't expected to enjoy fishing, but it was a beautiful day, and there was something so relaxing about sitting with a line in the water and just waiting for that exciting tug on the line.

The hours passed quickly and the sun was setting when we started heading home. We had three decent-sized fish for dinner. My score ended up at three, though none of them were big enough to keep. Ruby was claiming she caught one of the fish in the bucket – though I think it was mostly Cassie's efforts – and Joe caught the other two. Skye had turned her nose up at the fishing rods and protested that she wouldn't eat the poor fish. Joe and Cassie exchanged a look.

"Skye's a vegetarian at the moment," Cassie told me.

"Unless you put a hamburger in front of her," Joe said. "Apparently she's not so precious about cows if you grind them up and put them between some bread."

"Dad!" Skye snapped. "The cow had already died and you cooked too many burgers. I didn't want it to die for nothing."

"It'll be something else next week," Joe whispered.

"I heard that," Skye said. "Just because *you're* unprincipled."

Joe rolled his eyes and returned his attention to navigating the boat.

"That's Elephant Rock," Ruby said, sidling over to me.

I squinted into the setting sun, following her finger to the red rock formations.

"The one that looks like an elephant," Skye said, giving me a cheeky look. I wasn't sure if they were winding me up. "It looks like a trunk at the end," she explained.

"Oh yeah! It does look like an elephant, doesn't it? There's some very imaginative names around this place – Elephant Rock and Celebrity Tree Park."

Skye leaned into me. "You've not seen Hidden Valley yet have you?"

"Or Kelly's Knob!" Cassie chimed in.

"What?" I asked.

Cassie and Skye erupted with giggles and Joe turned to Ruby. "Come here," he said, holding a hand out to her. "Come and sit with Daddy and don't listen to their filth. My poor innocent baby!" She grinned and climbed into his lap.

"What on earth is Kelly's Knob?" I asked. "Do I even want to know?"

"It's a lookout," Joe told me as Cassie and Skye calmed down. "A big rock that you can walk to the top of. The best view of the town."

"We'll have to take you up one evening," Cassie said.

Joe caught my eye. "Sunset's nice up there."

"But why's it called Kelly's *Knob*?" I asked after a moment. No one seemed to know.

***

Back at their home – a blue house built up on sticks – we were greeted at the front gate by their dog, Charlie. He looked vicious and growled at me for a minute before his face relaxed and he gave me big puppy-dog eyes. He jumped all around me like an excited kid.

Skye laughed at him. "You're such a dork, Charlie, you big wuss!" He jumped up, almost knocking her backwards as he licked her face. "He's still a pup really," she told me, fighting him off. "Or at least that's what we say to hide the fact that he's the dumbest dog ever!"

Ruby looked wounded. "You're mean. He *is* a pup – he's not dumb!"

As though he knew she was defending him, Charlie bounded over to Ruby to lick her face in thanks. She was quickly knocked to the ground and lost under a sea of slobbering dog.

Cassie expertly body-checked Charlie with one arm and found Ruby with the other. "We have to watch him around Ruby. He's a big softie but he doesn't know his own strength."

"Dumb dog!" Ruby shouted through tears.

"Welcome to the madhouse," Cassie called over her shoulder, carrying Ruby up the front steps and into the house.

In the open-plan living room, an aquarium dominated one wall and the hum of the filtration system mingled with the noise of an overhead fan.

"I'm gonna put some chips on," Cassie told me. "Joe will sort the fish. Why don't you go out the back with the girls? Ask Skye to show you where the beers are."

"I probably shouldn't."

"Oh, go on. It's Saturday! Grab me one while you're at it."

I followed the girls' chatter through the back door and found them jumping happily on a trampoline. The grass at the back of the house had been scorched by the sun, leaving a dull and dusty yard. I moved to the sheltered patio area, which gave shade to a solid wooden dining table surrounded by assorted chairs. Potted plants gave some colour to the area.

I located the outdoor fridge, which mainly contained beer, and took a bottle in for Cassie before grabbing one for Joe and moving around the side of the house. He was busy in the garage, unloading the boat and putting away the fishing gear.

"Thanks," he said when I passed him a beer. "So you do have your uses! Maybe we'll keep you around." Laughter lines appeared round his eyes when he smiled. He was a nice guy – just what I'd have wanted in a dad. It annoyed me that Mum had kept me from him. I could've had holidays here. There was a whole family here that I'd been denied.

"I better do something with those fish," Joe said, his voice dispersing my thoughts. *I'll have to talk to him soon. I just need to find the right moment.*

When the girls nagged me, I set my beer down and climbed up on the trampoline with them. Ruby got bored before long and went to watch Joe. Skye was trying to teach me tricks, but there was no way I could replicate her perfect somersault. Not without causing myself serious injury.

When I finally climbed down with wobbly legs, I caught sight of Joe sitting beside Cassie. He whispered and nuzzled her ear until she pushed him away, giggling. My heart dropped to my knees. They were such a lovely couple, but all I could think of was my mum and all those years she spent alone.

"Fish won't be long," Joe said. I realised I'd stopped in the middle of the yard and he was looking at me awkwardly.

"Great," I said, swallowing hard and moving to sit with them. "I'll probably head off after that. I'm really tired."

"The heat's hard to deal with, isn't it?" Cassie remarked. "You get used to it after a while."

"I feel like it's just zapping all my energy," I said. *That and the emotional rollercoaster I'm on.*

The fish and chips were served on a big platter.

"We're kind of feral, aren't we?" Skye said. "Maybe when we have guests we should use plates."

"Saves the washing up this way," Joe said, jabbing his fork into a piece of fish.

"I can get you a plate," Cassie offered.

"It's fine," I said, amused as I watched them dig in. "I don't mind."

"I promise, it's just fish and chips! We're more civilised with everything else."

"Eat quick," Joe said. "It's survival of the fittest round here."

He was right; I ended up tussling with Skye over the fattest chips. "Let me have it," she complained. "You've got fish to eat too."

"You can eat fish," I said.

"Just not this one," Ruby said, having taken one whole fish to her side of the platter. "I caught it. It's mine!"

"You're all crazy," I said, laughing as we fought over the chips.

When I was full, I leaned back into my chair with a feeling of contentment. I wasn't in a rush to leave any more. In fact, when Cassie started telling Ruby it was time for bed, I felt really sad that the day was coming to an end.

Chapter 43

LIBBY – August 2017

When Joe drove me home, I found the silence unbearable. I contemplated what to say to him. It only took a few minutes until we were outside the Croc. I had my hand on the door, wondering whether to keep quiet and talk to him another time.

"I don't know why Mum didn't tell me about you before," I said, attempting to jump-start a conversation.

He looked confused. "What does your dad think about you coming over here?" he asked.

I spluttered and emitted a strange noise, stuttering as I tried to find words. Any words would do. "I don't have a dad. I mean, I never knew my dad. That's why I came here."

He looked at me but he didn't get it.

"That's why Mum wanted me to find *you* . . ."

"You've lost me somewhere," he said, his voice level.

My heart pounded and I wanted to be anywhere but there. "When Mum left here . . ." I took a deep breath, trying to keep my emotions under control.

"When she got home she was pregnant with me. She never told anyone who my father was. Not until she was dying, anyway."

Joe turned away from me. His arms draped over the steering wheel and his gazed fixed somewhere in the distance.

"Sorry," I said when I couldn't take the silence any more. "I don't know why, I always thought you knew about me. She didn't really explain what happened . . ."

He leaned his head to his hands and rubbed his temples. "She said I was your dad?"

"You must be really shocked?" I said, tears filling my eyes. "Maybe we can just talk tomorrow."

I was reaching for the door handle when he finally turned to me. "I'm sorry, Libby. I don't understand why she told you that."

"She was dying," I said. "She just wanted me to know the truth."

"That's the thing," he said, eyes full of sympathy. "It's not the truth."

"I don't want anything," I said quickly, tears coming in a steady and uncontrollable flow. "If you think I'm just after money or something, I'm not."

"It's not that," he said sadly. "I wouldn't have any problem if it were true, but it's not."

"Mum wouldn't lie to me," I said, suddenly angry. "You're just worried I'm going to mess up your perfect little family, aren't you?"

"I'm not saying she lied. I just don't know why she would say that to you."

"I just wanted to meet you," I said, pulling on the door handle. "I shouldn't have bothered."

I walked quickly to the gates of the Croc and heard Joe's door open and close behind me. "Libby. Wait a minute," he called.

"It doesn't matter," I shouted. "Just go."

"Libby!" His hand caught my elbow and he swung me towards him. I instinctively yanked my arm from him and he raised his hands defensively. "Just slow down. We can talk about this."

"But you're not going to acknowledge that you're my father?" I asked, rooted to the spot and glaring at him. "You're just going to call my mum a liar?"

"Libby!" He threw his hands up and paced a few steps before he spoke again. "We were never together, Evelyn and me. Not in that way. Things just never worked out for us. I can't be your father – it's not possible." Silence hung between us for a moment and he raised his eyebrows. "It's really not possible."

A sob escaped me as I turned and continued into the gardens, desperately wanting to get to my room and be alone. I needed to get away from Joe Sullivan.

"Libby!" he called. "Don't go off on your own. Wait!" I could hear his footsteps behind me and I sped up, almost crashing into Kai as I reached the hostel.

"Hey," he said cheerily. "Slow down." He placed his hands on my shoulders and his face filled with concern when he saw the state of me. "What's going on?"

Joe called my name again as he approached. I wriggled away from Kai and hurried up the steps.

"Go away," I shouted behind me. When I reached my room, I glanced down to see Kai with a hand on Joe, blocking his path. Joe looked up at me with confusion and sympathy.

305

My face was soon buried in my pillow and I cried quietly. Thank goodness there was no one else in the room. I'd made such a fool of myself. It was tempting to get on the next plane and pretend none of this had happened. I couldn't get my head around it. Nothing made sense. The worst thing was, I'd never know now. I couldn't ask Mum, and I didn't know who else to ask. Why did she leave such a mess?

My phone must have connected to the Wi-Fi and new messages beeped in. I replied to Uncle Rob, since he was obviously desperate to talk to me. I told him I was fine and I'd call soon. I didn't want to speak to anyone yet; I'd tell them everything later, once I'd got used to the news myself.

A knock on the door came ten minutes later. "It's Kai," he called through the door. "Why don't you come out and talk?"

"I don't want to see Joe," I replied.

"He's gone. Come out. I'm worried about you."

Slowly, I opened the door and followed Kai. We sat side by side at the top of the stairs, listening to the chatter and laughter coming from the bar.

"Don't you need to work?" I asked.

"They'll be okay for a while. Jakob said he'd keep an eye on the bar!"

"You're brave."

"Jakob's pretty boring and sensible. Though I heard you led him astray at the pub last night!"

"That doesn't feel like just last night," I mused.

"Did you have a good day on the boat?"

"Yeah," I said, my eyes welling up again. "It was great."

Kai looked thoughtful. "Joe filled me in."

306

"Is he really not my dad?" I asked.

He shook his head. "Joe wouldn't lie."

"But neither would my mum," I argued. "Why did she say that? I came all the way out here just to make an idiot of myself!"

"Don't be daft. No one thinks that."

"What happened then? You were here. Don't you know anything?"

"It's a bloody long time ago." He paused, deep in thought. "It's all a bit vague now. I remember everyone was surprised when she left. She didn't say goodbye, you know? Just left without a word. I was pissed off at her. We were good friends. Or so I thought."

"Why would she leave without saying anything?"

"I don't know. Joe's ex came back to town out of the blue. But he was over her by then. It never made any sense. Joe couldn't even figure it out."

"But why did she get me to come all the way out here? I don't get it."

He looked at me sadly. "I don't know."

Chapter 44

EVELYN – February 1995

When I kissed Joe for the last time, I had no idea that when our lips parted they would never touch again. So many times, I pondered what I would do differently if I could go back to that night. I could have clung to Joe and refused to leave. I could have told Beth to go away or insisted that Joe walked me home. I could have gone and cried to Leslie. There were a number of options that could all have changed my fate.

I'd watched Kai leave and shouted goodnight to Cam and Leslie. I was a bit drunk and very happy when I put my arms around Joe's neck and moved my lips to his.

Beth called out to Joe as she walked over to us. I was confused; she was supposed to be in Sydney, not standing here looking radiantly beautiful. Joe looked as surprised as I was, but there was something else too. There was concern in his eyes and maybe something more. *Was he still in love with her?*

Her voice wasn't its usual silky-smooth tone, but raw and desperate. "I'm so sorry." She glanced at me before looking to Joe. "I really need to talk to you."

He was never going to say no. Joe was too nice, and Beth had always had him wrapped around her little finger. I couldn't shake the feeling that he might still love her. Joe looked at me apologetically and I wanted to cry. Instead, I glared at Joe, who opened his door for Beth before turning back to me.

"I'm sorry," he said, looking frustrated. "I better just check she's okay."

"Are you serious?" I asked, tears springing to my eyes. "She reappears and you drop me? I thought she was in Sydney. I thought she was out of the picture."

"She is," he insisted, reaching to take my hand. "It's not like that. But she's still my friend, and she obviously needs someone to talk to."

"Are you really that stupid?" I asked. "She wants you back. And when she waltzes back you ask me to leave?"

"Evelyn," he said with a sigh. "I'm with you. Let me just see what's wrong with her—"

"You'd still be with her, wouldn't you? If she hadn't gone to Sydney."

"No. Of course not. I'd be with you. I only want to be with you. Why do you think I went to so much effort to figure out how you could stay?"

He made a good point, but I'd had too much to drink to think rationally, and seeing Beth had brought all my insecurities to the surface.

When Joe reached for my hand, I pulled away. "I'll see you tomorrow."

"I should walk you home . . . ."

"I know the way!" I shouted without looking back.

The little town that I'd come to love so much

suddenly threatened to close in on me. *Why did she have to turn up? Why isn't she in Sydney? How could I possibly compete with her?* Suddenly, it seemed like she'd always be there, and Joe would always choose her over me.

I was suffocating. Gulping down my tears and spluttering on my sobs, I hurried down the road at a quick pace.

Joe *should* have walked me home. Kununurra by night was a different place altogether, and it wasn't always friendly. I wasn't worried though; I was too busy crying to pay any attention to my surroundings. That was until I walked past a couple of men scuffling on a driveway, lit up by a bright security light. They stopped fighting as I passed, their words slurring as they invited me in. They were having a party, they told me, I should join. I picked up my pace and kept my head down, hoping they wouldn't follow me.

The light from a cigarette danced in the dark night air in front of the hotel, and I could tell from the silhouette that it was Todd. I had no energy for him and his weird conversations so I hunched further over and carried on my way.

When I felt someone following me, I wished it was Joe coming after me.

It wasn't though.

The voice that called my name definitely belonged to Todd.

HANNAH ELLIS

Chapter 45

LIBBY – August 2017

I think I managed a few hours of sleep, but I was lying wide awake when the gentle tapping came at the door. There was another girl in the opposite bunk who'd I'd not properly met yet. When she'd come in the previous evening, I'd turned towards the wall and pretended to be asleep. She didn't stir when I hopped out of bed to answer the door.

"Did I wake you?" Joe asked quietly.

I shook my head. "I couldn't sleep."

"Me neither. Can we talk?"

"I'll get dressed," I said, shutting the door again.

He was sitting on the bottom step when I went outside. I followed him to the car and didn't ask where we were going. It was only just getting light and the town was empty. The motion of the car was soothing, and I could've fallen asleep easily. When Joe parked below an imposing red rock formation, I followed him out and along the jagged path upwards.

"It's worth it when we get to the top, I promise."

"Kelly's Knob?" I asked.

He smiled and gave a slight nod. "It's the best

view of the town."

We were both puffing by the time we reached the top. Sunlight rose on the horizon and the town looked wholly different from that vantage point. Everything glowed in red and gold. It was stunning.

"I forgot what a workout it is," Joe said, sinking onto a wooden bench.

"It's beautiful up here."

"Your mum liked it."

"I don't understand why she told me to come here," I said, sitting beside him and staring out to the emerging sun. "I'm so confused and I feel like I'm never going to get any answers."

"I wish I could help."

"What happened with you and her?"

He shrugged. "For most of the time that Evelyn lived here, I was seeing someone else. We only just got together and then she left." He paused. "She didn't tell anyone she was leaving. She was just gone one morning."

"There must have been a reason?"

"We were at a friend's place, drinking, chatting, the usual. At the end of the evening my ex turned up wanting to talk to me. Evelyn said she'd talk to me the next day. She wasn't happy, obviously, but the next morning she'd left."

"And you didn't see her again? Didn't you try and find her?"

"Technology wasn't such a big thing back then," he said, smiling. "There weren't twenty ways to get in touch with people. I only had an email address for her and she didn't reply . . ." His voice trailed off and I thought that was all he was going to be able to tell me.

While his mind raced back twenty years, I wished he could project his memories so I could see what she was like back then. It would be even better if I could jump in there and ask her what on earth had happened.

"I saw her one more time," he said softly. "I flew to Sydney and waited at the airport the day she was due to fly home. I didn't even know if I'd find her."

"What happened?"

"She was like a different person. She practically laughed at me – said it was just a holiday fling and we both knew that. Everything was weird. She was cold and distant. She said there was no point in keeping in touch. That we both had lives to get on with and it'd been fun while it lasted."

The hurt was still there in Joe's eyes more than twenty years later. Why had she done that to him? "It doesn't sound like her."

"It wasn't like her," he said. "She was mean. I'd never seen her like that before."

"Something must have happened to make her leave so suddenly. She had this old photo album full of pictures of you and her."

"You must have talked to her about your father before? You must have asked when you were younger?"

"She told me she had a fling. That it was just the two of us and that was all we needed. I was okay with that. I don't know why I wasn't curious, but I just didn't care. We *were* fine, just the two of us."

"So why did she suddenly start talking at the end? And why didn't she get in touch with me then?"

"She wasn't always herself," I said. "She was on

strong medication. Sometimes she didn't make sense."

"Maybe that explains it then. Maybe sh—"

"No," I said, cutting him off. "My Uncle Rob said that too – he didn't want me to come here. He said she didn't know what she was saying. She was clear though. She wanted me to know the truth. She said . . ."

I trailed off as my mind took me back there. Mum was having a good day. She told me she needed to explain something. She'd been tearful and apologetic. "I lied to you," she said, looking me right in the eye. "About your father. I'm so sorry. I should have told you the truth. Joe deserved the truth too. But I thought he'd be better not knowing. I wish I could see him again. I should've gone back to Kununurra while I had the chance. You'd love it there."

"Who's Joe?" I'd asked, panicking that she'd lose her train of thought or need to rest. I needed to hear everything she had to say.

"My Joe!" she said with a smile. "Joe Sullivan. There are photos in my wardrobe. I wish I could tell him I'm sorry."

"Oh, God!" I said, looking up at Joe as everything became clear. "It was two different conversations. Uncle Rob was right. She told me she'd lied about my dad and then she spoke about you. I thought she meant . . ." Tears fell down my face and I dropped my head into my hands. Joe's hand landed heavy and reassuring on my shoulder. "She didn't ask me to come here. She said she wished *she'd* come back. She didn't ask me to come at all. She didn't want me to find my father. She just said she was sorry that she'd lied."

As one piece of the puzzle became clear, more questions arose. What had she lied about? She knew who my dad was? It wasn't just a fling? Why didn't she want me to know him? I was back to square one. I'd never know.

"I think it's good you came," Joe said. "Maybe you just needed something to focus on."

"I think I wanted you to be my father. I never cared before because I had my mum. Then she died and I had no one. I just wanted to have some family, somewhere."

He smiled sympathetically. "Stay in town for a while. We'll show you around. There's still a lot to see."

I frowned. "You don't have to feel obliged to look after me."

"I *am* obliged though. Evelyn was my friend. She'd want me to look out for you."

"What did she want to say sorry for?"

"For leaving and breaking my heart," he said with a sad smile.

I thought of the photo album full of memories and of the look in Mum's eyes when she spoke about Joe.

"I think maybe it broke her heart too."

Chapter 46

EVELYN – March 1995

It was three weeks after I left Kununurra that I got a taxi to Sydney airport bound for a flight which would take me to London. In those three weeks, I'd roamed the streets of Sydney, losing weight by the day and doubting my decision to leave without saying goodbye. Joe sent me emails which I read and reread in various internet cafes, torturing myself. His words alternated between worry, anger and sadness. It was such an effort not to reply. I yearned to tell him how much I loved him and that I needed him so badly I was in physical pain. Then I would think of that night before I left and knew things were broken beyond repair. If I spoke to Joe, I would have to tell him everything, and I couldn't bring myself to do it. Guilt and shame followed me everywhere. The best thing was to go home, live my life and never look back.

I hadn't for a moment considered he might come and find me. He knew the date I was due to fly out. It never occurred to me that he might turn up at the airport, but there he was. Just as I was approaching security, he called my name. A cold shiver ran through me at the sound of his voice. I almost couldn't bring myself to look at him, and it crossed my mind to ignore him and hurry on through the security gate. He was owed an explanation and in a split second I decided to give him one – even if it wasn't the truth. At least that way he'd have some closure and move on with his life. I'd fade to a distant memory and he'd go on being the happy, carefree guy he was supposed to be.

When I turned to face him, I buried my emotions and set my features to cold and unfeeling. It was one of the hardest things I'd ever done. As soon as I saw him, I just wanted to run to him and tell him everything and hold him while I cried.

"What are you doing here?" I asked, making sure the only emotion I displayed was puzzled. *Ignore the fact he's turned up at the airport. Don't think about how romantic that is or how much he must love you. Don't pay any attention to how amazing he is or think about what you're about to do. Just do it, quick, and move on. He deserves so much better than you. Let him go.*

"Looking for you, of course," he said, his own features perplexed, searching mine for some clue as to what had happened. "You just left . . . What's going on?"

"I'm not great at goodbyes," I said, aloof, cold, awful. "And I wanted to see a few more places before I flew out so I thought I'd make the most of my last few weeks."

He stared at me, looking for the Evelyn who he'd been friends with for all those months. He wouldn't find her though; she was hidden, pushed down into

320

this empty shell of a person who was desperately trying to appear as hard as nails.

"What about us?" he asked, his brow furrowed and his eyes full of hurt and confusion. "I thought you wanted to stay?"

"Oh come on, Joe!" I said, my voice sounding like it belonged to someone else. "We both knew that was never going to work out. It's been fun, but let's be serious, I was never really going to relocate my life to a hot-as-hell, dusty outback town in the middle of nowhere."

"Evelyn," he whispered desperately. "I don't understand. What happened? Is this about Beth? Becau—"

"No," I said, sharply. I was suddenly so clear. I couldn't leave him with any hope, and I also couldn't leave him thinking this was anyone else's fault but mine. It would be easier if he hated me; he'd be able to move on and live his life without thinking of me. I'd never get through this if I imagined he was out there somewhere thinking of me.

"It's nothing to do with Beth. It's just time for me to go home." I tilted my head to one side, forced an arrogant tone into my voice. "This was a nice holiday romance but it's time to move on." I shrugged and then made the mistake of taking his hand. It sent shockwaves through my body. There was still time to tell him the truth. Everything could be okay. We could still be together.

"Don't leave like this," he said, pulling me gently to him.

If he put his arms around me, I'd dissolve into a blubbering mess and he'd demand the truth. I took a step back. The hurt in his eyes was torture. "I got you something," he said, pulling a small velvet bag from his pocket. "I got it ages ago, I just didn't find the right time to give it to you."

"I don't want it," I said coolly.

"It's so you won't forget me, even when we're apart."

"I have to go," I said, but he pushed the plush drawstring bag into my hand and I gave in and took it. I slapped on a smile before I turned. "Say goodbye to everyone for me."

"Evelyn . . ." It was the last time I heard him speak my name and it echoed around my head as I walked away. I didn't turn back. He didn't need to see the tears which poured down my cheeks.

I managed to make it around the corner before I slumped against the wall and sobbed, my chest heaving as I gasped for air to fill my lungs.

"Are you okay?" an older woman asked, her concerned husband by her side.

Swallowing hard, I forced a smile onto my lips and stood straighter. "I'm fine," I said, pushing my hair off my face with trembling hands. "I'm fine."

Chapter 47

LIBBY – August 2017

"Can you stay and play with me?" Ruby asked on Monday afternoon, her eyes wide and difficult to resist.

"She's just been swimming with you," Cassie said. "Give her a break."

I'd been concerned that Cassie would be angry after she found out why I'd really come to Kununurra. I'd spent a whole day with them, thinking they were my family, without saying anything. I felt as though I'd deceived them, but Cassie had come to see me at the Croc. She was warm and sympathetic about the situation and we'd had a good chat. When I'd offered to take Ruby swimming one afternoon, both Cassie and Ruby had jumped at the suggestion.

"It's okay," I said, looking at Ruby. "I can play for a little while."

She took my hand and pulled me to the back of the shop and into a tent. We'd been pretending to be camping for about ten minutes when the bell tinkled over the shop door.

Cassie's voice drifted through the shop, chatty and

friendly. When I heard my name, I stood, looking down through the assorted items, a strange feeling rushing through me. I couldn't see who Cassie was talking to but when I heard his voice, chills ran down my spine. *It couldn't be.* My feet moved quickly to the rhythm of my quickening heart. He stopped mid-sentence as our eyes met.

Had he always been that gorgeous? "Andrew!" I blurted out, moving towards him. "What are you doing here?"

His eyes lingered on me and the momentary pause seemed to stretch out forever.

"I was in the area," he said, his smile making my stomach lurch. "I thought I'd look you up."

"It's nice to see you," I muttered.

He reached into his pocket. "I wanted to bring you this too."

My heart was in my throat as I reached for my necklace. "Oh my God!"

"It was caught up in my hoodie."

My hand brushed his as I took it. Words failed me.

"Is that the one you were looking for?" Cassie asked.

"Yes," I whispered, overcome with emotion. I didn't think I'd ever see it again. "Thank you," I said, finally managing to look up.

"You're welcome."

A little hand slipped into mine and I looked down. "Are you coming to play?" Ruby asked.

"You can come and help me now, Ruby," Cassie said. "I've got some jobs for you."

Ruby looked up at Andrew. "Who are you?"

"I'm Andrew," he told her.

"How do you know my Libby?" she asked, making us all smile.

"We met a couple of weeks ago," he explained.

"We're playing camping," Ruby told him.

"That sounds like fun," he said before shifting his gaze to me. "I'm staying at the backpacker place across the road. Maybe I'll see you later?"

Cassie took Ruby by the hand. "Libby's got to go now," she told her gently.

My brain wasn't functioning and when Cassie's eyes bored into mine, I looked blankly back at her. "Jeez!" she said. "He brought your necklace back. Buy the poor fella a drink!"

"Oh!" I looked up at Andrew. A smile played on his lips and there was amusement in his eyes. "Yes! I should buy you a drink." I glanced from Cassie to Ruby. "We can play again another day," I promised.

"Go!" Cassie said. "Have fun." I was just walking out the door when I heard Cassie mutter, "And I think a drink is the least you owe him!"

The blush hit my cheeks as I stepped outside.

"She seems like a character," Andrew remarked.

"She is!"

"She's probably right though," he said as we ambled in the direction of the Tav. "You owe me more than a drink . . ."

I smiled up at him. I couldn't believe he'd turned up in Kununurra. "I might stretch to lunch too."

"That would be a good start."

There were a few people in the Tav but no one I recognised. I'd half expected to find Jakob and Sylvie propping up the bar. We ordered beers and found a table.

I reached for the silver feather pendant and enjoyed the feel of it, back where it belonged. "I thought I'd lost it for good," I said. My joy at being reunited with it was tinged by a slight annoyance. "I'm sure you could've got in touch and let me know you had it."

"Some thanks I get for bringing it all this way!"

"Sorry. I appreciate it. It's sentimental – I was upset about losing it."

His face creased into a frown. "You're right, I should have got in touch when I found it." He paused, looking bashful. "But I thought you might just tell me to post it. I wanted to see you again."

There was only a brief moment before my mouth twitched involuntarily into a smile. I couldn't stay annoyed with him. "In that case, I suppose you're forgiven."

He grinned back at me. "It was a nice excuse to travel a bit more too. I was jealous of you exploring the outback. Plus, I kept wondering how things turned out for you. I felt like I'd pushed you to come out here and started to feel responsible. Did you find him?"

I took a sip of beer and suppressed a sudden bout of giggles. "I found the guy I was looking for but it turns out he's not my father!" I started laughing then. It was so absurd.

"What's so funny?"

"It's just so embarrassing. It's one of those laugh or cry situations, and I've had enough of crying."

"So what happened?"

"It's a long story. He's lovely, just not my dad. Cassie, in the shop, is his wife. They've been very understanding about it. But it was just a big mix-up."

"So who is your father?"

"No bloody clue!" I said. Laughter hit me again.

"Sorry."

I dabbed at my eyes. "It's fine. So I guess you expect me to show you around Kununurra now?"

"How much is there to see?"

"More than you'd think."

"It seems pretty quiet."

"You'd be amazed at how much fun this place is. It's surprisingly lively at times. You won't believe how busy this place gets on a Friday night. And the bar at the hostel is lively every night."

"I'm not sure I believe you."

"We can check it out tonight . . ."

"It's a date."

I met his gaze and raised my eyebrows. "How long are you expecting to get free drinks out of me?"

"My treat tonight," he said, his eyes sparkling in amusement.

I nodded and ignored the fluttering in my stomach.

Chapter 48

LIBBY – August 2017

We found Sylvie and Jakob at the Croc and sat to have a drink with them. A young guy was working behind the bar and I kept catching sight of Kai, coming and going in the office and doing odd jobs. I was laughing loudly at Andrew – who'd been scared by a passing lizard – when Kai appeared and placed a pint of water in front of me without a word. He winked at me and walked away again.

"What's his deal?" Sylvie asked. "He's always watching you. I think it's creepy."

"Kai is a nice guy," Jakob said again.

"He knew my mum when they were young," I explained. "He's just a bit protective, that's all."

"He could have brought *me* water too," Sylvie said, heading for the bar.

"Come with me," I said, pulling a relaxed Andrew off his sunlounger. He jumped again when a lizard shot across our path in front of the office.

"It's tiny," I said. "How can you be scared of that?"

"They're so fast!" he said. "And they come out of

nowhere. Creepy little things."

The office was quiet and I stood in front of the photo wall with Andrew. "That's my mum," I said, pointing.

Andrew moved closer. "Who's the guy?"

"That's Joe. Nice guy. Not my dad!"

Andrew ignored my light-hearted tone and draped an arm around my shoulder. I leaned in, enjoying the feel of his toned chest.

"You look like your mum," Andrew remarked.

The office phone rang and Kai appeared a moment later, prompting us to move back outside. I jumped into the pool, leading Andrew and Jakob to have a mock-serious conversation evaluating my diving form. I couldn't help it; I always bombed into the water hugging my knees.

Kai wandered over. "Joe and Cassie are having a barbecue at the Swim Beach. We're all invited. You fit to drive, Jakob?"

"Always," he replied.

"Good," Kai said. "Grab a crate of beer from the back and I'll pick up some meat and see you up there."

Skye and Ruby were doing cartwheels on the sand when we pulled up, and smoke wafted from Joe's barbecue. Cassie stood to greet me with a big hug. Jakob knew everyone already and Sylvie and Andrew introduced themselves while I went to say hi to the girls. I swung Ruby around when she ran at me.

Skye came close to me and whispered, "Mum said some hot guy turned up looking for you."

"That's Andrew," I said, nodding over to where he was chatting to Joe.

"Nice!" Skye said.

"Don't embarrass me, will you?"

"Me?" She grinned mischievously. "Never! I'm going to go say hi."

I followed her back up the beach with Ruby's hand in mine. She climbed into my lap when I slumped into the camping chair beside Cassie.

"We like him!" Cassie said out of the corner of her mouth.

"You guys are going to embarrass me, aren't you?"

"Never!"

"That's just what Skye said." I caught Andrew's eye and he grinned at me as Skye chatted away to him.

"He's so sweet," Cassie said. "Bringing your necklace back. So romantic."

I felt myself blush. "He's just a friend."

"I don't like boys," Ruby announced. "They're all yucky."

Andrew came over and handed me a beer, taking a seat beside Cassie.

"Nice to see you again," she said.

"You too. Your daughter's just interrogated me and told me my hair's thinning!" He frowned and felt around at the top of his head.

Cassie grinned. "Did she suggest you should wear a hat?"

"Cowboy hat," he said. "I'm twenty-four. I'm not really going bald, am I?"

I grinned and shrugged.

"Thanks!" he said.

"I like your hair," Ruby said, leaving me to sit in

331

his lap instead. She ran a hand through his hair. "You're not bald."

"Thank you!"

She nestled into him with no sign of moving.

"Traitor," I said. "I thought all boys were yucky?"

"He smells nice," Ruby said flatly.

Andrew looked thoroughly pleased with his new friend.

"Who's coming swimming?" Jakob called as he walked down the sand, closely followed by Sylvie. I shook my head while Andrew shuffled Ruby off his lap, pulling his T-shirt off as he stood.

"You not coming?" he asked.

"It's full of crocs."

"Only freshwater crocs," Cassie said. "You won't get much more than a nip from them."

"Oh my God," I said. "So there really *are* crocs in there?"

"Probably," she said. "They won't come near with so many people splashing around though."

"Unless they fancy a snack!" Joe shouted over.

"Can I go?" Ruby asked.

Cassie sighed. "We only just got out of the water."

"He'll look after me," Ruby said, taking Andrew's hand.

"Do you mind?" Cassie asked.

"Not at all. Sure you're not coming?" he said to me.

"No chance!"

"Just stay near me," he said. "The crocs won't bother with you. I'm the one who smells good!"

"Thanks, Ruby! He's never going to shut up about that now."

They wandered off hand in hand.

"She's a good judge of character, that kid," Cassie said.

"He's still got to get my seal of approval," Joe shouted, bringing me a hot dog.

"He's just a friend," I insisted again.

"Good of him to bring your necklace," Joe said. A strange look passed over his face, and I reached for my necklace when his eyes lingered on it. "Sentimental, is it?" he asked.

"Mum gave it to me. I can't believe I lost it."

"It found its way back to you," he said with a smile.

Cassie kept a beady eye on Ruby, but she looked to be in good hands with Andrew, Jakob and Sylvie, who splashed around with her. She climbed repeatedly onto Andrew's shoulders to jump into the water.

We stayed until long after the sun had set, eating, drinking and laughing. It was peaceful and relaxing.

I felt like I'd known them all forever.

Chapter 49

LIBBY – August 2017

"What shall we do today?" Andrew asked after breakfast. I liked the assumption that we'd do something together.

"I don't know. We can ask Kai to recommend something."

Kai was in the office and I didn't even have time to say anything before he threw an envelope at me. "Boat trip round Lake Argyle," he said as I opened the envelope to find two vouchers for just that. "Joe's treat. He left you his ute for the day too." He turned for the keys and handed them to me. "It's out on the road."

I looked down at the car key with its worn fob in the shape of a pickup truck. "That's so kind of him."

"Cassie did you a picnic," he said, nodding at a cool box by the door. "Have fun!"

"Kai!" I called as he began to walk away. "Where's Lake Argyle?"

"There'll be a map in the ute. It's easy though. Victoria Highway and then Lake Argyle Road."

We found the ute out on the road and climbed in.

"It feels like ages since I've driven."

"D'you want me to?" Andrew asked.

"Nope!"

"Worth a try."

"Maybe on the way home," I said. "If you're good."

"If you decide you fancy a beer, more like!"

Once we were out of town, the open road seemed to stretch on forever. The stark dry landscape was ruggedly beautiful. I could see why my mum had fallen in love with the place. We found the turn on to Lake Argyle Road and arrived at the lake half an hour before the boat tour was due to leave. To kill time, we walked along the lakeshore, skimming stones as we went.

"How long do you think you'll stay here?" Andrew asked. "Have you got any plans?"

"I haven't really thought about it. I was all set to do a runner when I found out Joe wasn't my dad, but everyone's been so lovely and I'm having such a good time." *And now that you're here, I've no desire to leave at all.* A thought occurred to me. "How long will you stay?" I asked. "You've got a flight home from Sydney, right?"

"Yeah. My flight's in two weeks so I can't stay too long. Maybe a few more days. Simon's in Cairns with Yvonne so I'll go back and see them before I fly out." He threw a stone and it skipped across the surface of the water, causing ripples as it went. I'd be sorry to see Andrew go but tried not to dwell on it.

The tour guide on the boat was a larger-than-life character who talked us through the wildlife and the history of the dam and lake. At one point, he stopped to point out crocodiles lazing in the sun on the rocky shore.

"I won't be swimming then," I whispered to Andrew.

"Just stay by me, they won't bother y—"

I laughed. "Are you ever going to shut up about how good you smell?"

"I've got to take the compliments where I can get them."

"From a five-year-old?"

"That kid knows what she's talking about." He leaned into me, jutting out his chin, and I inhaled deeply. *Heaven.*

I wrinkled my nose. "Not too bad, I suppose."

When the boat stopped for a while in the middle of the lake, the sun was directly overhead and the water was hard to resist, even for me.

"Come on, then," Andrew coaxed when we were the only ones left on the boat.

"If I lose a limb, I'm blaming you," I said as I lowered myself into the water ahead of him. I pushed myself away from the boat and Andrew followed. The water was so refreshing I completely forgot about crocodiles and floated happily on my back.

Andrew disappeared under the water as he swam further away from the boat. I followed leisurely after him. It took longer than I expected for him to resurface, and when he did he was so close that my heart rate increased dramatically. The grin he gave me notched it up even more, and I was sure it would cause ripples in the water. I made the mistake of looking around.

The lake was vast and intimidating, the murky

water hiding whatever lurked beneath. Now that I was sufficiently cool, my mind wandered. Crocodiles, I thought. *How many? Hundreds? Thousands? Could they smell fear or was that sharks? Maybe they're circling my legs.* I glanced at the boat, which was further away than I would have liked, and then down at the water. *Any second now my leg will be ripped from me.*

"You okay?" Andrew asked, staring at me.

"I need to get back to the boat," I said, suddenly breathless. My legs kicked furiously below the surface – probably the last exercise they'd get before they were taken for a snack. Terror gripped me when Andrew's leg bumped into mine. My throat constricted. *Swim! Swim away! Get back to the boat.* My body wouldn't listen to me.

"What's wrong?" Andrew asked.

"Crocs," I whispered, as though they might hear me. Andrew laughed like I'd told a joke but stopped abruptly when I looked at him. I swallowed hard in an attempt to widen my airways. Breathing was an effort.

"Think about something else," Andrew said gently.

Great advice. Idiot. How haven't I noticed before what an idiot he is? And how did I have a crush on him? I'm about to lose a limb and he tells me to think of something else?

His body bumped into mine and I was surprised by the feel of his soft lips on mine. My heart rate slowed. *Inhale*, I told myself as he pulled away. *Exhale. And repeat.* Our legs knocked together as they worked methodically below the surface. My heart rate settled to a more normal rhythm, and Andrew's green eyes sparkled when he moved to kiss me again. There were no more crocs. There was no more anything. There was only Andrew. When my legs forgot to keep working, I slipped under the water and came up laughing.

"Sorry," Andrew said. "Promise I'm not trying to drown you."

The boat was suddenly beside us. *How did that happen?* Andrew raised an arm to hold the side of the boat and our legs slowed. I kept a hand on his bicep.

His fingers lightly brushed my skin. "I thought you were going to have a panic attack,"

"Sorry." My face flushed and I moved away from him.

"No worries," he said with a deliberate Aussie twang. He held the rail of the ladder and waited while I climbed back up onto the boat.

The rest of the tour went in a blur. Andrew took my hand in his and I found it difficult to concentrate on anything else. We saw wallabies and kangaroos hopping about on one shore and were back at the boat dock before I knew it. We set up the picnic on the lakeside and I found myself nervous in Andrew's company. Without shade, it was too hot to stay long so we ate and then headed back to the car. I let Andrew drive back while I relaxed in the passenger seat. Gazing at his profile, I was aware of the fact he'd be leaving soon. I shouldn't get too attached. My eyelids were heavy and were just starting to close when Andrew slowed the pickup to a stop.

"Look at that."

I sat up and peered through the windscreen. A long snake meandered easily across the road and into the bush. I'd never seen a snake in the wild before, and I was mesmerised by its graceful movements. "This place is incredible, isn't it? It feels like every day I see something new and amazing."

"This place suits you," Andrew said, looking at me seriously.

"What do you mean?"

"I don't know. You seem so at home here. I can imagine you staying here."

I laughed nervously. "No way. It's stinking hot. And the crocs give me the creeps."

"You're starting to sound like a local too!"

"What? No way."

"Stinking hot!" he mimicked.

Before I could reply, he moved over and kissed me again, sending my stomach into an elaborate gymnastics routine.

Chapter 50

LIBBY – August 2017

There was a buzz about the town for the rodeo and I laughed when Andrew strutted out in his brand new Akubra. Skye would no doubt be getting her iPhone soon.

"What do you think?" he asked.

"Looks like I've got myself a cowboy," I said, reaching up to kiss him. He was flying out the following day, but he'd been easily persuaded to stay for the rodeo. I wished he were staying longer. I felt so comfortable with him and we'd hardly been apart for the last week. Sometimes we'd sat and talked for hours. I felt like I could tell him anything. We'd become so close so quickly, and I was dreading saying goodbye to him. He promised we'd keep in touch and meet up once we were back in the UK. I kept reminding myself that was only a few weeks away.

My time in Australia had flown by. Having Andrew back in the UK would make leaving much easier. I was also looking forward to seeing Aunt Mel and Uncle Rob and the boys. And Heidi, of course, who'd been bombarding me with messages and emails. She now had purple hair, she told me, but I knew that could change again before I saw her.

Jakob drove us out to the rodeo and the atmosphere was magical as soon as we arrived. Cassie and the girls were sitting on picnic blankets spread along the fence line with a good view of the action. Real-life cowboys wandered with their dusty jeans and spurred boots. I loved the rodeo before it had even begun. It was like being on a film set.

"We got you a present," Joe said, dropping an Akubra onto my head.

"I love it," I said. "Thank you!"

"You're welcome," Cassie said as I joined her on the blanket.

"So, this is your first rodeo?" Leslie asked, pouring fizzy wine into a plastic cup for me.

"Yes! It's amazing," I said, taking it all in with awe.

"Cheers to that!" she said.

Ruby wandered over behind Leslie. "I like your hair today, Mrs Cooper," she said, twirling it round her finger.

"Thank you, Ruby, but it's Auntie Leslie when we're not at kindy, isn't it?"

"Oh yeah," Ruby said, giggling. "It's very confusing."

"You teach?" I asked.

Leslie nodded and ruffled Ruby's hair. "And this is my star pupil."

Ruby beamed before her attention drifted somewhere over my shoulder and she took off at a run, darting past me.

"Uncle Cam!" she squealed as she ran towards the guy walking casually over to us. His cap shielded his face, but I recognised him from Mum's photos nonetheless. He threw Ruby up in the air and showered her with kisses until she wriggled to get away from him. He embraced Joe in a hug that lifted him off the ground before slapping Kai on the back and finally catching my eye.

"You must be Evelyn's kid?" he said, a nervous smile spreading across his face.

"Libby," I said, standing, unsure of how to greet him.

His eyes searched my face. "Joe called and told me about you. Thought I better come and check you out for myself. It's crazy!" He looked at Joe with a huge grin. "Evelyn's kid!"

"Look what the cat dragged in!" Cassie said, moving to hug him.

"Nice to see you too," he said with a laugh.

Andrew moved over to me as the events of the rodeo began. Over the course of the evening we watched bull-riding and barrel-racing, calf-roping and bronc-riding and lots more. It fascinated me, and I was glued to the fence for every event, occasionally moving back quickly when the action got too close. The rodeo clowns were my favourite, jumping in with their bright clothing and putting themselves in harm's way to make sure the competitors were safe after a fall.

Between events, I mingled round our little group, chatting and laughing and hearing lots of stories about Mum. Some of them I refused to believe; surely my mum hadn't really drank and partied as much as they were suggesting. For the first time, I found myself remembering her without getting upset. It was so much fun to hear new stories about her.

I was standing by the fence at the edge of the group, enjoying watching everyone having such a good time, when a figure appeared beside me.

"So you're still in town?"

I searched the face under the hat with a puzzled smile until I realised it was the guy from the hotel: Todd. "I decided to stay around for a while," I told him. "I quite like the place."

"I thought you might come back to the hotel and look at the photos again. You're welcome to take any that you'd like."

"Thanks, but I think I'll leave them where they belong."

"It was weird how she left," he said. "Without a word."

"I'm sure she had her reasons." I didn't want to think about it. Thankfully, Cam came over, scaring Todd off with a scowl and a nod of the head.

"Was he bothering you?"

"Not really," I said. "I just find him a bit odd."

"He's always been odd. Not a bad guy though, really."

Chapter 51

EVELYN – February 1995

"Wait," Todd called, jogging up beside me in the darkness. "Are you okay?"

"I'm fine." I was so upset about Beth turning up, but I really didn't want to talk to Todd about it. "Please just go home and leave me alone."

He kept quiet and slowed his pace but didn't leave. Eventually, I turned on my heel and snapped at him. "What are you doing? Why are you following me? Just go home! Go away!" When he looked hurt, I felt guilty on top of everything else. "I'm sorry, Todd. I'm fine though, honestly, I just want to be alone."

"I only want to make sure you get home okay," he said, earnestly.

I frowned, annoyed by him but also feeling sorry for him. He was such an oddball. No wonder with his strange family life. "Okay," I said as shouts drifted eerily from a nearby house. "You can walk me home." I paused and set off again. "Thank you."

He kept quiet and strolled along beside me. I was already drunk, but when we reached the Croc, I insisted that Todd have a drink with me to thank him for walking me back. At least he cared, I thought to myself. Joe was too busy with Beth to worry about me.

"You did a good job with this place," Todd said, as we walked through the dimly lit grounds of the Croc.

"It was mostly Kai," I said, remembering how different it had been when I arrived. "It does look good though, doesn't it? I just need to get Stan to install a pool in the next month and my work here is done!"

"You only have a month left?"

Sadness overcame me once more. "Less actually."

I used my key to the office and let us in. My valuable items were kept in the office fridge – chocolate and alcohol.

"It'll be weird without you around," Todd said.

"I left you something," I blurted out. Todd looked puzzled and I grinned at him. "I hid it a while ago. One day, when I'm long gone, you'll find it and think of me. You'll laugh!"

"In the hotel?"

I nodded. I'd been thoroughly amused when I'd sneaked around hiding photos in the hotel. There was always a way to get round Arthur.

"You should laugh more," I said, suddenly concerned about Todd. He had a funny old life, and I wondered what sort of person he'd be if he didn't live in his father's shadow.

"You should go to bed," he said, looking at the beer in my hand and shaking his head. "I better get back. See you at work."

"Thanks for walking me home," I called as he left.

346

Chapter 52

LIBBY – August 2017

Kai kindly lent me his car to drive Andrew to the airport.

"I'll see you soon," Andrew said, wrapping his arms around me as we stood before the security gate.

I pouted and pulled him closer to me. "I don't want you to go."

"I don't want to go either."

"Message me when you get to Cairns?"

"Of course!" He took my face in his hands and kissed me tenderly. "You could just come with me . . ."

"Don't tempt me." It had crossed my mind to head back to Cairns just to have a couple of extra days with Andrew. I wasn't sure when I'd make it back to Kununurra though, and I just didn't feel like leaving yet. Everyone had been so welcoming: I hadn't found the blood relatives that I'd hoped for, but I felt like I'd found a family nonetheless.

"I'll see you in a few weeks," I said, trying to be positive as I fought off tears.

He kissed me again and squeezed me tightly

before releasing me. "I'll call you later."

I watched until he'd disappeared through the security gate and then headed back to the car.

My emotions were a jumble when I pulled up outside of the Croc. I missed Andrew already, but I felt so at home in Kununurra and was glad I'd made the decision to come to Australia. Nothing had worked out how I'd planned, but I'd had the most fantastic adventure of my life.

My phone connected to the Wi-Fi and when it buzzed with a call, I stayed in the car to answer it.

Uncle Rob appeared on the screen. "Why don't you ever answer your phone?" he said, a look of surprise on his face that I'd actually answered.

"Hello!" I said. "Nice to see you too! You always call when I'm asleep, that's why!" I'd been messaging them often, and they were up-to-date with the Joe situation.

"How are you?" he asked. "You look nice and tanned."

"I'm fine," I said. "It's been a weird few weeks but I'm fine."

"I told you not to go over there. You're too far away. What if you need us and we couldn't get to you?"

"Uncle Rob," I said, feeling emotional. "I just needed to do this."

"You don't need anyone else though – you've got us."

It dawned on me why he'd been so against me going. "You know that no one could ever replace you, don't you?" I said. "You're like a dad to me and that won't ever change."

"I just worry about you when you're so far away." I could see him getting emotional, and the screen turned briefly to the wall while he shouted for Mel. He'd composed himself when he reappeared with Aunt Mel hovering over his shoulder. It was nice to see her face.

"I'm sorry you didn't find your father," she said.

"It doesn't matter," I said sniffing. "It really doesn't. I've had such a great time. When Mum died I thought I would never make any more memories of her and never know any more about her. But I met all these people who remember her, and they've told me all these stories that I never knew."

"That's amazing," Mel said, tearfully. "I can't wait to hear them all."

"You're being looked after then?" Rob asked.

"Yes!" I told him, laughing through tears. "Stop worrying!"

"And you're still coming home in a few weeks?"

"Of course. I miss you!"

"We miss you too," Rob said. "And you need to come and sort Heidi out. She's round here all the time complaining about her love life! She's driving me mad." Mel gave him a slap on the arm.

"Give her a hug from me! And the boys too. I better go."

"Love you!" they shouted before they disappeared from the screen.

My face was blotchy from tears when I walked into the Croc, but I was smiling nonetheless. I was surprised to see Cam, sitting alone at the bar. "Kai not around?" I asked.

"He just nipped out," he said, eyeing me intently.

349

Cam had seemed like a lot of fun at the rodeo, but I wasn't sure what to talk to him about now we were alone. Plus, he looked like he'd just crawled in after an all-night party. Maybe he had.

"I was looking for you, really, anyway."

"Yeah?" I said, sitting beside him.

"It's such a blast from the past," he said, shaking his head. "You've just taken me back twenty years!"

"It's been so much fun meeting you all. I think it's helped me a lot."

He was quiet for a moment, and I was just starting to feel awkward when he spoke. "It took me a long time to get over Evelyn leaving," he said, a sad glint in his eye. "Our little gang fell apart for a while. I got a job out at the diamond mine – I'd fly out there and be gone for weeks at a time. Things just weren't the same around here." He paused, lost in his thoughts. "Joe moved on eventually. When Cassie arrived on the scene."

It was incredible the impact she'd had on people's lives, and I wondered if she'd had any idea of the effect of her leaving the way she did.

"I can't believe how much people remember of her," I said.

"Some things stay with you," he mused. "And guilt is hard to shake."

His words confused me as he pulled his wallet from his back pocket, flipping it open as he passed it to me. There was a photo of a boy and a girl. "They're my two," he said. "Jess is fourteen and Daniel's ten."

"Cute."

"They're a handful," he said lightly.

He didn't take the wallet when I tried to pass it

back but leaned onto the bar. After a moment, he turned to look at me. "I'm fairly sure they're your brother and sister."

My eyes darted between the wallet and Cam. I frowned, trying to figure out if he was making some weird joke. "What?"

"I didn't know about you," he said, his eyes begging me to believe him. "I promise, I never knew Evelyn was pregnant." He was silent for a moment and my head spun. "But she left because of me."

"I don't understand," I said. "I thought she left without telling anyone . . ."

He shook his head miserably. "I drove her to the airport. Watched her leave." I looked at him and waited for him to go on. I was finally getting my answers. "I don't have a good excuse. Joe's ex turned up one night. Evelyn was upset. We were drunk. One thing led to another . . ." I felt sorry for him as he battled with a mistake he'd made so long ago. "I didn't want her to leave but she said it was for the best. She said Joe could never know."

"You didn't tell anyone?"

"Not a soul," he said. "All this time, I never told anyone." When he turned, his eyes were filled with tears. "I'm so pissed off that she didn't tell me about you. How could she not tell me?"

"You don't even know for definite," I stammered.

"I knew as soon as Joe rang and told me you'd come around asking if *he* was your father. I know because that's exactly the sort of person Evelyn was. She'd keep it to herself just so she didn't hurt anyone else. She was so worried about coming between me and Joe."

"But you can't be su—"

"I *am* sure," he said gently. "I knew as soon as I saw you." He pointed at the photo of the girl in my hands. "I know because you look exactly like my other daughter."

Tears rolled down my face.

"I'm sorry," he said. "I didn't mean to upset you. But I couldn't not say anything."

"Thank you," I said. "I'm glad you told me. You could've just kept quiet."

"No, I couldn't," he said quietly. "How could I keep quiet? All this time I've lied to Joe and now it's all going to come out."

"You don't have to tell him," I said, crying and realising why Mum kept me to herself. She loved Joe, and she must have loved Cam too, in some way.

"I do have to tell him," he said, his features softening. "You're my daughter. Everyone's been telling me how great you are, and I just spent one evening with you and I can see how amazing you are. I don't want to keep you a secret. I want everyone to know you're my daughter. At least, if that's okay with you?"

"It's okay with me," I said, wiping at my tears. "I just wish people would stop making me cry!"

"I've gotta go and talk to Joe now," he said. "I might be back to cry with you in a bit!" The worry must have been clear on my face. "I'm kidding! He'll be right."

"Really?"

"We've been friends forty years. This is going to be one awkward conversation! But it'll be fine." He stood and looked down at me. "I still can't quite believe all this myself."

"I'll see you later?"

"Definitely," he said, grinning.

Chapter 53

EVELYN – February 1995

When Cam appeared in the doorway, I was crying with my head on the desk.

"So Beth's back," he said, wincing at the sight of me. "Leslie wanted me to check on you. You okay?"

"No," I spluttered. "I think meeting Joe was the worst thing that ever happened to me."

Reaching into the fridge, I got a beer and held it out to Cam.

"I reckon I've had enough," he said.

"It's my hour of need," I said, pushing it at him. "Don't leave me to drink alone."

He dutifully cracked the can and took a swig, sinking into the chair opposite me.

"I really wish I'd never met him," I said.

"You don't mean that."

"I do actually. Because I should have spent the year travelling all around Australia and meeting all sorts of different people, but all I've done is hang around here and wait for him."

"You're just drunk," Cam said. "You've had an ace year. And you *did* meet all sorts of people."

355

"But how can he just go back to Beth?" I asked, my voice raised.

"He hasn't. She's just upset. They're not getting back together. He loves you. He's moved on."

"No!" I snapped. "His ex turns up and he asks *me* to leave. They'll be together as we speak!"

"It's not like that," Cam insisted. "You've had too much to drink. Just go to bed. Everything will seem better tomorrow." He moved to the fridge and handed me a bottle of water. "Drink that or you'll have a killer hangover."

There was no avoiding the hangover at that point, but I did as I was told, drinking the water and moving in the direction of my room.

"What happened with Leslie?" I asked at my door. "I thought things were looking good at the New Year's party."

"Who knows?" he said, slumping against the doorframe. "She went cold again. I guess it was just a drunken thing."

"Why don't you just ask her how she feels?" I said, beckoning him inside and closing the door behind him.

"Because it's quite nice to live in hope," he said, flopping back on the bed. "And if she knew how I felt and she didn't feel the same then things get weird. I've thought it through."

I sat beside him and squeezed his knee. "Well that's crap."

"It is, isn't it?" he said, smiling. "Aren't we a sorry pair?"

I didn't move my hand from his leg when he sat up, and in my inebriated state, kissing him seemed completely natural. The surprise was how much I enjoyed it. I could sense his hesitation and knew that part of him wanted to stop. We didn't though; we sat kissing, my heart rate steadily increasing. My hands finally moved from his hair and trailed down his torso before tugging at his T-shirt, desperate for skin contact.

"Evelyn . . ." He stood to pace the room. "We can't." His eyes pleaded with me. "I should go." He didn't move towards the door, but just stopped and stared at me. I didn't want him to leave. *Why should I be alone when Joe's with Beth?* I didn't want to be alone.

When I moved and put my hand on his chest, looking up at him longingly, I knew he wasn't going anywhere. "We can't," he said again, sounding pained as he looked towards the door. I knew I should tell him to go; he needed me to kick him out.

My hand on his cheek brought his face to mine and our lips met again. Soft for a moment, slow. He pulled away and I was sure he would leave. His hand was on the door. He opened it and closed it again. There was no going back then. He was all over me in a second, kissing me harder and faster. We were on the bed, pulling at each other's clothes.

I closed my eyes and forgot all about Joe.

HANNAH ELLIS

Chapter 54

EVELYN – February 1995

The light was still on when I woke. Outside, it was dark and everything was still. I didn't move a muscle, and it took a moment for things to come into focus. Calmly, my eyes trailed over Cam's tattooed skin, his body tangled with mine. I closed my eyes. Maybe when I opened them again, he'd be gone and none of this would have happened. I didn't want to open my eyes, but when I did they filled with tears. I nudged Cam; his mouth twitched to a lazy smile and he ran a hand through my hair, pulling me closer to him.

"Cam," I said, my voice a croak.

His eyes snapped open and he shot away from me like I was poison. "Oh my God," he groaned, burying his head in his hands. "What did we do?"

I pulled at the sheet to cover myself and tears fell down my face. Cam hastily grabbed at his clothes. For a moment, I thought he was just going to leave. Then he inhaled deeply and sat beside me on the bed. "I'm sorry," he said. *Why's he apologising? It's my fault.* "I'm so sorry."

I felt horrible and leaned into him, crying on his

shoulder. "What do we do now?" I asked. *How can I fix this?*

"Joe's never gonna speak to me again," he said, before letting out a string of profanity. "Why didn't I just go home? What's wrong with me?"

"It was my fault," I said. "I kissed you. I'm so sorry."

He rubbed his temples, every muscle tense. "He's my best mate."

"I thought he was with Beth," I said, searching for my defence but knowing I had none. "Why did she have to come back?" *I should be waking up with Joe. I'm supposed to be lying in his arms now, happy and glowing. This isn't how things are supposed to be.*

"I'll never be able to look him in the eye," Cam said.

I felt sick. "It's my fault," I said again.

Cam ignored me. "This is gonna kill him."

"Joe can't know," I said, as my brain whirred to life and I fought to make a plan. To make everything right again.

"We can't just pretend nothing happened!" Cam said with anger in his voice. "We have to tell him. You reckon we can just carry on as though nothing happened?"

"I don't know," I said desperately. "I've no idea."

Cam leaned onto his knees and we sat in silence for a moment.

"I should leave," I said eventually.

He straightened up. "What?"

"I'd be leaving anyway." A plan began to formulate in my head. *I can't face Joe. He can't know about this.* "I'll just go now." I glanced at the clock and made my calculations. "I can get the eight o'clock flight out. I'll be gone before anyone notices. All you have to do is keep quiet. Don't tell Joe."

"Well that's insane," he said with wide eyes. "We'll talk to Joe. He'll forgive you and you can stay."

Tears flooded my eyes and I knew he was right; Joe *would* forgive me. That's the sort of person he was. "He might forgive *me*," I said. "But I'm not sure he'll forgive *you*. And you really think the three of us can still hang out and everything be fine?"

He rubbed at his eyes. "I don't know. Probably not."

"One way or another he'll lose me anyway. He doesn't need to lose his best friend too."

"I can't just not tell him."

"Leslie will know you didn't come home," I said, remembering she stayed at Cam's.

He shook his head. "She was drunk off her face. She'll have passed out and won't wake up until lunchtime."

"Good," I mused, mulling things over. "Then you just need to get your car and drive me to the airport." I was crying as I spoke but knew it was the best option.

"No," Cam said, spitting out a laugh. "You're being ridiculous."

"Fine! I'll hitch a ride." I clutched at the sheet around me as I stood to find clothes. "I'm going whether you drive me or not."

"You can't just run away!"

"I can't stay here and be the girl who ruined everything."

"You didn't ruin everything."

361

"You were just a happy little group of friends until I came along and messed everything up."

He shook his head sadly. "Don't be like that."

"Please drive me to the airport."

Realising I was going to leave anyway, he finally relented and left, saying he'd be back in ten minutes.

I didn't have much, so packing didn't take long. Everything was shoved into my backpack haphazardly, and when I had everything in, I stopped and looked around the bare room. My heart ached.

It occurred to me that if I left without a trace, people would think I was dead in a ditch somewhere and Cam would be forced to confess. Scribbling a quick note to Stan, I thanked him for everything and told him he better have a swimming pool next time I came to visit. It was heartbreaking to leave without saying bye to Stan. Kai would look out for him though and that was some comfort.

I left enough cash to cover what I owed him for my room and then took a deep breath, hauling my pack onto my shoulder and slipping out into the early morning light.

"You shouldn't do this," Cam said in the car park at the airport. "I'll drop you back at the Croc and we won't mention this to anyone."

"No," I said as tears welled once more. "I can't be with Joe now. It's not fair on him."

"But you can't leave without saying goodbye. Everyone's gonna be hurt – Leslie, Kai, Stan . . . And I'm supposed to look them in the eye and pretend I don't know anything?"

"I left Stan a note."

"That hardly helps! There must be another way.

Don't just leave. You're leaving me to deal with it all."

"It will be worse if I stay," I told him, opening the car door. "Everyone will forget me soon enough."

I pulled my backpack from the back and looked up to find Cam gazing at me. "No one's going to forget you."

"They will," I said, fighting off tears. "You all will."

He shook his head. "*I* won't."

I dropped my backpack to hug him. He was the only one I got to say goodbye to, but I couldn't find any words, just squeezed him tight. "Go to work," I said. "Carry on as normal. Look after Joe for me."

"I don't want to do this," he said.

I kissed his cheek. "It'll be better for Joe in the long run."

"If you need anything," he shouted after me, "just call me, won't you?"

I nodded through tears and went into the tiny airport. Cam was still in the car park when I walked out to the plane. I could see him standing at the fence, watching me go. I hoped he wouldn't tell Joe what happened. And that they would all get on with their lives and be none the worse for having had me around for a while.

As the plane soared above Kununurra, I was in agony. I'd tainted all my wonderful memories. I missed Joe and Leslie already, and I wanted to turn around and tell them what I'd done.

But I wouldn't. Because deep down I was sure they were all better off without me.

Chapter 55

EVELYN

The three weeks between leaving Kununurra and getting my flight home were torture, and when I thought things couldn't get any worse, I'd joked with myself that I could be pregnant. As soon as the thought entered my head I knew it would be true. I thought about telling Cam. His parting words to me filled my head: *If you need anything, just call me.* With great effort, I resisted. Then Joe turned up at the airport and I wanted to tell him everything.

I hated myself for a while, telling myself I'd got exactly what I deserved. It wasn't until Libby was born that I realised I'd really got far more than I ever deserved.

Going home had been awful, and I'd hidden the pregnancy for as long as possible. I was in denial and spent my nights out drinking and partying. Everything seemed so terrible and I sank to a pathetic self-pitying mess. Then one day, she kicked me; this tiny foot poked through the stretched skin of my belly. I grunted my annoyance and discomfort, but she did it again. "Hey!" I said, but a laugh escaped me and I pushed at the little foot inside me. She pushed back.

"What do you want?" I asked as tears sprang to my eyes. She kicked again. "I'm sorry," I whispered, filled with a love I'd never known possible. "I'll be better," I promised her. "I'll be better for you."

I stopped drinking and partying. I even started eating healthily. My baby was my first concern and I concentrated on her. Sometimes, I thought of Cam and Joe, but I convinced myself I was doing the right thing by not telling them.

When Libby arrived, everything changed. My life was all about her. It was so hard but so worth it. She was only a few days old and I was an emotional wreck when I looked down at her and realised what I was denying Cam. All this time, I thought I was doing him a favour by not telling him, but he was missing out on this beautiful baby girl. During the pregnancy, I'd dialled his number so many times, always hanging up before it rang. That day I let it ring; I was going to tell him all about his perfect baby girl and how that huge mistake we made wasn't a mistake at all. The phone rang and rang. I imagined him sitting outside with Joe, drinking and laughing while the phone rang in the background. I hoped that was what they were doing.

I hung up and never called again.

Rob and Mel were fantastic. For a while I was worried about denying Libby a father, but then I watched Rob with her and was certain she would never want for anything. He adored her from the first time he held her. Mel too. They were her family, always there to step in for me when I needed them to, and I knew my little girl would always be loved and cared for.

I often wonder if I did the right thing, and how things could have been different. In these finals days, my mind wanders often to my time in Kununurra. I've thought of telling Libby about Cam but I've left it too late. I'm worried about what might happen if she decides to track him down after I'd gone. I should have told her the truth long ago, but it's too late now . . .

Chapter 56

LIBBY – September 2017

The week before I was due to leave Kununurra, Joe organised a barbecue at his place. It was a Thursday and there seemed to be some secrecy surrounding it. Any time it was mentioned, knowing glances were exchanged. I wasn't sure if it was someone's birthday or some tradition that no one was telling me about. I hoped it wasn't a going away party for me.

The weekly sausage sizzle was underway when I walked downstairs to find Kai giving instructions to the guy behind the bar.

"You ready?" he said when he saw me.

"Yeah," I said, following him and Leslie to the car. "Why didn't everyone just come here for the barbecue?"

"It's family night!" he said with a cheeky grin. "Don't want bloody customers ruining the fun!"

"I feel like I'm missing something," I said. "Everyone's being secretive. I don't like it."

They exchanged a look and their eyes sparkled in amusement.

"See?" I said. "What're the weird looks for?"

They said nothing, just ushered me through the gates and into the car. When we arrived at Joe and Cassie's house, it was the usual banter. Cam gave me a wink as he sat chatting to Joe, who was busy manning the barbecue. Cam had confessed everything, shocking everyone, but he'd assured me everything would be fine. I wasn't sure if he was just telling me that to make me feel better, but they were putting on a good act for me, if that's what it was.

Cassie was tossing salad and shouting at the girls to come and help her. They were splashing in the paddling pool and ignoring her completely.

"We can help," Leslie offered.

"Great. Start carrying stuff outside, will ya?"

After a couple of trips, the outside table was loaded with salads and side dishes. It was a lively meal and everyone was in high spirits. Looking round the table, I could see how difficult it must have been for Mum to leave. I was even struggling with the thought of leaving, although I knew I'd be back sometime. It definitely wouldn't be goodbye forever.

Joe stood up after we'd finished eating. "Right, let's do a quick tidy up and get going."

He started clearing plates and everyone followed his lead. Again, I had the distinct feeling I was missing something.

"Where are we going?" I finally asked when we all congregated on the driveway. Everyone climbed into cars, and Joe gestured for me to get in his ute.

"It's a surprise," he said.

"I knew you were up to something," I said, sitting with Ruby and Skye in the back. "I don't like surprises!"

"This is a nice surprise," Ruby said as she struggled with her seatbelt. "Unless you're scared of fireworks."

A groan rippled around. "Who told her?" Joe asked. "Big mouth!"

"Sweetheart," Cassie said gently. "Remember we talked about surprises and keeping them secret?"

"Yes!" Ruby said, defensively.

"But you just told Libby," Skye pointed out, impatiently.

"No!" Ruby snapped. "The fireworks aren't the real surprise. We're going to do something special fo—"

"Aaaarrrrgggh!" Joe growled, drowning her out as Skye gagged her with a hand over the mouth.

"Oh yeah," Ruby said, giggling when Skye released her. "It's a secret!" She beamed at me and made a zipping motion over her lips.

"Really?" Joe said, smiling at Cassie as he pulled out of the drive. "You thought she could keep a secret?"

"But what's going on?" I asked.

There was no reply.

We turned into Celebrity Tree Park a few minutes later, and Joe pulled on my arm as I followed the rest of them to the water's edge. "Come with me," he whispered, breaking away from the group. I looked suspiciously at the screwdriver in his hand but decided it wasn't worth asking. All would be revealed.

Since I had a moment alone with Joe, it seemed like a good time to quiz him.

"Are things really okay with you and Cam?" I

asked, desperate to know how he really felt about the fact Cam was my dad.

He rolled his eyes. "I still feel like I wanna knock him into the middle of next week! I don't know how he didn't tell me. All those years, he knew why Evelyn left and kept it a secret."

"I think he had good intentions," I said, feeling the need to defend him. I'd spent a lot of time with Cam over the past week and felt suddenly protective of him.

"That's what I keep telling myself," Joe said. We walked in silence. "It's hard for me to be too angry with him," he said after a moment. "I've got Cassie and my girls and when I look back, there's nothing I'd really change about my life. I loved Evelyn but maybe things worked out as they were supposed to."

I nodded as we reached the small hill in the middle of the park. "Are you ever gonna tell me what we're doing here?"

Joe cleared his throat. "Your mum once joked that she was gonna be famous and have her own little plaque here."

I smiled as we reached the bench at the top of the hill. The sun was setting over the water and the sky was streaked with glorious reds. "I love it here."

"We got the bench after Stan died," Joe told me. "He owned the Croc before Kai. Your mum and Stan were close."

"That's nice," I said, looking at the plaque dedicating the bench to Stan.

"I thought we might add to it, if it's okay with you?" He pulled a shiny plaque from his pocket and handed it to me.

My fingers trailed over the engraved letters: *Evelyn*. Grief enveloped me in a way that I'd managed to avoid since the first few weeks after she'd died. My insides felt like they would rip me apart, and all I wanted to do was scream. *She should have been with me.*

"Is it okay?" Joe asked cautiously.

My throat was so tight I couldn't speak, but I nodded. Tears streamed down my face when I handed the little plaque back to him.

As Joe drilled the plaque into place, I let out a sob. When my legs felt as though they would give way, I knelt in the grass and cried. I couldn't stop. Joe made no move to comfort me and I was glad; I just needed a few minutes to cry.

Finally, I focused on my breathing and fought to get my emotions under control. "Sorry," I whispered to Joe automatically. There were tears in his eyes when I moved to the bench to admire the tribute to my mum. "It's perfect."

When I dragged my gaze from the plaque, Joe was looking at me. "The back of your necklace is engraved, isn't it?" he asked.

I reached to turn the feather pendant over and ran my thumb over the engraving: *Always with you* x.

"How did you know that?"

"I gave it to Evelyn," he said. "The last time I saw her, at the airport." He smiled at the memory. "I was sure she was going to throw it in the nearest bin."

"She kept it all that time?" I said, surprised by the story behind the necklace. "I never saw it until a few days before she died. She didn't tell me anything about it."

His gaze moved away from me and we sat in silence for a moment, looking out over the water.

"I don't know if this is going to come as a surprise or not," Joe said, smiling slowly, "but Cam brought fireworks!"

The laughter was a welcome relief as I wiped the remaining tears from my cheeks.

I stayed on the bench with Joe Sullivan as fireworks lit up the sky and threw a cascade of colours onto the lake. The silhouettes of Mum's old friends could be seen gathered at the water's edge. When I closed my eyes, I could imagine her sitting between me and Joe, the fireworks reflected in her eyes and her wonderful laughter echoing all around us.

THE END

Acknowledgements

Back in 2005, I was backpacking around Australia and took a job as a nanny in the beautiful outback town of Kununurra. I spent about eight months there and have the most amazing memories of that time. Arlene and her girls welcomed me into their home and treated me as part of the family. Their house was always full of fun and laughter and I'm so grateful to have been part of their lives for a little while. Arls – you are my friend for life. I'm so happy we've stayed in touch over all these years. One day we will meet again and I know it will be like we've never been apart.

As always, I have many people to thank for helping me with this book.

Firstly, Mario. None of this would be possible without your support and encouragement. I'm so grateful for all that you do.

Anthea Kirk for being so enthusiastic and helpful with my earliest drafts. Your input is so important to me.

My amazing team of beta readers and proof-readers: Sarah-Jane Fraser, Dua Roberts, Fay Sallaba, Ki Anglesea, Kathy Robinson, Sue Oxley, Sarah Walker and Meghan Driscoll. I couldn't do it without you. Thank you so much.

Thanks to my mum and dad, for always making time to help and support me, no matter what else is going on.

Thank you to Aimee Coveney for a stunning cover. You are so talented and it's always a pleasure to work with you.

A huge thank you to Katherine Trail for a fantastic editing job. I look forward to working with you again in the future.

To all my friends at CLCHQ, many thanks for all your help. It's so great to be part of such a wonderfully supportive online community.

And finally, a special thanks to my readers. You really are the best.

Made in the USA
Coppell, TX
19 October 2021